P9-ELT-523

Books by Rita Mae Brown
with "Sister" Jane Arnold in the Outfoxed series

Outfoxed
Hotspur
Full Cry
The Hunt Ball

Books by Rita Mae Brown with Sneaky Pie Brown

Wish You Were Here
Rest In Pieces
Murder At Montecello
Pay Dirt
Murder, She Meowed
Murder on the Prowl
Cat on the Scent
Sneaky Pie's Cookbook for Mystery Lovers
Pawing Through the Past
Claws and Effects
Catch as Cat Can
Cat's Eyewitness
Sour Puss

Books by Rita Mae Brown

The Hand That Cradles the Rock
Songs to a Handsome Woman
The Plain Brown Rapper
Rubyfruit Jungle
In Her Day
Six of One
Southern Discomfort
Sudden Death
High Hearts
Started from Scratch: A Different Kind of Writer's Manual
Bingo
Venus Envy
Dolley: A Novel of Dolley Madison in Love and War
Riding Shotgun
Rita Will: Memoir of a Literary Rabble-Rouser
Loose Lips
Alma Mater

THE HOUNDS AND THE FURY

THE HOUNDS AND THE FURY

A NOVEL

RITA MAE BROWN

BALLANTINE BOOKS
NEW YORK

The Hounds and the Fury is a work of fiction. Names, characters, places, and incidents are the products of the author's imagination or are used fictitiously. Any resemblance to actual events, locales, or persons living or dead is entirely coincidental.

Published in the United States by Ballantine Books, an imprint of The Random House Publishing Group, a division of Random House, Inc., New York.

Library of Congress Cataloging-in Publication Data
Brown, Rita Mae.
The hounds and the fury : a novel/Rita Mae Brown.—1st ed.
p. cm.
ISBN 0-345-46547-4
1. Fox hunting—Fiction. I. Title.
PS3552.R698H63 2006
813'.54—dc22 2006042768

Printed in the United States of America

www.ballantinebooks.com

2 4 6 8 9 7 5 3 1

First Edition

This novel is dedicated to the members of the Oak Ridge Foxhunt Club, some of the best people to ever throw their leg over a horse. As to what else they may have thrown their leg over, that is a subject upon which I prefer not to dwell.

ACKNOWLEDGMENTS

Special thanks to David Wheeler, who took the time to make me aware of "GAAS," generally accepted auditing standards. His experience and insight, as he is an accountant, proved invaluable. As he is joint-master of Oak Ridge Foxhunt Club he is truly invaluable.

As always, Mrs. Mary O'Brien, MD, helped me understand insurance issues, medical terms, and procedures. She is honorary whipper-in to Oak Ridge Foxhunt Club.

CAST OF CHARACTERS

HUMAN

Jane Arnold, "Sister," is the master of foxhounds of the Jefferson Hunt Club in central Virginia. She loves her hounds, her horses, her house pets. Occasionally she finds humans loveable. Strong, healthy, vibrant at seventy-three, she's proof of the benefits of the outdoor life.

Shaker Crown is the huntsman. He's acquired the discipline of holding his tongue and his temper most times. He's wonderful with hounds. In his early forties, he's finding his way back to love.

Crawford Howard, a self-made man, moved to Virginia from Indiana. He's egotistical and ambitious and thinks he knows more than he does about foxhunting. But he's also generous, intelligent, and fond of young people. His great disappointment is not being a father, but he never speaks of this, especially to his wife.

Marty Howard loves her husband. They've had their ups and downs, but they understand each other. She is accustomed to sweeping up after him, but she does this less than in the past. He's got to learn sometime. She's a better rider than her husband, which spurs him on.

Charlotte Norton is the young headmistress of Custis Hall, a prestigious prep school for young ladies. Dedicated to education, she's cool in a crisis.

Anne Harris, "Tootie," is one of the brightest students Charlotte Norton has ever known. Taciturn, observant, yet capable of delivering a stinging barb, this senior shines with promise. She's beautiful, petite, African-American, and a strong rider.

Valentina Smith is the class president. Blonde, tall, lean, and drop-dead gorgeous, the kid is a natural politician. She and Tootie can clash at times, but they are friends. She loves fox-hunting.

Felicity Porter seems overshadowed by Tootie and Val, but she is highly intelligent and has a sturdy self-regard. She's the kind of person who is quietly competent. She, too, is a good rider.

Pamela Rene seems burdened by being African-American, whereas for Tootie it's a given. Pamela can't stand Val and feels tremendously competitive with Tootie, whom she accuses of being an Oreo cookie. Her family substituted money for love, which makes Pamela poor. Underneath it all, she's basically a good person, but that can be hard to appreciate.

Betty Franklin is the long-serving honorary whipper-in at JHC. Her judgment, way with hounds, knowledge of territory, and ability to ride make her a standout. Many are the huntsmen who would kill to have a Betty Franklin whip-in to them. She's in her mid-forties, a mother, happily married, and a dear, dear friend to Sister.

Walter Lungrun, MD, joint-master of foxhounds, has held this position for only a year. He's learning all he can. He adores Sister, and the feeling is mutual. Their only complaint is that there's so much work to do they rarely have time for a good talk. Walter is in his late thirties. He is the result of an affair Raymond Arnold, Sr., had with Walter's mother. Mr. Lungrun never knew—or pretended he didn't—and Sister didn't know until a year ago.

The Bancroft family. Edward Bancroft, in his seventies, ran a large corporation founded by his family in the mid-nineteenth century. His wife, Tedi, is one of Sister's oldest friends. Tedi rides splendid thoroughbreds and is always impeccably turned out, as is her surviving daughter, Sybil, who is in her second year as an honorary whipper-in. The Bancrofts are true givers in terms of money, time, and genuine caring.

Ben Sidell has been sheriff of the county for three years. Since he was hired from Ohio, he sometimes needs help in the labyrinthine ways of the South. He relies on Sister's knowledge and discretion.

Garvey Stokes, mid-forties, president of Aluminum Manufacturing, has been on an acquisition spree. He now needs an extended line of credit from Farmers Trust Bank. He foxhunts and gets along with everyone.

Iphigenia Demetrios, "Iffy," at thirty-six, is being treated for lung cancer. She is the treasurer at Aluminum Manufacturing, where she has worked since graduating from college.

Jason Woods, MD, a lung cancer specialist, keeps close tabs on Iffy and his other patients. They are devoted to him.

Donny Sweigart, Jr., mid-twenties, likes to hunt deer. He works for Sanifirm, owned by his uncle, which picks up waste from the hospital. Although he's not a bad guy, he doesn't much impress folks.

Alfred DuCharme, mid-sixties, is one of Jason Woods's success stories. Free of ambition, Alfred runs the huge family estate, Paradise, as best he can, given the scarcity of funds. He loathes his brother, Binky.

Binky DuCharme, early sixties, doesn't speak to Alfred. He owns a small gas station and lives on Paradise with his wife, Milly. They live in a dependency, a house originally built for the help, since the main house is uninhabitable.

Margaret DuCharme, MD, specializes in sports medicine. She gets along with her uncles and acts as go-between. She also lives on the estate in her own little cottage.

Frederika Thomas, "Freddie," at thirty-four, is a stunning-looking woman and surprises people when they learn she is an accountant. She winds up on a pressure-cooker job with Gray Lorillard.

THE AMERICAN FOXHOUNDS

Sister and Shaker have carefully bred a balanced pack. The American foxhound blends English, French, and Irish blood, the first identifiable pack having been brought here in 1650 by Robert de la Brooke of Maryland. Before that, individual hounds were shipped over, but Brooke brought an entire pack. In 1785, General Lafayette sent his mentor and hero, George Washington, a pack of French hounds whose voices were said to sound like "the bells of Moscow."

Whatever the strain, the American foxhound is highly intelligent and beautifully built, with a strong sloping shoulder, powerful hips and thighs, and a nice tight foot. The whole aspect of the hound in motion is one of grace, power, and effortless covering of ground. They are "racier" than the English hound and stand perhaps two feet at the shoulder, although size is not nearly as important as nose, drive, cry, biddability. The American hound is sensitive and extremely loving, with eyes that range from softest brown to gold to sky blue. While one doesn't often see the sky-blue eye, there is a line that contains it. The hound lives to please its master and to chase foxes.

Cora is the strike hound, which means she often finds the scent first. She's the dominant female in the pack and is in her sixth season.

Diana is the anchor hound, and she's in her fourth season. All the other hounds trust her, and if they need direction, she'll give it.

Dragon is her littermate. He possesses tremendous drive and a fabulous nose, but he's arrogant. He wants to be the strike hound. Cora hates him.

Dasher is also Diana and Dragon's littermate. He lacks his brother's brilliance, but he's steady and smart.

Asa is in his seventh season and is invaluable in teaching the younger hounds, which are the second "D" litter and the "T" litter. A hound's name usually begins with the first letter of its mother's name, so the "D" hounds are out of **Delia**.

THE HORSES

Sister's horses are **Keepsake,** a thoroughbred/quarter horse cross, written TB/QH by horsemen. He's an intelligent gelding of eight years.

Lafayette, a gray TB, is eleven now, fabulously athletic and talented, and he wants to go.

Rickyroo is a seven-year-old TB gelding who shows great promise.

Aztec is a six-year-old gelding TB who is learning the ropes. He's also very athletic, with great stamina. He has a good mind.

Shaker's horses come from the steeplechase circuit so all are TBs. **Showboat, HoJo,** and **Gunpowder** can all jump the moon, as you might expect.

Betty's two horses are **Outlaw,** a tough QH who has seen it all and can do it all, and **Magellan**, a TB given to her by Sorrel Burrus. Magellan is bigger and rangier than Betty is accustomed to riding, but she's getting used to him.

Czpaka, a warmblood owned by Crawford Howard, can't stand the man. He's quite handsome but not as quick as the thoroughbreds, and when he's had it, he's had it. He's not above dumping Crawford.

Matador, a gray thoroughbred, six years old, sixteen hands, was a former steeplechaser. Sister buys him.

Bombardier, Sybil Bancroft's thoroughbred, has great good sense.

THE FOXES

The reds can reach a height of sixteen inches and a length of forty-one inches. They can weigh up to fifteen pounds. Obviously, since these are wild animals who do not willingly come forth to be measured and weighed, there's more variation than the standard cited above. **Target;** his spouse, **Charlene;** his **Aunt Netty;** and **Uncle Yancy** are the reds. They can be haughty.

A red fox has a white tip on the luxurious brush, except for Aunt Netty, who has a wisp of a white tip, for her brush is tatty.

The grays may reach fifteen inches in height, be forty-four inches in length, and weigh up to fourteen pounds. The common wisdom is that grays are smaller than reds, but there are some big ones out there. Sometimes people call them slabsided grays because they can be reddish. A gray does not have a white tip on its tail, but it may have a black tail as well as a black-tipped "mane." Some grays are so dark as to be black.

The grays are **Comet, Inky,** and **Georgia.** Their dens are a bit more modest than those of the red fox, who likes to announce his abode with a prominent pile of dirt and bones outside. Perhaps not all grays are modest, nor all reds full of themselves, but as a rule of thumb, it's so.

Earl is a gray fox, two years old, living at Paradise.

THE BIRDS

Athena is a great horned owl. This type of owl can stand two feet and a half in height and have a wingspread of four feet. It can weigh up to five pounds.

Bitsy is a screech owl. She is eight and a half inches high with a twenty-inch wingspread. She weighs a whopping six ounces, and she's reddish brown. Her considerable lungs make up for her stature.

St. Just, a crow, is a foot and a half high. His wingspread is a surprising three feet, and he weighs one pound.

THE HOUSE PETS

Raleigh is a Doberman, who likes to be with Sister.

Rooster is a Harrier and was willed to Sister by her old lover, Peter Wheeler.

Golliwog, "Golly," is a large calico cat and would hate being included with the dogs as a pet. She is the Queen of All She Surveys.

OTHER ANIMALS

Bruce and Lisa are otters who live at Paradise along with their many merry children.

Old Flavius is a forty-pound bobcat, quite fierce.

A wild boar over four hundred pounds, who if he had a name wouldn't tell anyone.

THE HOUNDS AND THE FURY

CHAPTER 1

Silvered with frost, the geometric patterns on the kennel windowpane displayed Nature's gift for design. Sister Jane Arnold stared at the tiny, perfect crystals, then turned back to the large old oak desk in the middle of the office. In warmer weather the back door of the office would be open to the center aisle in this, the main kennel. She found it comforting to inhale the odor of her hounds, to hear them breathing as they slept on their raised beds. Today, Boxing Day, December 26, Monday, the mercury clung to twenty-eight degrees Fahrenheit. The office felt warm at sixty-eight degrees, and she gave a small prayer of thanks that she'd found the money to put in a new heat pump and venting for the main building. The hounds, nestled in their straw-filled beds, threw off body heat, so the thermostat in their portion of the building was kept at forty-two degrees. The actual temperature hovered near fifty. The two medical rooms were warmer. Fortunately, no one was in sick bay.

Christmas culminated in such frenzy that Sister wished Joseph and Mary had been sterile. Sister found Boxing Day one of the happiest days of the year. In England, thousands would turn out in the villages and along country roads to witness hundreds of vigorous folk riding to hounds. The ban on foxhunting, voted by Parliament in 2004 and coming into force February 2005, was a sorry work of class hatred. The first Boxing Day after the ban was 2005, and British foxhunters rode out to a man. Local authorities declined to arrest these men and women. Constables knew that foxhunting benefited the livelihoods of their communities. The bizarre aspect of the foxhunting ban was that not even the most fervid Labor Party members pretended they wished to save foxes. It was perfectly fine with them if the farmers shot the beautiful creatures. The whole point of the ban was to punish those suspected of wealth or title from enjoying themselves. The fact that most English foxhunters were middle-class people was lost in this revenge on the wealthy few. As the Labor Party had created seven hundred new criminal offenses under Tony Blair's leadership, the fact that noncountry people tolerated these infringements on their rights shocked Sister.

She wondered whether Americans, no longer conversant with country life—and worse, feeling superior to it—could become as illiberal as the Laborites. The political push to ban foxhunting in America would start on one of the coasts, but Sister believed it wouldn't succeed. Americans still retained vestiges of common sense. Better yet, Americans did not hunt to kill the fox. They were content to chase the highly intelligent creature until he finally eluded them—easy enough for the fox.

Sister's study chair had rollers on it, and in a burst of enthusiasm she propelled herself around the room and spun backwards.

Shaker Crown, the huntsman, opened the front door at this moment. "Someone's happy."

"Three hundred and sixty-four days until next Christmas. Thank you, Jesus." She braked, putting both feet on the ground.

"Amen, Sister."

They burst out laughing.

"Hounds had a wonderful Christmas. Nothing like warm stew. I remember watching my father cook it up outside. The pot was large enough to hold three missionaries."

He smiled. "Horses liked their treats, too, as did I. Thank you for my Dehner boots and my bug guard."

"Do you think they really work?"

"Bug guards?" He paused. "Not now."

"I deserved that." She rolled her eyes at his droll remark. They wouldn't work now because it was winter, hence no insects were flying around outside.

"Sure they work. That curve at the top sends the bugs away from the windshield."

"Maybe I should get one for my GMC. You know, I'm still getting used to it. Drove the other one 287,000 miles and buried it with honors." She smiled at him. "I actually considered parking it in front of the kennel and making a huge planter out of it."

"You cut the bed off the truck and use it for a wagon." He pretended to think hard. "Could still fill with dirt and spring bulbs."

"No point wasting something that can be useful. All I had to do was sand the edges so we wouldn't cut ourselves, put a Reese hitch on it. If nothing else, we can put a big old water tank up there, and I can water my trees on the drive if another drought comes." She crossed herself as if warding off the evil eye, for droughts caused terrible damage.

"Heard anything?" After crossing himself, Shaker changed the subject.

"Not a peep."

He sat on the edge of the desk as she rolled back to it, replying, "He'll be vicious."

"Marty can't calm him down?" Shaker named Crawford Howard's wife.

"Crawford was publicly humiliated. Even the ministrations of his good wife won't help. His ego is in a gaseous state, ever expanding." Sister threw up her hands, exasperated.

"He deserved it, loading hounds up like that, then setting them loose during the hunt ball."

"Of course he did! After you belted him, he knew he couldn't stand up to you, so unleashing hounds was his revenge. And a damned sorry one. He wasn't entirely sober, which only made matters worse. He's lucky I only slapped him."

"Hard. Everyone in the room heard that crack." Shaker relished the recollection.

"Too bad I didn't have a roll of nickels in my palm. Then I'd have broken his jaw. Now, that's a happy thought, Crawford Howard with his jaw wired shut."

"Strange we haven't heard anything. Betty hasn't, either. I called her."

"You surprise me." Sister didn't expect him to call Betty Franklin, one of her best friends, an honorary whipper-in.

He folded his arms across his chest. "I didn't get us in this mess, but I made it worse."

"When a man pulls down your fiancée's evening gown, even if he was pushed and tripped, most of us can understand the response."

"Poor Lorraine. She's still embarrassed."

"Honey, any woman with that rack should never be embarrassed. Entire careers have been built on less."

He smiled. "She's a beautiful woman."

"She is. You two are a good pair and a good-looking pair to boot."

He walked over to the kennel-side door. "Sound asleep."

"I often envy them. They are loved, have the best of care, and do what they were born to do. Think of the millions of people in this world struggling at jobs that aren't right for them. They might be flourishing financially, but deep in their hearts, they know this isn't what they should be doing with their lives—and, oh, Shaker, how fast the time slips away."

"Got that right." He returned to the desk. "Hope we can hunt tomorrow."

"Me, too, but feel the storm coming? Truth is in the bones."

"Seen the sky in the last hour?"

"No, I've been in here rooting through the old stud books."

"Look." He opened the front door, and they both stepped out into the biting air.

Gunmetal-gray clouds stacked up behind the Blue Ridge Mountains.

"Moving faster than the Weather Channel predicted." She noticed the tops of trees swaying slightly. "Going to be a big one. We'd better get all the generators in place, just in case."

"Already did. Up at your house, too."

Relief filled her voice. "Thank you."

"Rather deal with snow than ice."

"Me, too."

"Boss, you think Crawford will sue?"

"He doesn't have much of a case. It would be a hardship on us, of course, but ultimately it would be worse for him. My hunch is he'll forego that and do something where he can use his wealth as leverage."

"Like withdraw his support to the club?"

"That's a given." She rubbed her shoulders. "It will hurt, too. His largesse covered about 25 percent of our annual budget."

"He'll go to Farmington Hunt or Keswick, maybe even Deep Run, and throw money at them. If he can keep his ego in check, he might even get along with most of them. What master doesn't need money for the club?" Shaker put his arm through hers, and they stepped back into the office. Sister settled back into the warmth of the office, glad the door was closed. "Ego is the key word."

"Hard on Sam."

Sam Lorillard of the Lorillards, an African-American family that had been in the country since before the Revolutionary War, possessed both intellectual and athletic brilliance. Unfortunately, a tendency toward alcoholism had also passed from generation to generation among both the white and black Lorillards. Gray, Sam's older brother and Sister's boyfriend, had escaped it. Sam had not. He was currently sober after much suffering. Attending Alcoholics Anonymous Meetings helped.

The black Lorillards had taken the name of their owners, common enough in the Old South. Not even the pull of convention or ideology could keep the two sides of this vast family apart. A Lorillard stayed a Lorillard.

Before sobriety, Sam had wreaked so much damage throughout the Virginia horse world that he'd descended to living at the train station downtown. He and the other drunks sucked up Thunderbird, panhandled, took odd day jobs. Eventually, he got clean and, with Gray's financial help, back on his feet. But no one would hire him. Crawford Howard, however, who was relatively new to the town and the club, did. He had no preconceived notions. Sam was loyal, drunk or sober. Sister knew he'd stick with Crawford even if he cringed at Crawford's revenge. Shaker knew it, too.

Shaker glanced out the window again. "We're in for it."

"In more ways than one." She pulled on her fleece-lined old bomber jacket and wrapped her red scarf around her neck. "Bring it on. If nothing else, we'll find out who is the stronger."

"My money is on you."

"Funny, I was going to say the same thing about you. We're in this together."

"Hey, if there's a fight, you're the one I want at my back." He threw his arm around her shoulders.

Since Sister was six feet tall and Shaker five ten, he reached up slightly. She was strong in her early seventies, smart as the foxes they hunted. He was thirty years younger, quick and muscular. They made a sensational team as master and huntsman, each intuitive concerning the other.

Outside the wind was rising.

"You know, we might get a foot out of this."

"Plow's on the old 454." Shaker mentioned the old Chevy with the mighty engine.

"Sometimes I welcome a storm."

"Nature's pruning."

"Clears the air. Trouble's easier to deal with if you see it coming. We see this coming."

Sister was right in that. Trouble that creeps up on little feet is far worse. That was coming, too.

CHAPTER 2

Like white molasses the winter storm moved so slowly that by the afternoon of Wednesday, December 28, the last bands still spit snow over the mountains and valleys of central Virginia. The power stayed flowing, a miracle under these conditions. If the storm didn't knock down lines, some fool going sixty miles an hour in an SUV usually skidded off the road, taking out a utility pole. The snow, heavy and steady, kept even the owners of sixty-thousand-dollar SUVs at home.

Until midnight, every couple of hours, for two days, Shaker fired up the Chevy 454 to plow the farm roads and the paths to kennels and stables. By morning's light he was back at it again while Sister fed and checked the hounds and horses. The horses when turned out played in the snow. The hounds in the big kennel yards frolicked as well until worn out, when they snuggled down into their condominiums raised off the ground. The wraparound porches on these eight-foot-square, four-feet-high buildings glistened with snow. Before winter's onset, Sister and Shaker had bolted on an addition to the large openings, blocking most of the frigid air. The opening, facing away from the northwest, could accommodate two hounds passing through. Sometimes in early morning Sister would walk out into the quarter-acre yards to see the steam floating out of the condos from the hounds' body heat.

She'd started at five-thirty this morning, accompanied by Raleigh, her Doberman, and Rooster, the harrier. Golliwog, the long-haired calico, felt that the deep snow would clump on her luxurious, much-groomed coat. She elected to lounge on the leather sofa in the den as the fire crackled in the simple, beautifully proportioned fireplace.

Sister returned every three hours to toss hardwood logs on that fire, put logs in the kitchen walk-in fireplace, and cram full the wood-burning stove in the cellar. The heating bills stayed down, thanks to the stove and fireplaces. The split hardwood logs came from dead trees on her property or the property of friends. Country neighbors helped one another in this fashion. Someone usually had an excess of fallen timber somewhere.

Sister told Shaker to keep plowing. She'd do the chores. Trudging through deep snow wearied her legs. Even with the paths cleared, in no time there'd be a bit more snow. Double-checking the condos was what told on Sister's legs, even though hers were strong. At least her feet stayed warm in her Thinsulate-lined high work boots.

Another squall sent tiny flakes down. The big flakes looked pretty, but the tiny ones stuck. Little bits stung her cheeks, touched her eyelashes.

She'd put out kibble for the foxes on the farm in three locations. She figured Inky and Comet, gray foxes, brother and sister, and Georgia, Inky's grown daughter, were toasty in their straw-lined dens. Each fox had only to go a few yards to the five-gallon bucket with the hole drilled in so they could pull out food. The small hole kept larger marauders from raiding the buckets, although raccoons and possums could fish out the small kernels of food. Once the snows subsided, walking would be easier. She'd move the feed buckets farther from the dens.

Shaker chugged along. He stopped outside the stable as she came out.

"How's it going?"

"Pretty good. Did you check the Weather Channel lately?"

"Two hours ago when I filled up the fireplaces. Should end about five."

"Jeez," he whistled.

"You've got your girlfriend in the cottage." Sister nodded at the smoke barely rising from the chimney before flattening out. "Bet she's making barley soup."

He smiled underneath the lumberjack cap pulled low over his auburn curls. "Want some?"

"I'll be by later. Who could pass up Lorraine's soup?" She rubbed her hands together. "While I remember, Delia's looking a little ribby. I fed her separately and threw in some extra vits. Let's not hunt her until she puts the weight back on." She paused. "Starting to show her age a little." Then she sighed. "She's a good solid hound."

"Old Piedmont blood."

"Yep," she agreed. Delia's blood went back to a hunt established in 1840 that had used hounds bred for Virginia conditions by the Bywaters family, one of the great names in American foxhunting.

As he rolled up the window, slowly pushing snow again, she whistled for the house dogs, busy trying to catch a mouse in the feed room. The mouse would have none of it.

"Come on, boys. Come on, let's have a cup of hot tea, and then we'll come back and bring in the horses. Sun will set around quarter to five. Going to be a bitter night."

No sooner had she stepped into the kitchen, the oldest part of the house, than the phone rang.

"Sam." She recognized Sam Lorillard's voice. "How are you doing over there?"

"Okay."

"What can I do for you, Sam?"

"Crawford's still in a rage."

"Crawford's not taking this out on you, is he?"

"No, no"—his voice lowered—"he's really good to me. Marty, too. Politics," he said, assuming she'd understand he needed to stay out of it, which she did. "The reason I called is before the storm hit, early Monday morning, I drove up to Green Spring Valley Hunt in Maryland to look at a timber horse, a balanced, sixteen-hand, flea-bitten gray. Good mind. Smooth, bold over fences. Crawford was interested, but the horse is too small for him. Crawford's packing on weight again. This is your kind of horse: bold, kind, beautiful."

"How much?"

"Twenty thousand."

"That's a lot of money."

"It's a lot of horse and only six years old. Duck Martin knows the horse. Sheila Brown, too, and I think Ned Halle is friends with the owner." He named the three masters of Green Spring

Valley Hounds, all tremendous riders. Green Spring Valley was one of the great hunts in this or any country.

"Why doesn't one of them buy it?"

"Full up. You've got good horses, too, but you could use another made horse. You could throw a leg over him right now and go. He's that good."

"Why is the owner selling?"

"Getting out of the 'chasing game.' "

"All right, give me the number and I'll see what's what. I sure thank you for thinking of me."

"Sister, you've been good to me, and well, I know things are going to be tense for a while. I don't want to lose my job, but I'll keep you posted."

"Everyone knows you need the job, Sam. No one will criticize you for it. And I'll never reveal my source." She chuckled.

"This is Virginia." A note of sarcasm crept into his voice.

"You're right. Some will criticize you, but they'll end the sentence with 'Bless his heart.' "

"Right," he agreed.

"Sam, what's the horse's name?"

"Matador."

"Bold name." She liked it.

Sam lowered his voice, even though Sister was sure he was alone. "One other thing, Crawford's always been on good terms with Jason Woods. Better terms now."

"Oh." Sister wondered what Crawford's real interest was in the good-looking doctor. "Maybe he's sick."

"No. But Jason, Crawford, and the Bancrofts are the big-money people in Jefferson Hunt. No secret that Crawford will leave."

"We all figured that." Sister actually felt some relief that Crawford would be out of the club.

"I suspect he'll pull Jason with him. I know the doctor hasn't been in the club but so long. He's the kind of member people want. Rich."

"Yes." Sister paused. "And often those members will give more as they settle in, really become part of the club."

"All I know is Crawford is up to something." He waited a beat. "See you on Matador."

After the call, Sister checked each of the fires as the water heated. She poured herself a restorative cup of orange pekoe. While the tea warmed her she called the number in Maryland. Once she learned that the top line of the gelding went back to War Admiral and the bottom line traced to Golden Apple, a chestnut mare born in 1945, she made an appointment to have a vet check the horse. There are some people with whom you do business on their word; Sam was one. If he said it was a good horse, it was. Add the "staying" blood, and Matador was probably more than good. She made a note to send Sam a finder's fee if this worked out. Sam needed all the money he could get. Next she called a vet she knew in Carroll County, Maryland. The sky had darkened; she piled her gear back on and went out to bring in the horses.

Raleigh and Rooster tagged along.

"You'll be cold, paws wet, I'll be warm as toast," Golly called after them.

"You're a big hairball the devil coughed up," Raleigh replied over his shoulder.

Incensed, Golly grabbed Raleigh's big knotted rawhide chew, but it was too big for her to damage it. She shredded one of Sister's needlepoint pillows instead.

. . .

As Sister and Shaker finished the day's chores and hurried in for barley soup, Samson "Sonny" Shaeffer, president of Farmers Trust Bank and a dear friend of Sister's, received a phone call.

"Sonny, it's Garvey Stokes."

"How are you doing in this storm?"

"The kids love it," Garvey replied. "They've worn me out."

"By tomorrow every house in the county will have a snowman."

"Yeah," Garvey agreed. "I called to do a little business."

"Sure. Anything I can help you with now?"

"Well, I've got a shot at tying up fifteen tons of aluminum, very high grade at $1,680 per metric ton. The Chinese are snapping up everything. I think by spring the price per metric ton will top out at $2,300. Of course, you never know, but despite the slowdown in demand by the auto makers for aluminum, I still think prices will climb. So I was hoping for a modest expansion to the business line of credit."

"We should be able to accommodate you."

"Business has been great, booming," Garvey added.

"Once we can all get back to our offices, I'll send over the paperwork."

"Okay."

After a few more pleasantries, Sonny hung up. He was glad to have Garvey's account, Aluminum Manufacturers, Inc. The company made everything from window frames to the small caps on top of broom handles. It was one of the largest employers in the area. For the past five years Garvey had been buying up smaller companies in Virginia as well.

A good businessman, he hired competent people and

trusted them to do their job while he concentrated on creating more business, seeking greater opportunities for profit.

Garvey, a foxhunter, rode the way he hired: bold with brio, if occasionally too impulsive. Better to have impulsiveness as a fault than to be too cautious in both business and foxhunting, although sooner or later one would tumble. Garvey trusted he'd get right back up again, and so far his trust had not been misplaced.

CHAPTER 3

The Blue Ridge Mountains stood like cobalt sentinels, reminding those who knew their geology of the time before human time when Africa and part of South America slammed into this continent during the Alleghenian Orogeny, pushing up what then were the tallest mountains in the world. These collisions had occurred between two hundred fifty million and three hundred million years ago, knocking into rock already over one billion years old.

Time's unchallenged power affected Sister Jane. Each time she beheld the beautiful Blue Ridge Mountains, she paid homage to the forces of nature and to the brevity of human habituation: only nine thousand years by the Blue Ridge. At this exact moment, she was paying homage to the wisdom of the red fox, *Vulpes vulpus.*

Target, a healthy red in luxurious coat, had traveled too far from his den on After All Farm, the neighboring farm. He graced Sister's Roughneck Farm. The Bancrofts, Sister's beloved friends, owned After All. Hounds gaily shot out of the kennels at nine in the morning, skies overcast. Hunting in snow presented interesting tests for a pack of American foxhounds. The glowering skies, perfect for hunting, presaged well, but the snow would release scent only as the mercury climbed up from thirty-two degrees Fahrenheit. Today it stuck at thirty-eight degrees. Little snow melted. In the shade of towering pines and spruces, the mercury shivered below thirty-two degrees. But a fresh line is a fresh line, whether on dirt, sand, soft wet grass, or snow. A fresh line allows hounds to get on terms with their fox, and this morning highlighted both Sister's and Shaker's own good hunting sense. The hounds did the rest.

The small field, nine people, trotted behind the thirty-two couple of hounds gaily working what was called the wildflower meadow, a half mile east of the kennels, east of the sunken farm road that wound its way up to Hangman's Ridge.

The two whippers-in, Betty Franklin and Sybil Bancroft Fawkes, rode at ten o'clock and two o'clock in relation to the pack. Shaker rode at six on the clock dial. They'd already moved through the mown hay field, which had been treated to a good dressing of fertilizer and overseeded before the hard frosts. The snow couldn't have been better for the hay field.

On level ground the white blanket was piled to a foot. Wind kicked up deep drifts. Other spots had but two or three inches, thanks to the winds. Trouble was, you couldn't readily tell the depth of the snow just by looking at it. If the temperatures remained low and another front passed through, this packing of snow would become the base for more powder. Weeks might pass before it melted in the deepest folds of ravines. Sometimes the snows in those places wouldn't melt until April.

Sprays of white powder followed the hounds. Clods of snow popped off the horses' hooves. The chill air brought color to everyone's cheeks.

On Thursdays, Sister's joint-master, Dr. Walter Lungrun, could join them. Tedi and Edward Bancroft, Gray Lorillard, Charlotte Norton, Bunny Taliaferro, Garvey Stokes, Henry Xavier (called "X"), and Dr. Jason Woods filled out the field this Thursday, December 29.

Diana, anchor hound, paused by a low holly bush. She inhaled deeply before moving to a dense bramble patch, which even without leaves was formidable.

A small tuft of deep red fur fluttered on a low tendril replete with nasty thorns. Large pawprints, rounder than a gray fox's, marked Target's progress. He'd meandered through in a hunting semicircle coming from the east.

"Target," Diana called out.

Cora, the strike hound, Asa, Diddy, Dasher, and Dragon hurried over. All hounds put their noses to the bluish snow. Just enough *eau de Vulpes,* fresh on the surface, kept hounds moving. Their long wonderful noses warmed the air as it passed through.

As hounds, sterns waving, eagerly pushed this line, Sister passed the brambles. Her sharp educated eyes noted the tiny red flag. She observed the fresh prints, fur showing around the pad, preserved in deep snow as perfectly as fossils in stone.

"Close." She thought to herself, echoing the assessment of her hounds.

Shaker still did not lift the horn to his lips.

"Let the young entry come up to the scent," he thought to

himself as four couple of first-year students joined the pack today, their very first hunt in snow.

Both Shaker and Sister liked hounds to figure things out for themselves, to be problem-solvers, a trait natural to foxhounds in general. It was one thing to call out in heavy coverts, or in ravines to give a toot just to let the hounds and whippers-in know where he was, but in open ground, he liked to be silent, with a word or two of encouragement to a youngster.

Both master and huntsman loathed noisy, showoff staff.

The "A" young entry looked ahead as the pack lengthened their stride.

Shaker smiled down at the gorgeous tricolored hounds and quietly said, "Hike to 'em, young 'uns."

Picking up their pace, ploughing through the snow, within seconds they filled in the pack. As yet no hound opened, spoke to the line, but all those gifted noses kept down.

Cora, the richness of years and high intelligence to her credit, wanted to make certain the line was growing stronger and fresher before she sang out. She didn't much like poking around old lines of scent when fresh ones could be found with diligent effort. Being head bitch as well as the strike hound, she occasionally needed to chastise younger hounds who, in their excitement and desire to hunt, opened too early. Sometimes they would babble on the wrong quarry. That would never do.

Dragon, proud, competitive, and desperately wanting to become the strike hound, pushed ahead of Cora and called out, *"Come on."*

Cora, livid that the younger dog hound had challenged her authority, bumped him hard, knocking him in the snow. As she passed him she bared her fangs. Even Dragon, arrogant as he was, knew better than to start a fight during hunting and certainly not with Cora.

The pack opened, the young entry lifting their voices. Mostly they knew what they were doing, but sometimes the excitement of it overcame them and they'd *"Yip, yip, yip"* in a higher pitch than the other hounds.

Target, hearing the hounds, picked up his handsome head and looked around. The wind, light, blew away from him in a swirl. Once out of the shallow bowl he happened to be in at that moment, the wind would revert to a steady breeze from west to east. He realized he hadn't smelled the hounds because of where he was. The little wind devils didn't help. Being lighter than the hounds, he could run on snow with a crust on it, but this fresh powder slowed him. Target was not in an enviable situation.

Perched high in a two-hundred-year-old walnut, St. Just, king of the crows, peered down with relish. Perhaps this would be the day when he would watch Target die. He hated this fox with a vengeance, for Target had killed his mate.

Also observing the hunt was Bitsy, the screech owl. Curious and tiny, but big of voice, she was returning to her nest in the rafters of Sister's barn when she heard the pack. Bitsy, social, liked to visit other barns and other owls. She'd enjoyed a night of feasting on various tidbits at Tedi and Edward Bancroft's barn with a regular barn owl who lived there. That particular bird also lived for gossip, just like Bitsy.

None of the owls liked St. Just or any of the crows. Crows sometimes mobbed them in daylight. The battle lines were clearly drawn. St. Just and his minions feared Athena, the great horned owl. In fact, any animal with sense kept on the good side of the Queen of the Night. She could hurt you.

She wasn't in sight, so St. Just, emboldened, began calling for his troops to rouse themselves. Within moments the edge of the nearby woods filled with cackles and calls. Those crows dozing in the walnut tree awakened, their bright eyes focusing on the laboring fox in the snow.

The sky filled with black birds circling the fox.

St. Just dive-bombed the big red, who snapped with his jaws.

Hounds were gaining, and the fox and crows heard Shaker blow one long blast followed by three short ones. Three times this sequence was played, which meant "All on." All hounds ran on the scent.

To those riding behind, their bodies as warm as the tears on their faces felt cold, the hounds flying together on the blue snows was a sight they would always remember.

Target hoped he'd live to remember.

Bitsy flew wide of the crows to stop and assess the situation from the top of the recently vacated walnut. She flew back, and since she was an owl she could fly slowly, the marvelous construction of her feathers' baffling silencing her approach.

"They're a quarter mile behind."

"Bitsy, help me," Target pleaded as he ran. *"See if the pattypan is open. Used to be an old den there."*

The pattypan, so named for its circular shape, had been a small forge built immediately after the Revolutionary War. After World War I it had fallen into disuse, although burrowing animals found it a wonderful place for a home.

The crows shadowed Target, the braver ones bombing him, slowing his progress. The edge of the woods, now one hundred yards ahead, could be his salvation, but he had to cross open ground—and therein lay the danger.

Cora could now see, dimly, the big red pushing through the

snow, his brush straight out. Sister, too, could see him and knew from his brush that he wasn't fatigued or beaten, but he was in peril. Target's stride, shorter than the hounds', was now, though not usually, a problem. He flattened his ears, his heart pumping, and he ran straight as an arrow.

A young male crow swerved right in front of him to slow him, but Target, quick as a cat, lashed out with his front paws and batted the bird down, then crushed its neck in his jaws. He bit into the body, kept the bird in his mouth, and trailed blood for ten yards before dropping the crow.

St. Just waxed apoplectic. *"Kill him, Dragon! Kill him, Cora!"*

The odor of fresh blood threw off even Cora for a moment. The intoxication of it slowed the pack down just a second or two, but that was enough for the fox to reach the woods.

"The old den is clear; you can get in." Bitsy noticed the blood on Target's jaws. *"The old deer path is better going. Not as much snow on it."*

The sheltering pines, oaks, hickories, black birches—the whole rich panoply of eastern hardwoods and pines—did keep the snows lighter on the deer path. Target sped along.

As the field rode along the narrow path the thunder of hooves brought down the snow on the boughs and branches. Showers of iridescent spray slid down collars, stuck to eyelashes, and secreted themselves into the tops of boots.

Target spied the thick walls of the redbrick forge ahead. He lunged forward, skidding into an old woodchuck den whose entrance was at the outer wall of the forge. Over the centuries this den had developed into a labyrinthine maze worthy of a tiny minotaur. Safe, he flopped on his side to catch his breath.

Dragon vaulted through a long window four feet off the ground, the glass long ago pulverized. Diddy, Dasher, and Cora followed, Asa last over the windowsill.

"There's got to be more denholes!"

Cora looked around. The interior was intact. *"There are plenty of holes, Dragon, but he's not going to pop out."*

"We can dig him out," Diddy, young and excited, squealed.

Shaker blew three long notes, then called, "Come back."

"Better go," Asa advised as he also heard the rest of the pack baying, digging at the outside den entrance.

As the five hounds turned to obey their huntsman Cora lifted her head. She trotted over to another window where snow streaked across the floor. A raspberry, congealed lump the size of a tin of chewing tobacco, glistened. She drew close, inhaled deeply. *"Human."*

Asa joined her, putting his nose close to the lump. *"Indeed it is."*

Calling again, Shaker half-sang the words, "Come along." He blew "Gone to Ground," which should have excited them as well as the hounds outside.

"What's this mean?" Diddy asked, puzzled.

Dragon, having given up on a promising denhole, now stood by Diddy's side. *"Don't know. Someone could have cut themselves."*

"But there's no footprints. And no scent." Diddy, young though she was, already displayed formidable powers of logic, powers necessary to a good foxhound.

"Scent's long gone by now." Asa furrowed his brow, wrinkles deepening between his ears. *"And the storm blew snow over whatever footprints there might be."*

Diddy inhaled again, her warm long nasal passages helping to release what scent remained. *"I've never smelled human blood before. Since this is frozen, it must be very strong when it's fresh."*

" 'Tis," Asa simply replied.

"Sure a big glop." Dragon, too, was baffled.

"Human blood is never a good sign. Never." Cora, voice low, turned from the blood against the snow to leap through the window, followed by the others.

Bitsy sat on the spine of the slate roof, almost as good as the day it had been put on in 1792. She'd watched everything, and her amazing little ears had picked up tidbits of the conversation inside the pattypan forge. St. Just then dive-bombed her.

"One of these days, Bitsy, I'll get you!"

She blinked, ducked, then opened her little wings to scuttle through a window. St. Just flew in after her. She emerged on the other side only to be confronted with the whole angry mob of crows.

Shaker knew Bitsy. When Cora, Dragon, Asa, Dasher, and Diddy had rejoined the pack, he praised his hounds, patting them on the head.

"Bitsy, come down toward me." Then he called to the little brown owl, badly outnumbered.

The hunt staff, as well as some of the other humans, recognized Bitsy, for her curiosity lured her into their company. She'd watch people disembark from the trailers, she'd sit on the barn weather vane, or she'd hang out in the big tree opposite the kennel door. Every now and then she'd emit the screech for which her type of owl was named. It could freeze one's blood as sure as that frozen lump in the forge.

Bitsy, not as fast as the crows, kept her head down, which was pretty easy for her, and she flew to the edge of the slate roof closest to Shaker and the den entrance.

Target, inside, heard the commotion. If the pack hadn't been out there he would have helped his friend. Under the circumstance, his emergence meant instant death.

The crows, wild with rage, ignored the human underneath them. They continued to attack Bitsy.

A huge pair of balled-up talons knocked one crow out of the throng. Then another. The people below, the horses and the hounds, looked up to behold Athena, her huge wingspread out to the full, her talons balled up like baseballs, wreacking havoc among the crows.

St. Just cawed loudly, then sped off, his squadrons with him. Two dazed crows lay in the snow.

Tinsel, a second-year hound, started for one.

"Leave it," Shaker said quietly.

Tinsel quickly rejoined the pack.

"Never saw anything like that in my life." Walter was gape-jawed.

"Me neither, but I know enough not to mess with a great horned." Sister, too, was dazzled at the winged drama. She spoke to Shaker next. "Pick them up. It was a very good day for the young entry." She smiled down at the pack. "Very good day for the Jefferson hounds."

As they walked back, Sister motioned for Charlotte Norton to ride up to her.

The attractive young headmistress of Custis Hall, an elite preparatory school for girls, came alongside Aztec, Sister's sleek young hunter.

"What a beautiful sight, the pack running together over the field." Charlotte was radiant.

"Do you ever think of what we see? Things most folks never see. They see the tailpipe of the car in front of them." Sister marveled at the patience of people for sitting in traffic as they shuttled to and from their jobs.

"We are very, very lucky. One of the things I try to impress upon the girls is how we have to work together to preserve farmland and wildlife. They're receptive, for which I'm grateful."

"You're a good example," Sister complimented her. "Do you ever regret being an administrator instead of faculty?"

"No. I really love being at the helm of our small ship." Charlotte felt passionate about education, particularly at the secondary level.

Although many of her peers were climbing the ranks at major universities and some had already been named as presidents of smaller colleges, Charlotte felt fulfilled.

"Have you been having a good Christmas vacation?"

"I have. Carter had a few days off from the hospital. We drove up to D.C. to the National Gallery, to the Kennedy Center. I like being reminded of why I married him in the first place. He's such fun, and I'm always intrigued by his observations. It's that scientific mind of his."

"I miss the girls." Sister mentioned the Custis Hall girls who had earned the privilege of hunting with the Jefferson Hunt. "Tootie and Felicity e-mail me. Val has once."

Bunny Taliaferro, riding instructor at Custis Hall, rigorously selected the toughest riders for foxhunting. The prettiest on horseback competed in the show ring, since there was high competition among the private academies. But the toughest, some of whom were on the show jumping team, foxhunted.

"They're so buoyant, so full of life and dreams. They make me feel young again," Charlotte beamed.

"Me, too, and I have more years on me than you," Sister laughed. "Funny though, Charlotte, I feel younger than when I was young. I love life and I love my life. Sometimes, I feel light as a feather."

"You look light as a feather. And you fool people. They think you're in your fifties."

"Now, Charlotte, that's a fib, but I thank you. You never met my mother, but she grew younger as she grew older. Energy and happiness just radiated from her. Dad, too, but he died before Mother. She made it to eighty-six, and if she were alive today, the technology is such that she'd still be here. But I think of her every day, and I'm so glad I had that model. It must be difficult for people who grow up with depressed parents, or drunks or angry people. Makes it harder to find happiness because you haven't lived with it."

Walter Lungrun, riding behind them and a colleague of Charlotte's husband, Carter, was head of Neurosurgery at Jefferson Regional Hospital. Riding with him was Jason Woods, a doctor in the oncology department; both men could hear them because the snow muffled the hoofbeats. "If you can't be happy foxhunting, you can't be happy, period." Walter smiled.

"Hear, hear," the riders agreed, toes and fingers throbbing with cold.

"Because of us." Aztec believed riding cured most ills for people.

"Hound work, that thrills 'em," Asa, the oldest dog hound in the pack, said with conviction.

As they neared the kennels Athena and Bitsy flew toward the barn.

"Mutt and Jeff," Sister remarked.

Tedi Bancroft, her oldest friend, also in her seventies, laughed. "You know, there are generations that never heard of Mutt and Jeff."

"Never thought of that—the things we know, silly things I guess, that younger people don't know. Well, they have their own references."

"References are one thing; manners are another. The boys still haven't written their Christmas thank-you notes." Tedi thought her grandsons lax in this department.

They really weren't. She had forgotten how long it takes to become "civilized."

"Tedi, they're good boys." Sister believed in the young. Her eyes followed the two owls. "I'll tell you, girls, let's stick together like Bitsy and Athena. A friend in need is a friend in deed."

Up in the cupola, Bitsy, thrilled at her near miss and by what she'd heard inside pattypan forge, breathlessly relayed all to Athena.

"H-m-m," was all Athena said.

"Let's go back and see for ourselves."

"No."

"Why not?" Bitsy, disappointed that her big friend showed so little interest, chirped. *"If someone hurt themselves, a deer hunter, say, it's over and done with. But what if someone is"*—Bitsy relished this—*"dead."*

"When the snows melt we'll know." Athena found hunting small game or raiding the barns more fascinating, most times, than human encounters.

"Maybe." Bitsy blinked. *"Sometimes they never find them, you know."*

"Bitsy, did it ever occur to you that that might be a good thing?"

"Well, no," the little owl honestly replied.

"Think about it." Athena's gold eyes surveyed all below. Then voice low, she sang, *"Hoo, Hoo,"* and paused. *"Hoo, Hoo, Hoo."*

The small brown screech owl knew her large friend would

not appreciate more questions, so she decided she would think about it. In time Bitsy would come to understand Athena's idea that it might be better, sometimes, if humans didn't know where the dead slept.

Before Sister could dismount, Dr. Jason Woods rode up to her. "Might I have a word?"

"Of course."

Handsome, reed-thin, he spoke low. "You know, when I was a resident I whipped-in at Belle Meade."

Belle Meade, located in Georgia, drew members from as far away as Atlanta as well as country folks closer to Thomson, Georgia.

Sister knew Epp Wilson, the senior master, so she knew Jason told the truth but not all of it, or he hadn't figured out his real position vis-à-vis Mr. Wilson. Given his ego, the latter was quite possible.

Before Jason had joined Jefferson Hunt two years earlier, she'd done what any master would do. She called the master of his former hunt. Epp gave a forthright assessment, no beating around the bush.

The young doctor rode tolerably well. To his credit, he was fearless and generous to the club with his time and money. To his discredit, he was arrogant and thought he knew more than he really did about foxhunting.

Jason was an outstanding doctor. He went to war daily against cancer, his particular specialty within oncology being lung cancer. He never gave up and encouraged his patients to keep a positive attitude. He had a special talent for tailoring treatments to the individual. He didn't practice cookie-cutter medicine. He also displayed an additional talent for self-aggrandizement, emboldened by the worship of many of his patients.

At Belle Meade Jason had whipped-in on those occasions when one of the regular whippers-in was indisposed. He confused riding ability with hunting ability. A whipper-in needs both.

"Yes." Sister had a sinking feeling about where this discussion was heading.

"I'd like to whip-in for you. You could use a man out there."

She bit her tongue. "I appreciate your enthusiasm. If you're willing to walk out hounds in the off season, to learn each one, then we can go from there to next season's cubbing."

This was not the answer he'd anticipated. "I could learn their names as I go."

"No. You need to know each single hound. You need to know their personalities, their way of going. How else can you identify them from afar on horseback?"

"Epp didn't ask me to do that." His face reddened.

She wanted to reply, "Epp didn't ask you to do that because you were a last-minute fill-in. He's a true hound man, and he'd not pick a whipper-in just because he could ride." Instead, she demurred, "He would have gotten around to it."

"Am I refused?"

"Delayed," she smiled.

He had the sense not to lose his temper. He was a highly intelligent man and he recognized that Sister was like the great horned owl: silent and powerful. Don't openly provoke her.

He rode back to his impressive three-horse slant-load trailer with its small, well-appointed living quarters, something rarely seen in foxhunters' trailers. This was pulled by a spanking new Chevy Dually, a mighty Duramax 6600 turbo-diesel V-8 under the polished hood. Coupled with an all-new Allison six-speed transmission, the 6.6 liter Duramax put out 360 horsepower and 650 pound-feet of raw torque.

Sister admired the brute of a truck. She gave Jason credit for buying a truck that could do the job. She also gave him credit for managing to buy this model months before it would be on Chevy lots. She hoped when it was made available it wouldn't be tarred and feathered with the Chevy ads that completely insulted women. They had to be seen to be believed.

Jason had money. He'd no doubt give more to the club if he could claim to be a whipper-in, a coveted position.

Many a master, strapped for cash, gratefully accepted a large contribution, then put the soul out where he or she could do the least harm. The other alternative was to couple the neophyte with the battle-hardened whipper-in for a half season or entire season and pray some of the knowledge would rub off.

Her method was to watch a candidate in the stifling hot days of summer. Were they quiet with hounds? Did they impart confidence with firmness? Were they helpful in the kennels if asked?

It was one thing to be on the edge of the pack, possibly attracting the admiring gaze of the ladies and the envious stare of the gentlemen. It was quite another to clean the kennels in ninety-degree heat with corresponding humidity.

Yes, many wanted to be whippers-in, to swarm about the tailgates once hounds were in the kennels or loaded on the party wagon. That, too, wasn't entirely proper. Staff shouldn't mingle until hounds were properly bedded down. If a hound happened to be out, the whipper-in should find him or her. This divided the professional whipper-in from the honorary. The honorary would leave the hunt to go to their jobs whether or not a hound was out.

Jason might actually make an honorary whipper-in. She

needed to see if he had hound sense and the even more elusive fox sense or game sense.

Her instincts told her he didn't have the patience. Nor would he shovel shit.

She thought she had time to work this out, to provide him with something for his ego but steer him away from thinking he could handle her sensitive American foxhounds. Deep down, she also knew that he'd not be able to handle Shaker.

What an interesting dilemma.

CHAPTER 4

The winter solstice on December 21 was the sun's fulcrum. The seesaw of light slowly moved upward from that date in the northern hemisphere. Sister watched light as she watched flora and fauna. Country people read nature the way city people read books.

The sun dipped behind the Blue Ridge Mountains before five o'clock Thursday evening, but with the cloud cover, the underside of the gray fleece darkened to charcoal. Hounds curled up in the kennels, and foxes wrapped their brushes around their noses down in their burrows.

Target, finally back in his den, pushed around a Day-Glo Frisbee he'd carried home at summer's end. A baseball cap, an undershirt, and two nice ballpoint pens bore testimony to his desire for material goods. Once he'd taken a class ring, but he later put it outside his den where Sister and Crawford Howard, then on excellent terms, found it.

Before turning in for the night, Sister drove over to Tedi's, parked her truck, and walked through the snow to Target's den. She inhaled deeply, smelling the big red secure within. Given his run for the day, she refilled a five-gallon plastic can of kibble, coating it with corn oil. This rested not far from his main entrance.

She knelt down, snow reflecting the fading lavender light. "Target, pay more attention. You're getting sloppy."

He barked back at the human he had known all his life, *"I know."*

She smiled when she heard his bark, took off her glove, reached into her pocket, and dropped a large milkbone into his den. As she walked back by the covered bridge she passed the grave of Tedi and Edward Bancroft's eldest daughter, Nola, buried next to Peppermint, Nola's favorite hunter, a big gray. Snow covered the lovely stone-walled enclosure. The marble grave markers were flat on the land and covered with snow.

Sister paused for a moment. One of the deep bonds she shared with the Bancrofts was that both had lost a child. Unfortunately, Sister had had but one son, whereas the Bancrofts still had Sybil. Sister envied people little in life, but she did envy those with healthy children. Her son, Raymond Jr., had died at fourteen in a tractor accident. He'd be forty-six now.

"You missed a good one today, Nola," Sister said to the grave marker. "Pepper, you would have loved it, too. We nearly chopped Target, God forbid, and the crows mobbed him across the wildflower meadow. There's a foot of snow on the ground. Feels like more coming." She lingered for a moment. A rustle in the bridge told her someone was returning to his winter nest, a brave little wren who had stayed out late. He was scolded by his mate, wrens possessing an infinite variety of scold notes. The spat soon dissipated. She smiled, then added, from Psalm 118:24: "This is the day that the Lord hath made; let us rejoice and be glad in it."

As she started the truck Sister hoped that Nola's soul, for all her wild ways when she was alive, had found peace and joy in whatever lay beyond.

The formidable and incredibly snotty Mrs. Amos Arnold, Sister's mother-in-law, F.F.V. (First Families of Virginia), had insisted that Raymond Jr., who'd died in 1974, and then Sister's husband, Raymond, who'd died in 1991, be buried at Hollywood Cemetery in Richmond, a place where a president rested as well as numerous generals, admirals, senators, and other worthies. Sister, although she preferred having her loved ones near, had not protested. It wasn't that she feared Lucinda Arnold as much as she pitied her. All the old woman had was her bloodlines and her pilgrimages to her own husband's grave, then that of her son and grandson. In her mid-nineties, she had let these visitations become an obsession, although she seemed in no hurry to join her three beloved men.

Sister turned east after passing through the simple gates to After All Farm. The roads, even the back roads, were clear. Within seven minutes she had turned down the winding dirt road, snow packed, to the old Lorillard place.

She parked the truck and knocked on the faded red door. She laughed to herself that the color could be named "Tired Blood" in honor of the old vitamin ads promising to pep up your tired blood.

"Come on in," Sam Lorillard's voice called out.

She opened the door, welcomed by the fragrance of wood burning in the fireplace.

Sam, emerging from the kitchen, brushed off his hands. "Let me take your coat."

"You've accomplished a lot since my last visit."

"Thanks. Next task, rewire the whole joint. Then replumb. Little by little, Gray and I are getting it done. I'm glad he gave up his rental and moved in with me. We get along most times."

"Good," she remarked. During Sam's long tenure with alcohol the brothers had barely spoken.

"Coffee?" he asked.

"Tea. If you have any. Something hot would be good. Where is Gray, by the way? He left after hunting this morning with Garvey Stokes. I barely had time to speak to either of them."

"Running late."

"Ah." She sat down, her hand gliding over the porcelain-topped kitchen table like the one from her childhood. She traced the red pinstripe along the edge. "Don't see these anymore."

"Too practical." Sam smiled. "Everything today is made to self-destruct in seven years. Our whole economy runs on obsolescence."

"Is that what you learned at Harvard?"

"Actually, what I learned was to drink with style and abandon."

She noted all the cookbooks on top of the shelves. "Sam, if you remove those cookbooks I reckon your roof will cave in."

"That's our spring project. Rebuild the whole kitchen. No choice but to rewire, then." He placed a large, dark green ceramic pot of tea before her, along with a bowl of small brown sugar cubes. Then he sat down and poured her tea into a delicate china cup at least one hundred fifty years old. The pale bone china had pink tea roses adorning its surface. "Great-grandmother's."

"M-m-m, the Lorillards knew good things. White Lorillards, too."

"They knew enough to buy us," Sam joked. "And we knew enough to buy ourselves free, too."

"Ghosts. So many ghosts." She sipped the bracing tea. "Sam, what is this? It's remarkable."

"Yorkshire. A tearoom called Betty's, which has the best teas I've ever tasted—and the cakes aren't bad either. I love the north of England."

"I do, too. And Scotland."

A silence followed, which Sam broke. "Funny, isn't it? The chickens come home to roost. I'm lucky to have a roost." He stared into his teacup, then met Sister's eyes. "You know, you were one of the few people who would talk to me down at the train station. You spoke to me like I was still a human being."

"Sam, no one asks to be born afflicted, and I consider alcoholism an affliction even if there is an element of choice to it. You threw away your education, your friends, but you've come around."

"Rory, too." Sam mentioned his friend from his train station days who had cleaned up his act, thanks to Sam, and now worked at Crawford's alongside Sam. "We finished up early today, which is why I called. Thanks for coming over."

"Visited Target, so it wasn't far to visit you." She smiled.

He brightened. "Heard you had a good one."

"Did. Target damn near got himself killed. So what's the buzz, Sam?" She got to the point.

"Let me preface this by saying that Crawford can be a peculiar man. He's egotistical and vain, and it's difficult for him to realize other people know more than he does in specific areas. On the plus side he's generous, actually does learn from his mistakes eventually, and he treats me better than most other people would. He's a good boss. He comes down to the stable, bursting with ideas from whatever he's just read, but if I take the time to point out what's commercially driven in those articles along with what has always worked for me with horses, he listens. He's like most people who didn't grow up with horses; he thinks he can read about them and become a rider."

"Woods are full of those." Sister shook her head. She, like other masters, had seen it all and heard it all.

The hunt field usually sorted people out in a hurry. No matter how bright they were, no matter how much they could talk about staying over the horse's center of gravity, either they could stick on the horse or they couldn't. And sometimes even a fine rider couldn't stick. Sooner or later even the best would eat a dirt sandwich.

"He's going to start his own pack. He's found a pack in the Midwest that's disbanding, and he's buying the whole works: the hounds, the hound trailer, even the collars. He's also called Morton Structures to put up a kennel."

"In winter?"

"He's clearing out the old hay shed for temporary kennels."

"Jesus Christ!" She whistled.

"He'll hunt his own land, obviously, but he'll poach your fixtures." Sam was referring to land hunted by Jefferson Hunt; Sister, as master, lovingly nurtured the relationships with the landowners, people she quite liked. "You know, Sister, most landowners don't understand the rules of the MFHA. They figure if it's their land they can have anyone hunt it." He named the Master of Foxhounds Association of America.

"Well, they can. It is their land. What they really don't understand is what an outlaw pack can do to the community: tear it up."

"Overhunts the foxes. Creates accountability problems. If a fence is knocked apart or cattle get out, who did it? And it sure puts hunt clubs at one another's throats." Sam felt terrible about this.

"I know," Sister grimly replied. "But I will bet you dollars to doughnuts, Jefferson Hunt will acquire the lion's share of the blame precisely because we are accountable. Let a hound pass over someone's land, especially someone new to the area, and they assume it's one of ours. You wouldn't believe the calls I receive, not all of them friendly. Shaker or I dutifully go out, we catch the hound, often a Coonhound or a Walker hound, we explain to the caller that it isn't our hound but we will try to find the owner. And then we spend hours on the phone doing just that. If we don't find the owner, we find a home for it because people have strange ideas about hounds. They don't adopt them from the shelters. It's sad because hounds are such wonderful animals and so easy to train."

"Can you imagine what this pack will be like?" Sam raised an eyebrow.

"No. Do you know what kind of foxhounds they are?"

"No."

"M-m-m, puts you in a bad spot."

"He asked me to hunt the hounds, and I told him I can't. I don't know anything about hunting hounds, and that's the truth. He's going to hunt them himself."

"Sweet Jesus."

"He'll need Jesus," Sam laughed.

"So will I, Sam, so will I. No Jefferson Hunt master since 1887 has had to deal with an outlaw pack." She paused, then changed the subject, since it made her feel dreadful. "Getting Matador vetted. I'll let you know."

They heard the rumble of Gray's Land Cruiser. Then the door opened. "Hello."

"Hi back at you," Sister called out.

Gray walked in. He removed his lad's cap and hung it on the peg by the back door along with his worn but warm old red plaid Woolrich coat. He kissed Sister on the cheek, his military moustache tickling slightly. "Tea still hot?"

"Yep."

Gray grabbed a mug from the cabinet and sat down. "Sam, didn't you offer Sister anything to eat?"

"Uh, no."

"Worthless."

"Honey, would you like a tuna fish sandwich, a fried egg sandwich, or a variety of cookies which Sam had stashed in all those tins on the counter unless you ate them all?" He directed his gaze at his younger brother.

"The double chocolate Milanos."

"Sam," Gray grumbled. "My favorite."

"Well, they're mine, too, and I didn't have time to stop by Roger's Corner on the way home. I'll buy some tomorrow."

"I can't tempt you?" Gray asked Sister.

"Not with cookies." She smiled.

Gray poured honey in his tea and smiled sexily back at her. "Sam tell you the latest?"

"There will be hell to pay before it's all over," she responded.

"I expect." He nodded.

"How'd your day go?"

"After a glorious start hunting, then going to Garvey's plant, I met with an architect." He looked at his brother. "I finally broke down and hired one. We can't do this ourselves, Sam. It's just too big a job. I spent three hours there. We both need to go back." He sipped his tea. "Garvey Stokes wants an independent audit of his books. Meant to tell you that straight up. The architect is on my mind. Anyway, I told Garvey I'd be happy to perform the audit. So now I'm semi-retired instead of retired," he joked. Gray had been a partner in one of the most prestigious accounting firms in Washington, D.C. Two former directors of the IRS graced the firm's roster.

"Garvey should change the name of his company from Aluminum Manufacturers to Metalworks. He can work with anything: copper, iron, steel, titanium. Can you imagine working with titanium?" Gray added to Sam's information.

Sister laughed. "I wish he would make a titanium stock pin."

"Now there's a thought. Even the steel-tipped ones eventually bend," Gray agreed.

Sam turned on the stove to heat more water. "Why does Garvey want an independent audit?"

"The usual in these situations; he's not a detail guy. And he feels something isn't right. Also, just in case, he wants to be prepared for an IRS audit. We'll see." Gray truly liked accounting, but he realized most people found it boring.

"Iffy's Garvey Stokes' treasurer. How's she going to take this?" Sister wondered.

"She's a glorified bookkeeper, and she wasn't happy to see me," Gray said good-naturedly. "I assured her the audit was not a reflection on her skills but good business practices. I didn't feel right pulling rank on a woman in a wheelchair." He paused. "But I will if she forces me."

"Wheelchair?" Sister exclaimed. "I saw her last month and she was walking with a cane."

"She can get around just fine." Sam endured Iffy. "She glories in the sympathy."

"The good Lord didn't grant Iffy the best personality in the world. It, too, has deteriorated. But hey, we don't suffer from lung cancer. She's battling it. Let's give her a little room to be testy."

Sam countered his brother's comment. "Gray, Iphigenia Demetrios was born a bitch. She'll always be a bitch, lung cancer or not."

"I expect," Gray agreed, with resignation.

"The New Year looks like it will start out with a bang. Crawford's buying an entire pack of hounds, and Jefferson Hunt will pay for his every mistake. The club loses a boatload of money as he closes his wallet. Iffy will not be Miss Sweetness and Light as you go about your business," Sister said. Then she looked down from Gray to Sam. "And if Crawford thinks you favor me or Jefferson Hunt, he'll crack down on you. He's a hard man that way."

"True. No middle ground with Crawford. You're either with him or against him." Sam nodded.

"Those are the problems," said Gray. "Here are the good things for the New Year. The three of us are healthy. I'm back in the saddle again in all respects." He laughed an infectious laugh. "And we'll solve problems together. Who wants an easy life? No glory there."

"Honey, we'll be covered in glory." Sister loved his enthusiasm.

CHAPTER 5

A few lazy snowflakes twirled to earth at nine in the morning, Friday, December 30. Iphigenia Demetrios, at her office before anyone else, heard the front door open and close repeatedly as three officers of Aluminum Manufacturers came to work. Three assistants also arrived. It was a cozy office, in contrast to the large plant with high windows that housed the machinery and workers. To date no women worked in the pit, as Iffy called it.

Hearing Garvey's cheery voice, she waited a beat, then hit the button on her motorized wheelchair. Before he had time to check his e-mail, Iffy rolled into the sparse office, the whirr of the wheelchair motor noticeable.

"Good morning, Iffy."

"Morning." She had a file folder in her lap. "Here." She came alongside, handing it over.

"What's that?" He glanced at the folder.

"The invoice from Tiptop Trucking for the copper delivery. I stopped by when I was in Richmond yesterday. Paid the bill while I was there."

He opened the folder. "Okay," handing it back.

"Stopped by Farmers Trust main office, but I also popped in Wachovia, BB&T, and Crestar, too. Never hurts to keep the relationships fresh; right?"

He smiled. "Those last-Thursday-of-the-month trips to Richmond probably keep other relationships fresh."

A warm smile crossed her face. "I wish."

"You need to get out more."

"I'm going to the patient support group. Tonight's our New Year's celebration. No booze. No outlandish behavior, but we are celebrating Alfred DuCharme's two-year anniversary. So far he's cancer free."

"That is a celebration." Garvey paused. "Really, there's no liquor?"

"Some of our people are in chemo."

"Can't drive?" Garvey inquired.

"Some can. Funny, too: radiation and chemo affect people so differently. It nauseated me, but my hair didn't fall out." She paused. "After our little party I expect a few of us will toast our health."

"You know Alfred won't miss the chance to celebrate," Garvey mentioned, for Alfred was known to like a stiff drink.

"No, he won't." She thought a moment. "It's the uncertainty, Garvey. You think you've banished it, then a few days before your check-up, fear creeps in. Getting the all-clear is such a relief. Two years and his cancer hasn't returned."

"Yours won't come back either."

"I hope not." She tapped the arm of her wheelchair. "I just

had a bad reaction to some of the treatments. I know the strength will come back to my legs. Still, it's queer." She brightened, naming another member of her group. "But Macey Sorensen lost all feeling in her left hand after radiation. Came back."

"See," he said encouragingly as he leaned his rear against his desk, facing her.

Iffy abruptly switched subjects. "What's the big idea hiring Gray Lorillard? That's a slap in the face."

"We haven't had an independent audit of the books in ten years. It's time. It's good insurance."

"I keep an eye on all that. We're in good shape if the IRS ever calls us in. Besides, he's overpriced."

He glanced out the window. "You know, it's coming down harder."

Iffy kept up with the latest radar pictures. "More snow, a stalled low-pressure system." She waited a beat. "Cash flow's good. Course, if you go forward with this, Gray's fees will suck some of that up."

"I know." He then returned to the subject at hand. "He'll have the use of Angel's old office."

Angel had left this earth to become one at the ripe old age of eighty-four. Garvey let her keep working because he knew she would have died ten years earlier had she stopped. Angel loved being Garvey's right-hand woman. Like many elderly people she'd had some heart problems. Walter Lungrun, her doctor, noted that apart from her irregular heartbeat she was incredibly healthy. Garvey missed her terribly, not only because her fierce wit kept him thinking as well as laughing but because she could sweep her years for dustings of knowledge. Angel had known generations of the quick and the dead. That long memory helped Garvey when she'd tell him an anecdote or character trait concerning the family of a supplier, customer, or employee. He could never replace her.

They'd found her slumped over her desk, a can of cold Mountain Dew next to her notepad. Walter, as her physician, signed her death certificate.

"At least that office will be used. You've kept it as a shrine."

"One of these days I'll hire a new personal assistant, but I haven't had the heart to look."

"It's been a year, Garvey. She couldn't live forever." Iffy had loathed Angel because the older woman often questioned her.

"She gave it a good try," Garvey replied.

"An auditor is going to take up a lot of my time, and the end of the year is when I have to get everything in order—an entire year's worth of stuff." She emphasized "stuff."

"I appreciate that, but I think it's good timing otherwise. The year is over. The books are closed, so to speak."

"I think it would make more sense to bring him in right after April 15. The tax work would be done. He'd have all that in front of him."

"Iffy, we're going to do this my way," Garvey replied firmly but without rancor.

She glowered at him. "I'll provide Gray with whatever he needs, but don't expect me to fool with him. Or to humor him."

"I reckon Gray Lorillard can take care of himself."

"Certainly seems to be taking care of Sister Jane. Can you believe it. She's at least ten years older than he is!"

Sister was only five years older than Gray.

"And beautiful. She could wear out two men half her age."

"Face-lift."

"I don't know about that, but she's kept herself in shape."

"Boobs don't sag. Probably got those tucked up, too."

"Iffy, what have you got against Jane Arnold?"

She pulled off her black-framed glasses, the latest fashion. "She's an imperious bitch. Just look at the way she walks."

"Ah." The five-foot eight-inch Garvey finally pushed away from his desk to sit in his leather chair.

"Ah, what?"

He shrugged. "Nothing."

"You think I'm jealous because I hobble around when I'm not in this wheelchair, and I'm overweight."

"You're not that overweight. If it worries you, go to Jason and get him to put you on a program. Go to physical therapy. You're going to live, Iffy. Think of it this way: you're one of the few people to endure chemo and radiation and gain weight."

"Very funny."

"Jason said you beat it. He's the best. It hasn't been easy for you. I'm sorry for that. But you're getting mean."

Iffy and Garvey had grown up together, as had many of the people in this part of central Virginia. No reason to mince words.

"Just because I don't like Sister Jane, you think I'm jealous because she still has a great body and I don't. I never did."

"You weren't fat."

That did it. "Fuck you!" She wheeled around as he bit his lips.

"Dammit," he whispered under his breath as he listened to her wheelchair roll toward her office. The light flickered on his phone. "Hello."

"Sonny here. How you doing?"

Garvey smiled at the sound of the banker's deep voice. "All right. Iffy just blew up at me."

"How's she doing?"

"Just told you."

"Lot on her plate," Sonny said simply.

"Oh well." Garvey's tone lightened. "What's the point of having friends if you don't see them through? What's up?"

"I'm sending over the papers to amend your line of credit. Naturally, I'll review everything, but then I have to send it down to North Carolina. Gone are the days when I could do business on a handshake. You'd better brighten Iffy's mood because this falls in her lap."

"You have our corporate report and our tax information. Of course, we haven't done this year's yet, but neither has anyone else."

"The way it is now—thank the federal government for this—I pretty much need to know what you spend for toilet paper on an annual basis."

"If I had back all the time I waste on paperwork, regulations, insurance, and workers' comp red tape, I'd double my profit, I swear." He sighed.

"Brother, be glad you aren't a banker," Sonny simply replied. "I used to love this business. Last night I told Liz I'm retiring at sixty-five. Gone."

"You've got a few years left."

"Not many," Sonny replied. "Oh, before I forget, Custis Hall has begun the search for a new director of alumnae relations and a new head of the theater department. Let Charlotte Norton know if anyone comes to mind."

"I will. Be a nice place to work. If nothing else, think of the vacations."

"Another reason to retire. Liz and I can travel."

They chatted for a few more minutes. Once finished, Garvey walked down to Iffy's office.

Hunched behind her oversized computer screen, Iffy, gold earrings dangling, peered up at him. "Now what?"

"Paperwork from Farmers Trust will be walked over this morning."

"What are you trying to do? Bury me in paperwork?"

"It is all coming down at once, I know." He slid his right hand into his pocket. "If I don't buy aluminum now at this price, I'll pay through the nose by spring. Between the Chinese and Hurricane Katrina's aftermath, I'm lucky to get this price. Everyone needs aluminum."

"I'll get right on it." Her tone was conciliatory, but she didn't apologize for her earlier surliness. "If for some reason this isn't feasible—I mean that in terms of the interest rates, of course—we'll get more credit, but it might make sense to float a short-term loan for the purposes of buying the aluminum. I'll call around and check the interest rates. Could have asked yesterday when I was down in Richmond." She mumbled, as if to herself. "No point paying more interest than needs be."

"Good idea, but bear in mind we want to keep our relationship with Farmers Trust strong."

She turned her wheelchair away from the screen. "Money talks. Bullshit walks."

"Right." He left the office, but they did smile at each other.

That evening, the snow, having fallen steadily all day, although not heavy, accumulated six more inches. The sun set just before five. The long twilight, enlivened by flakes turning from white to pink to blue, finally surrendered to darkness.

Raleigh and Rooster slept in their large fleece-lined dog beds in the kitchen while Sister fiddled with garden plans spread over the table, knowing that the best time to plan a garden is in the dead of winter. Colored pencils filled a white ceramic jam jar.

Humming to herself, she drew a purple line around a corner bed. "More iris. Masses of iris."

Golly, on the table holding down the papers, flicked her fluffy tail. *"Catnip. Don't forget to plant catnip."*

The phone rang. Sister rose to lift the receiver off the wall phone. "Hello."

"Sister, it's Tootie." None of Anne Harris's fellow students at Custis Hall called her anything but Tootie, nor did anyone else.

"How good to hear your voice."

"I wanted to hear yours." Her young voice betrayed her loneliness.

Sister heard the emotion. "The hounds will be glad to see you. Mrs. Norton and Bunny hunted yesterday. Great day, really. You would have loved it."

"We'll be back on Wednesday the fourth, so if Bunny says it's okay, I can hunt Thursday. I miss it. Hope Val and Felicity can come, too." She named her two best school friends.

"I'll cross my fingers," Sister replied.

Tootie said, "Wonder when we'll find out which colleges accepted us? Dad really wants me to go to Princeton."

"It's a great institution."

A long pause followed. "I know."

"Tootie, you have a little time to sort this out. I know you aren't too enthused about Princeton even though you applied. It will all work out, one way or t'other." She used the old pronunciation "t'other." She added, "And you can always talk to me."

"And Iota." Tootie mentioned her horse, already feeling better.

"Iota knows more than all of us."

Sister hung up and returned to her rough drawings. Golly, paw on colored pencils, was now sprawled over them. Judging from the teethmarks, Sister surmised the calico favored something yellow.

The phone rang again. It was Anselma Wideman, who with her husband a year ago had bought Little Dalby, a lovely old place of two thousand acres. The middle-aged couple dedicated themselves to refurbishing the house, restoring the outbuildings.

Once owned by the Viault family, it had been one of the main fixtures used by the Jefferson Hunt. When the last Viault died, the place, sliding downhill anyway, picked up speed, so the Widemans' efforts were welcomed by hunters as well as by those who valued architecture and history.

"Sister, Harvey and I agreed to allow Crawford to hunt Little Dalby. He said he wouldn't be here when you are, and Marty has been so good to us, I didn't see how we could refuse."

Marty Howard, Crawford's wife, had designed and helped renovate the house gardens at Little Dalby. She and Anselma had become friends in the process.

"I understand, and I'm sure Crawford and I can work out some accommodation." Sister hung up and cursed, "Goddammit, it's already started."

CHAPTER 6

Central Virginia Medical Center, although not part of Jefferson Regional Hospital, sat two blocks away from that highly respected institution. Many of the doctors at JRH, as they referred to it, rented space in the two-year-old complex.

A lovely black band of bricks in a diamond pattern halfway up the four-story structure broke up the red brickwork. The large double-paned windows allowed much natural light into the rooms.

What was distinctive about the offices was their layout. The developer, Melvin Sweigart, knew physicians liked to group together by specialty, if possible. He figured it was the same principle as car dealers setting up shop next to one another.

Melvin had created internal squares, small quads. The offices surrounded the quads, and hallways connected the various quads.

Garvey Stokes had made special stainless steel sinks and tables for the center, as some procedures could be performed in the office. This saved a patient money.

The cardiac quads were on the first floor. The cancer quads were on the second. The third floor was dedicated to sports medicine. The top floor, flooded with light from gorgeous pyramidal skylights, housed the plastic surgeons.

A further advantage of this arrangement was it allowed the doctors in the various specialties to pool their resources if they wished.

Walter Lungrun and his associates bought the highest-tech heart monitors available, just as Jason Woods and his associates purchased an x-ray machine for forty-two thousand dollars.

The sports medicine group on the third floor went so far as to buy a magnetic resonance imaging machine for eight hundred thousand dollars. The other physicians rented time on it.

While the hospital provided this equipment, too, the doctors at Central Virginia realized nine out of ten people never want to set foot in a hospital. The antiseptic odor alone upset people, and the impersonality of it added to the psychological discomfort.

The more procedures that could be performed in this pleasant environment, the better from the patient's point of view.

Business exploded. Walter had just hired another nurse, and Jason had to hire another head nurse and another secretary. Even with those expenses and the exorbitant insurance the doctors were forced to carry, they made money.

So successful was the design for Central Virginia Regional Center that Melvin Sweigart was buying up old houses downtown to build another. Crawford Howard was a partner in this enterprise. He was considering buying out the company that disposed of waste—biological hazards, as they were now coined—since he thought he could do this more profitably than Sanifirm.

While the snow continued to fall, the survivors' party hit high gear at seven in Jason's quad.

Birdie Goodall, a pert thirty-two, office manager for this quad, ladled out the nonalcoholic punch.

Iffy held out her glass cup. "Did you put ginger ale in for sparkle?"

"I did."

Alfred DuCharme tiptoed behind Iffy, reached around, and, holding a paper bag with a bottle inside, poured in a touch of something stronger. "Here's your sparkle, girl."

Birdie winked at Alfred. "Works for me."

He reached over and poured some into her own cup. "Say goodbye to your troubles." Then he held up his glass to the twenty partyers, all of whom had their hair again, "Here's to a New Year!"

"Happy New Year," they agreed.

Another raised his glass cup again. "And here's to Mr. Jason, without whom we wouldn't be here."

A clamorous cry filled the quad.

Jason demurred, then lifted his own glass. "You have fought the good fight. It was a team effort."

The patients all knew one another, if not before treatment, because of treatment. They were all in it together. Jason made a point of speaking to each person, wishing each one health and happiness.

Birdie called out at one point, "Hey, don't forget your insurance forms if you haven't turned them in! I promise no more business."

This brief interruption was followed by more partying. Iffy, using a cane, wearied of standing and sat behind the table of treats, so she enjoyed many conversations. Her demeanor, so different from that at work, was relaxed and warm. Among the other soldiers, as they thought of themselves, she flourished.

Birdie glanced out the window at eight-thirty. "Still coming down."

Alfred also noticed the heavier snows as he walked over to Iffy. "Would you like me to drive you home? I'm going to leave."

"No, thanks. I don't have as far to go as you do, and the plows have been pretty good."

"That they have. Now if only they'd plow the roads on the farm." He smiled. "Well, Old Bessie will get me through." He named his rusty four-wheel-drive truck.

"By the way, Al, whatever you put in my punch makes me feel warm all over."

He patted the flat bottle, still in brown paper, in his inside jacket pocket. "And here I thought it was me."

"You, too." She smiled.

He leaned down conspiratorially, kissing her on the cheek. "To health and wealth."

The small gathering broke up at nine. Birdie handed Jason three insurance forms.

"Paperwork." He sighed.

"Well, if you'd asked Alfred for his bottle you'd fly through it." She smiled.

"I would. Of course, whatever I wrote would be illegible."

"I'll see you next year."

"Next year, Birdie. And may it be a good one."

Fifteen minutes later, Walter knocked on Jason's open door.

"You missed the party," said Jason.

Walter smiled. "Special group. They didn't need an intruder. Hey, do you have a Tom Thumb Pelham I can borrow?" Walter mentioned a type of bit.

"Rocketman?" Jason smiled, for Walter's young horse could be strong.

Clemson, the older hunter who had given Walter confidence when he started foxhunting, went in a simple snaffle. The Clemsons of this world were worth their weight in gold.

"Thought I'd try it before buying one."

"I'll bring it by."

Walter stared down at the papers on Jason's desk. "Me, too. I'm determined to get the damn paperwork done so I can really enjoy New Year's. I love the bowl games."

"Even with Birdie, I can't keep up with this shit." Jason disgustedly pushed the papers away.

"Insurance."

"Biggest scam in America." Jason's dark eyebrows knitted together.

Walter folded his arms across his massive chest. "Remember when we thought forty thousand a year in insurance was a ripoff?"

Jason rose from his chair. "What I don't understand is why we put up with it."

"Two reasons." Walter obviously had thought about this. "Doctors are scientists, right? We aren't by nature businessmen. We don't have a lot of free time. Our work can be emotionally exhausting."

"Right. That's more than two reasons." Jason smiled at him, one eyebrow now quizzically raised.

"One. Let me go back to the fact that we are scientists. That means we aren't accustomed to banding together for political purposes."

"We have the AMA," said Jason, referring to the American Medical Association.

"And what have they done about these crushing insurance burdens?" Walter uncrossed his arms. "In my darker moments I think the AMA is in collusion with the insurance companies."

"No." Jason shook his head. "The AMA isn't corrupt. Ineffective sometimes."

"I don't know." Walter walked to the window, which looked out over the back of the building.

"One thing, we lose hospital privileges if we don't carry the insurance."

"Yep."

"Look on the bright side, Walter. We could be OB/GYNs."

Walter sighed but nodded in agreement, for gynecologists and obstetricians were bent double by their insurance load.

"Donny Sweigart, in the snow, picking up the trash." Walter looked sideways at Jason, who now stood next to him. "Ever notice that Sweigarts are either really smart or . . . really not?"

"We know where Donny falls. Funny how after his father died in that warehouse fire he demanded that no one call him Junior."

"Was." Walter watched as the younger man, of medium build and wearing heavy coveralls, lifted tightly tied plastic bags into the large truck.

"He's a good truck driver."

"Think Crawford will buy Sanifirm?"

"I don't know, but if he does I bet Donny still has a job."

"Not if he keeps poaching, he won't."

"Deer?" Jason wasn't a deer hunter.

"Donny will sneak on your property and pretty much shoot whatever he can, although deer are his preferred target. He'll do it out of season, too."

"He doesn't shoot foxes, does he?" Jason sounded scandalized.

"Sister put a stop to that."

"I'll bet she did." The corner of Jason's lips curled upward in a half smile.

"She's too much of a fox herself to crack on him. She pays him off."

"No kidding?"

"Out of her own pocket. No hunt club funds are touched. She asks him to tell her where the dens are, so he's a consultant."

"But she knows where they are."

"Like I said, Jason. She's part fox." What Walter wanted to add, but didn't, was "Never underestimate the old girl. Never."

CHAPTER 7

December 31 is St. Sylvester's Day, commemorating a pope who died in 335 AD. He tolerated all religions and is credited with building many churches, including the first St. Peter's in Rome.

St. Sylvester probably would have stayed inside this Saturday, for the snow lay deep on top of the foot-deep base. Occasional squalls still cast down flurries. Snow plows worked through the night, so the roads were reasonably decent if one drove prudently.

As it was the New Year's Hunt, the last of the four foxhunting High Holy Days, forty-two people braved the weather to gather at Beveridge Hundred, a Jefferson Hunt fixture since 1887, the founding year of the club. Beveridge Hundred remained in the Cullhain family. The current crop of Cullhains struggled on. Their money had disappeared in 1865 along with some of their men, dying agonizing deaths in America's worst war. The survivors had pulled themselves back up, only to fall destitute again during the Great Depression. In deference to their pinched financial position, club members brought dishes for the traditional hunt breakfast. Walter supplied the drinks, which eased the burden on this most genial collection of relatives.

Hounds got up one fox for a short burst and then another, but the deep snows kept foxes close to their dens. By noon, everyone had filled the old mansion, whose outside and inside were badly in need of paint. A few spots, plaster off, revealed laths stuffed with horsehair. The piano in the parlor was put to good use. Jason Woods, a clear tenor, paired with Walter's baritone. Soon everyone sang with them.

Hounds were already back in the kennels by the time the humans reached the desserts.

Hunt staff's first responsibility was the hounds or staff horses, depending on their position. Rarely did Shaker attend a breakfast, although he might be able to get to a tailgate once the hounds were in the party wagon, the small horse trailer outfitted to carry them. A quick sandwich or muffin before he pulled out, accompanied by hot coffee, kept him going until he could really replenish his body. Huntsmen burn calories the way prairie fire burns grass.

Betty Franklin and Sybil Bancroft Fawkes, although honorary whippers-in, not paid staff, still performed all staff functions. They too didn't attend the breakfasts until hounds were in the party wagon or in the kennel, horses cooled out, blankets thrown over them.

Later, back in the barn, Betty Franklin and Sister cleaned tack in the heated tackroom. Shaker, with Sybil's help and that of her two sons of grade-school age, had fed all the hounds and even rubbed soothing bag balm on their pads. No one's pads had been cut up, as there wasn't much ice, but Shaker figured an ounce of prevention was worth a pound of cure. The two boys felt important to help with a big job. Sybil appreciated Shaker's thoughtfulness. Her marriage, a disaster, had left her a single mother. She liked her sons to be around real men, and Shaker was about as real as it got.

Sari, Lorraine Rasmussen's daughter, and Jennifer, Betty's daughter, were home from Colby College on Christmas vacation. They washed down the staff horses and asked to clean tack, but Sister sent them on their way. She knew both girls wanted to primp for a big New Year's Eve party, although first they had to attend Betty's party.

As Betty finished washing the bits, hanging Shaker's bridle on a tack hook high over a bucket, she asked, "When does Gray start at Aluminum Manufacturers?"

"Tuesday. Thought Garvey might be with us today, but maybe the roads aren't as good out his way." Sister paused. "Iffy won't take kindly to what she considers a footprint in her garden."

"Iffy's been a pill since birth."

Sister laughed so hard she startled Raleigh and Rooster, who barked. "Oh, shut up. It's just me. Go back to sleep. Betty, savage but true."

"She isn't that bad looking. A bit of a dumpling, but pretty enough. She's so sour no man would have her."

"No woman either." Sister laughed.

"Who do you think is pickier? Men or women?"

"Men."

"See, I think it's women." Betty answered her own question.

"Maybe men and women are picky about different things. Men get very distracted by looks. Women get distracted by promises. And both get what they deserve."

"Ain't that the truth. You'd better go into marriage with your eyes wide open."

"Betty, you no more did that than I did. When you're young you can't possibly know the changes the years bring. Love is blind, for which I suppose we should give some thanks, or there'd be no next generation."

"Ha!" Betty wrung out a soft rag before rubbing it on saddle soap, her first step in cleaning the leather.

"Ha, what? I know that tone of voice."

"Sex. Nothing can keep the human animal from sex. No laws, no religion, not even the threat of death. In the old days it was syphilis. Now it's AIDS. We're fools breeding fools, and we always were."

"I did my share," grinned Sister, alluding to her very rich past.

"You did all right." Betty wiped down the leather after the saddle soap. "Back to Iffy. I heard she was seeing a lot of Alfred DuCharme. Hard to believe."

"Lord." Sister raised her eyebrows. "Hadn't heard that. Let's keep on the good side of Alfred. He allows us to hunt Paradise. Took awhile to bring Binky around to it, so we need Alfred to be especially happy with us. Iffy, on a whim, could toss a monkey wrench into the works. Especially if she gets mad at Gray. She'll take it out on the club."

Binky, Alfred's older brother, had stolen Alfred's girlfriend, Milly Archer, a west end Richmond girl, back in 1975. Alfred had never forgiven Binky.

Regardless of Binky's entreaties, Alfred refused to attend

the marriage. He wouldn't even wave to his brother or his sister-in-law if he passed them on the road.

When their father, Brenden, had died he'd kept the land intact. He thought this would force them to cooperate, and thus reconcile, without him alive to be a go-between. He figured wrong.

Instead, Binky and Milly's daughter, the bright and spunky Margaret, soon found herself filling in for her departed grandfather and mediating between her father and her uncle.

Embittered though he remained toward Binky and Milly, Alfred worshipped his niece, a sports physician at Jefferson Regional Hospital.

The brothers lived in separate dependencies, small houses, near the ruins of the main house. The one time they had been seen together willingly was at Margaret's graduation.

"Yep. Funny how people shoot themselves in the foot. Think of the happiness Alfred has missed. He doesn't stick with a woman long. Maybe that's why he's going out with Iffy. He thinks she'll be dead soon, so he won't have to dump her. Or vice versa." Betty giggled, finished cleaning Shaker's bridle. "You stripped your bridle. I didn't strip Shaker's. I washed it, then used saddle soap."

Stripping took more time as one used something like castile soap to wash it, then rub it even cleaner. After this, one hangs it up and reapplies a light leather oil with a clean cloth. Then one uses the heat of one's fingers to rub it again, lastly wiping all down once more with a clean dry cloth.

"I know. I'm being superstitious, so I went the whole nine yards."

"Any other superstitions besides cleaning way too thoroughly?"

"I count the spoons in the house."

"What?"

"I count the spoons in the house."

"Why?" Betty looked at her.

"I don't know. My mother did it and her mother did it every New Year's Eve. I know it's stupid—but hey, you asked me and I told you. What do you do?"

"Make resolutions. The usual. I will lose weight."

"You don't need to lose any more weight, Betty."

"I'm so used to making that as a New Year's resolution, I can't stop."

"See, that's why I have to count the spoons. I've always done it."

Another forty-five minutes passed between the two close friends, who could open their hearts to each other as well as talk about substantive issues sprinkled with the paprika of gossip.

The phone rang in the tack room.

"Hello. Hi, Walter."

"Jason Woods cornered me at breakfast after you left. He said you didn't think he knew how to whip-in."

"That's not what I said."

"I know. You'd be more diplomatic. He's taking this as"—a note of humor filled Walter Lungrun's voice—"a slur on his manliness."

"Jesus Christ, spare me a man who isn't one."

"He's okay, Sister. He's just one of those people who needs attention, adoration. He's very good at what he does."

"So are a lot of other people. If you aren't at the top 20 percent, you slide into mediocrity, I reckon. But that's not the point. The point is, what do we do with this twit?" She went on to explain her entire conversation with Jason concerning how Jefferson Hunt develops whippers-in. "And I apologize. I should have told you, but I thought he'd be smart enough to let it go. Or if not, then show up this summer to start walking puppies."

Betty listened, attention rapt.

"If he would do that, would you and Shaker work with him?"

"Of course, if he has aptitude. Look, I know he can ride. He has that beautiful chestnut gelding, Kilowatt. That's not the issue. It's the rest of it. I have yet to see him evidence any interest in even one hound, much less the pack, and he wants to whip-in?"

Walter, putting his feet on the hassock in his den, replied in a relaxed voice. "But if he does the real work, the hard work in the off-season, will you and Shaker work with him?"

"Yes."

"Do you mind if I call him and discuss this? I'll relay our conversation."

"No. I'm grateful. Gets me off the hook."

"Not if he shows up in April." Walter grunted when his Welsh terrier launched into his lap.

"Means early morning four-thirty or five o'clock wake-ups. We try to knock out the walks, the individual puppy walk, too, before ten in the morning. Once we cruise out of spring into summer, you know how fast that heat comes up. Stifling."

"Sticky hot." He thought for a moment. "The bait Jason dangled in front of me, so you know, is he will contribute ten thousand dollars annually to the Club."

She interrupted, something she rarely did. "Oh, if that's not a bribe!"

"Sister, with all due respect, Jason possesses considerable resources."

"Okay, Walter, you're managing me, but I get it."

He laughed. "I am. Bluntly put: Better to have Jason in the tent pissing out than outside the tent pissing in."

She exhaled through her nostrils. "You're right, but I'll be goddamned if I'm going to start creating whippers-in of people who write big checks. I just won't."

"Well, let's see how it plays."

After hanging up, Sister relayed Walter's half of the conversation to her curious friend.

"Who knows? He might turn out all right." Betty clearly supported Walter in this. "Since you, Shaker, Sybil, and myself might be working with Dr. Woods, let's list his good qualities."

A brief silence was followed by Sister saying, "Brilliant intellectually. Driven. Rich, although some of that wealth has to be inherited. We've never met his people, you know. He rarely mentions them except that they live in Newport Beach, California. Let's see. Well, he's handsome."

"Succumbs to flattery, especially from women," Betty added.

The two women looked at each other and laughed. "What man doesn't?"

"I'm on empty."

"By the time you know whether he really can make a whipper-in, you'll have figured out how to handle him," Betty said.

"Or he'll have figured out how to handle me."

"That's easy." Betty tossed her sponge in the bucket. "Do what you say."

CHAPTER 8

The glow of candlelight and the free flow of champagne improved everyone's complexions.

Betty and Bobby Franklin's modest, pretty clapboard house sat on forty acres. Bobby had wanted to name this patch of land Mortgage Manor, but Betty prevailed, and the name remained Tricorn Farm, for once a hatter had lived here who made tricorns in the eighteenth century.

The hunt membership plus flotsam and jetsam from town and country jammed into the traditionally decorated house. A time traveler from colonial Williamsburg would have felt at home. Jennifer and Sari, after dutifully greeting guests, sped away to a party where the median age was twenty. At the Franklins' the median age had to be forty, which for two girls in their freshman year at Colby College might as well have been one hundred and ten.

While the Franklins' daughter and Sari might have had no need of candlelight's soft glow, it added to Sister Jane's natural radiance. The soft glow didn't hurt Tedi and Edward Bancroft, either.

It most certainly didn't hurt Frederika Thomas, whose creamy cleavage pulsated in the light from the fireplaces, the candles flickering in the two-hundred-fifty-year-old chandeliers. Freddie's bosom, much admired, rose and fell at a pace she controlled. The more they heaved, the more she sought to impress upon the gentleman (it was usually a gentleman) with whom she spoke that she was deeply impressed with his conversation. Perhaps, given the height of the heave, she might even be sexually interested. When Freddie discovered the power of her mammary glands, she made certain to wear low-cut dresses or blouses. A snug cashmere turtleneck could be worn to good effect as well. Freddie had mastered this technique by eighteen. At thirty-four she had perfected it.

Speaking with Sister, a respectable 38C, which suited her six-foot frame, Freddie kept her glories at a moderate pace with the chat. Freddie admired Sister but had never thought of seducing her. Good thing, because Sister would have laughed herself silly.

"Poor Marty." Freddie's doe eyes widened further. "You just know she's dying to come. This is *the party.* Anyone not invited to the Franklins' winds up at the country club, I suppose. Well, at least Marty will be able to wear her major jewels. Crawford's no cheapskate."

Out of the corner of her eye, Sister saw Iffy in her motorized metal wheelchair festooned with party lights and sparklers, which Iffy intended to set off at midnight. "Marty needs a scooter like Iffy's. I'm surprised those rubies and diamonds don't bend her double."

"I'd kill for those rubies and diamonds."

"You'd have to."

Freddie, possessed of a good sense of humor, laughed at Sister's good-natured jibe. "Good as he is that way, Crawford's a brute to keep her from her friends."

"Once a man takes a position publicly, he rarely backs down or seeks a compromise. It's a particular failing of the gender, I'm afraid, and Crawford is more pigheaded than most."

"You don't think women can be stubborn?"

"I do." Sister's silver hair gleamed in the light. "But with great effort, especially from friends, most women can be brought around to seek a compromise. Maybe I'm making too much of it. I'm upset with Crawford, obviously, and I adore Marty. I miss her already. She was the most P.C. person in the hunt, and even though I often thought she was to the left of Pluto she made me think."

Jason Woods, intent in conversation with Walter, turned his head. Both Freddie and Sister noticed his classic profile simultaneously.

"Divine."

"I'd have to agree." Sister smiled. "But surely you've met him."

"In passing. There's never been enough time to talk, and I was usually stuck with my tick of an ex-boyfriend."

"Jason seems to have a refreshingly low opinion of monogamy," Sister remarked.

"These days so do I." Freddie laughed.

If a male stranger had beheld these two women together, he would have first fixed his gaze on Freddie. At thirty-four, lithe and voluptuous, she'd send the blood south. Eventually his eyes would shift to Sister. Standing there, completely unself-conscious, the older woman burst with raw animal energy. Maybe his blood wouldn't head south, although it would have when she was younger, but even a man half her age would be drawn to her. The energy would pull him—and it pulled women, too, in a different manner.

Some creatures possess this magnetism. Secretariat had it. Archie, Sister's late anchor hound, had it. You just *had* to look at him, the way you had to look at Sister.

Freddie wanted to be like Sister, but she was too concerned with her effect on others. Beautiful as she was, this made her vulnerable. She needed praise to feel feminine, to feel good. Sister woke up in the morning feeling good. If people liked her, fine. If they didn't, well, there were six billion people on earth. There ought to be someone out there they liked.

"I heard your parting with Mick was stormy."

Freddie pursed her lips. "I vented to all my girlfriends, and now I'm ashamed of myself. I should have kept my mouth shut."

The wind rattled the windowpanes. A downdraft sent spark showers flying up in the fireplace and glowing on the firescreens.

Jason made his way to the two women.

"Ladies."

"Jason, you've met Freddie Thomas before, I believe."

"That has been my pleasure, but"—he inclined his head toward the lovely woman—"she was always guarded by a two-toed sloth."

Freddie and Sister burst out laughing.

"You haven't been out hunting," Jason remarked.

"I've been so busy this season, I haven't been out once."

"Freddie has reached that critical juncture in her practice

where she needs to either take a partner or partners or cut back on work so she can enjoy life—which of course means fox-hunting." Sister leaned toward Freddie. "I mean it."

Freddie was a certified public accountant. Gray thought highly of her.

"I'm sitting at the crossroads being a big chicken." She sighed in agreement.

"If you don't get off the crossroads you'll be squashed. Listen to the sage of Roughneck Farm," Sister teased.

"Funny, my image of accountants is of someone dull. I was wrong." Jason assiduously avoided staring at her cleavage.

"I love accounting. I get to study businesses from the inside. I guess I'm a little like Sonny Shaeffer." She nodded toward the florid-faced banker. "I know a little bit about every business, but perhaps not enough to run one."

"Freddie, you could do anything you set your mind to because you're so intelligent." Sister meant that. She turned to make her exit so these two could discover one another but was nearly run over by Iffy, who hit her brakes.

Sister was pinned between Iffy on one side, Jason and Freddie on the other.

"Happy New Year." Iffy appeared festive, although resentment bubbled beneath the surface.

"Happy New Year," the others replied.

"Freddie, did you know that Jason is my doctor?"

"I did."

"He saved my life. If you ever feel a lump anywhere, go to him." She stared at Freddie's bosom.

"I'll bear your advice in mind, although I hope I never need it."

Jason put his hand on Iffy's shoulder. "I've never seen you so lit up."

"How do you mean that?" Iffy sounded a little testy.

"The lights." He pointed to her wheelchair. "If you all will excuse me, I'm going to find Gray."

"He's with Garvey." Iffy's lower lip jutted out. "And I'm mad at both of them."

"Don't stay mad long, Iffy; it's New Year's Eve. And I need you to back up."

"Oh." Iffy turned her head, beeped her horn, and backed up a tad as Binky and Milly DuCharme moved out of the way.

"Happy New Year," Sister greeted husband and wife.

Binky, golden hair laced with gray, wrapped his arm around her waist. "Here's to the two-faced god, Janus. He looks to the past; he looks to the future." With that he gulped his champagne.

Milly, a less enthusiastic drinker, clicked glasses with her husband and Sister. "You look divine in that color."

Sister, in royal blue, laughed. "Thank you, but I'm not divine, or I guess I'd be like Janus."

Leaning very close, Milly whispered, "I don't want to see the future."

"Me neither," Sister agreed.

"What'd you say, Honeybun?" Binky hadn't caught the whispered conversation amidst all the noise.

"That it's best for us not to know what tomorrow brings," Milly chirped.

"We know to not count our chickens before they've hatched." He laughed, then stopped. "One thing is consistent: Alfred."

"Sometimes old wounds are lovingly tended." Milly had lived with the situation since the middle seventies and felt justified in speaking her mind.

Sister, not wishing to criticize either brother, kissed both Binky and Milly on the cheek. "Whatever the year brings, I hope we stay healthy and thankful for our friends." As she sidled through the crowd she thought to herself that the statute of limitations on youthful traumas had run out.

When she reached Gray and Garvey she noticed Iffy doing her best to butt into everything Jason and Freddie had to say to one another.

Garvey noticed, too. "I think she's like a lot of women. She fell in love with her doctor."

"Perhaps," said Sister. Then she added, "Iffy's motto is, 'If I have made just one life miserable, I have not lived in vain.' "

Gray and Garvey laughed, for the sting of truth was in it.

"I'll get my share." Gray smiled.

"Hey, take mine, too. I've been on the short end of her stick for the last week."

"Hopefully Iffy will bow to the inevitable. She'll have her nose out of joint for a while about the audit, but it takes too much energy to stay angry," Sister sighed. "She needs a positive outlet."

"I thought Alfred was an outlet. Course he's not here tonight, since Binky is." Garvey looked over the room. Gray succinctly summed it up. "Iffy and Alfred are so used to being unhappy they don't want to upset the status quo. They're perfect for each other."

Sister held up her champagne flute. The men touched theirs to hers, and the crystal chimed, a high, clear note. "Here's to a New Year filled with new ways and old ways. Over solid bedrock the earth keeps shifting." She knew the Blue Ridge bedrock was granite more than one billion years old. However, no need for her to be pedantic.

"Hear, hear," the men toasted.

Then Garvey laughed. "I don't think I've ever heard a geological toast. Makes me wish I'd been in your geology class at Mary Baldwin."

"How about a toast from your profession?" Gray teased him.

"Put the pedal to the metal." Garvey raised his glass.

"That was too easy!" Sister laughed at him.

"You didn't say it had to be hard." Garvey then looked to Gray. "Your turn."

"Put your money in your head; no one can steal it from you there."

Sister and Garvey clicked their glasses once more.

Meanwhile, Iffy drove right under Freddie's bosom as if to find shade. It's doubtful Iffy could have found a toast for the occasion, but she could have wedged her champagne flute in Freddie's cleavage. Of course, Freddie could have used Iffy as an end table.

Ben Sidell, sheriff of the county, his back to Freddie, half turned and caught Jason's eye. "Dr. Woods, Happy New Year. Iffy"—and he included Freddie when she turned round—"Happy New Year."

"Why aren't you in uniform?" Iffy blurted out, oblivious to the fact that the sheriff was entitled to a private life.

"I worked Christmas Eve and Christmas." He smiled broadly. "Interesting hunt this morning."

"Interesting hunt tonight." The corner of Jason's mouth turned upward.

Ben looked at Jason, then Freddie, then Iffy, and thought this a strange triangle. "I was wondering if any of you could introduce me to the lady standing by the fireplace."

Champagne flute in hand, Dr. Margaret DuCharme leaned against the end of the fireplace.

Jason, unwilling to surrender his spot with Freddie, didn't move.

Nor would Iffy.

Freddie, happy to ditch both of them, took Ben's hand for an instant. "I'd be happy to."

Iffy and Jason were abandoned to one another.

Iffy smiled. Jason's eyes followed Freddie.

Meanwhile, Freddie, voice low, said, "She's a sports medicine doctor. I'm not exactly sure what that means, but she must be very good because the Washington Redskins send her their wounded. Professional golfers fly in to see her, too."

"Married?"

"To her work."

As they drew closer Freddie stepped forward.

Margaret, diminutive and attractive, extended her hand to Ben. "I didn't recognize you out of uniform."

The touch of her hand befuddled him. He stood there speechless.

Freddie, wise in such matters, chatted for a moment. "Everyone knows our sheriff."

Ben recovered, dropping Margaret's hand. She smiled. "If you two will excuse me." Freddie skillfully slipped away.

Jason watched her every move from behind Iffy's wheelchair.

People are like colors: they complement each other or they clash. Ben and Margaret complemented each other. Once Ben had regained his composure they talked easily, lighting up like the sparks flying in the fireplace. And the conversation veered from the superficial immediately. Their physical attraction was obvious. What a partygoer observing them couldn't have known was that their minds were on fire.

Driving home from the party, Sister and Gray noticed Donny Sweigart's truck by the side of the road a quarter of a mile from Crawford's entrance.

The headlights revealed blood on his camouflage fatigues as Donny walked to his truck.

Gray pulled over. Sister opened the window. "Donny, are you all right?"

"Yeah. Deer blood."

"If Crawford catches you here, he'll put the law on you."

Donny smiled slyly. "He's celebrating. Anyway, I'm out of here."

As they drove home, Gray, who planned to spend the night with Sister, said, "He pushes it."

"What I want to know is, where's the deer?"

"Could be down in the meadow."

"He can't drag it out by himself unless he dresses it in the field, and then he runs the risk of Crawford catching him. No deer in the truck bed."

"What the hell is he up to?"

Sister, lips taut: "I don't think we want to know."

CHAPTER 9

The New Year fell on Sunday. It was also the Feast of the Circumcision, a festival honoring the removal of the infant Christ's foreskin. No doubt the early church introduced this celebration to replace pagan New Year frolics whose devotees found other things to do with their foreskins.

Sister, up before dawn, as usual, left Gray in bed sound asleep under a down comforter. Not a drinker, she had enjoyed last night's champagne, but at this moment she enjoyed her hot tea even more.

After feeding the dogs and Golly, she pulled a heavy three-ply cashmere sweater over her head, wrapped a scarf around her neck, slipped her arms into her fleece-lined bomber jacket, and slapped on her cowboy hat.

She stepped outside into a charcoal-gray world and looked

east, where a faint sliver of lighter gray lined the horizon. The snow clouds had cleared out last night. Breathing in the cold air, she felt seventeen years old. Raleigh and Rooster plowed behind her as her boots sank deep into the snow. Hard going though it was, she told herself this was terrific exercise for her thighs.

Not one hound mumbled as she approached the kennels. They always slept well after a hunt, and yesterday's go had pooped them out.

Once inside the kennels, she put the two house dogs in the office. Removing her bomber jacket and draping it over the back of the office chair, she double-checked the clipboard on the desk.

Each hunting day, those hounds selected to go out had red checks by their names. She'd check their pads again, then note if anyone needed a little extra feed. She used the day's roster to determine who would go out next hunt. One of her favorite times was going over the draw list with Shaker. They rated each hound's work during the last hunt and each hound's condition. She loved few things in life as much as her hounds. Raleigh, Rooster, Golly, and all the horses ranked right up there, too.

Then she walked into the feed room, a large square room with a huge drain in the center of the gently sloping concrete floor. The room could be power washed in ten minutes. The temperature inside the feed room was forty-five degrees, but it would rise when the hounds came in, and it would also climb a bit as the sun did.

Keeping hounds at temperatures humans find comfortable produces a sick hound. Their body heat when they sleep together keeps them warm, as does good food. It's cruel to pamper a hound who, God forbid, might become separated from the pack and spend the night hunkered down in a covert or outbuilding somewhere. Hounds need to be hardy, fit, and resourceful.

The best thing any person who keeps animals can do is feed them properly, taking activity and season into account.

Sister filled the troughs with high-protein kibble: 26 percent during hunting season, 21 percent the rest of the time. She then poured a little hot water over it, along with corn oil.

First she pulled in the dog hounds. If the girls were fed first, their lingering enticing aroma could sometimes cause problems with the dog hounds.

Jefferson Hunt had separate housing away from the main kennels for gyps, the females, in season, connected by an arcaded walkway to the main kennel. Even when playing with hounds, Sister played with the dog hounds first. Sad to say, the girls evidenced much less interest in the boys than vice versa. After the dog hounds ate, she checked them. Everyone was fine—no bruised or cut pads, no barbed wire streaks on anyone's back.

She repeated the process with the girls. When those exuberant ladies finished, she brought in the youngsters, who cheerfully gobbled every morsel. Finally, she brought in Asa and Delia, two older hounds, fed separately to give them time to relax. She mixed in vitamin powder with their warm kibble. As Asa was stiff in the mornings, she let him eat Rimadyl out of her hands. He thought the medicine was a treat, it tasted so good.

"Asa, this is your last year hunting. After this, I'll need you to help me train puppies. If you don't like that, you can come on up to the house, but you have to put up with Raleigh and Rooster."

"It's Golly that plucks my last nerve," the gentlemanly hound smiled.

"Is that good?" Delia sniffed as Asa ate his Rimadyl.

"Candy."

"Here." Sister patted Delia on the head and let her eat one from her hand. "You don't really need it, Delia, but one tab won't hurt you."

Asa and Delia then ambled to their separate quarters.

Usually Shaker fed the hounds. Sister tried to be there as often as she could, but being a master took time. Landowners called, as did members, each needing information or wanting to impart the same to her. She and Walter both secured and opened territory—another time-consuming process.

Apart from foxhunting, Sister sat on the board of directors for Custis Hall, helped raise funds for the SPCA, and had her farm to run. Seed and fertilizer, if ordered early, often came with a 10 percent discount. Each year what the fields needed varied. Fences might need repair or replacing. A household chore would always pop up: a dying refrigerator, a crack in the wall. It never ended, but she was never bored.

Gardening, second to foxhunting in her passions, restored her spirits if they happened to be flagging. Even in winter, looking over glossy holly bushes and various conifers delighted her and inspired her to plant more trees, bushes, and flowers come spring.

Sari would return to Colby tomorrow. Today would be Shaker and Lorraine's last day with her until semester's end, which was why Sister fed the hounds. When Shaker roused himself in about a half hour, he'd find everything done: hounds fed, yards picked, the manure spreader full.

A long low pink ray of light fell over the snows. She left a note for Shaker, tacking it on the bulletin board in the office. She couldn't wait to get outside, for soon the world would be bathed in pink, then scarlet, and last, gold.

She put her bomber jacket back on. The dogs rose. The phone rang.

"Hello, Jefferson Hunt Kennels."

"Sister, you come over here this instant and pick up your goddamned hounds!"

She recognized Iffy's voice. "My hounds are in the kennels."

"Oh, sure, that's what you hunters always say. You pick up these hounds or you'll never pass through my land again." Iffy slammed down the phone.

"That girl needs charm school or Prozac. Maybe both." Sister replaced the receiver as she talked out loud to Raleigh and Rooster. "Well, let's crank up the party wagon. I don't know whose hounds are out there, but we'll pick them up."

She drove slowly. The road looked smooth enough, but black ice could flip you on your side in a skinny minute.

Fortunately, no traffic gummed up the works. No motorist impatiently hung on her butt in an effort to speed her along. A large portion of the county would be nursing hangovers. They wouldn't be out and about.

Iffy owned a small piece of land, thirty acres, give or take, south of Beasley Hall, Crawford's large, pretentious estate. Iffy's place rested twelve miles from Sister's farm, but twelve miles on treacherous roads could take a half hour or longer.

When Sister finally pulled down the plowed drive, the sun had fully cleared the horizon. Snows glistened bloodred.

Black and tan hounds aimlessly ran about.

She stopped the truck, put the hunting horn to her lips,

and blew three even long blasts. Hounds lifted their heads to stare at her. She blew the "come in" call again.

They trotted over the crusted snow toward her. A few heavier hounds broke through, leaping forward and up as snow sprayed in front of them.

"Good hounds," she called to them in a cheerful voice.

She opened the door to the party wagon. They hopped in.

"That's a blessing," she thought to herself.

If they'd been shy, she'd now be on a wild-goose chase. She put up three couple of hounds, then continued down the drive. No more appeared. She stopped and knocked at Iffy's back door. She could hear her thumping tread, then the door flew open.

"Happy New Year again, Iffy."

"Bullshit! Did you get those damned hounds?"

"I picked up six. How many did you see?"

"I don't know. Step in a minute. I'll catch my death of cold." Iffy motioned for Sister to step into the kitchen.

Sister noticed the .22 revolver on the kitchen table. She also noted that Iffy was moving along without her cane.

"I have never seen these hounds. They don't have tattoo marks in their ears, and they don't have collars either." Sister forced a smile. "Our pack is tricolor, Iffy. These are black and tans, but they're in good flesh. Someone has cared for them."

Iffy did not thank her for picking up someone else's hounds. "You're the hound queen. You'll find out who owns them before I do. I was ready to shoot them if one of them so much as bared a fang at me."

"Did it sound as though they were hunting?"

"I don't know. All I heard was my garbage cans knocked over."

"I'll pick up the mess," Sister volunteered. "No point in you going out in the snow."

"Some days are better than others. Most people stiffen up in the cold, but I have more trouble in the heat. Maybe it's the medicine. I don't know." Her features, a little puffy, brightened. "Jason's putting me on a new program for the New Year. He said my resolution is to build the strength back in my legs and"—she sucked in her breath—"lose the weight."

"He takes good care of you."

Iffy's lower lip quivered. "I'm not even forty. I want my old self back. Jason's lining up a physical therapist and a nutritionist." She brightened again.

Sister put her hand over the old brown porcelain doorknob. "If I find out who these hounds belong to, I'll let you know in case they come this way again."

"Do that." Iffy's voice was friendlier.

Sister walked outside, careful on the steps. She walked to the side of the house. One can, lid off, had garbage strewn about. The others, on their sides, had the lids on tight. She scooped up the debris: orange rinds, coffee filters and grinds within, soup cans, and one large bottle—no label, but a whiff informed her it contained something potent. She gave thanks for the freeze. Made the task easier, and easier on the nose, too.

Given that the road to the barn hadn't been plowed out, she trudged back there. No hounds.

As she drove out she pondered where to put these hounds. Since she had no idea as to their vaccinations or health records, she didn't want them near her hounds. She reviewed hunt club members who might have a vacant stall in their barns or a secure outbuilding. She saw, coming in the opposite direction, Sam Lorillard.

She flashed her headlights. He flashed. They both stopped.

The shoulders had snow piled up. They couldn't get off the road. Fortunately, there wasn't traffic on this back road.

One of the hounds yowled.

"Sister, where did you find them?"

"Iffy's. Three couple. Crawford's new pack?"

"A pack of escape artists. Got most back. Only one couple out now that you picked these up."

"You might suggest that the boss appease Iffy as well as anyone else."

"Yeah." Sam looked from her party wagon to his small trailer. "Think we could get them in the trailer?"

"Better not take the chance, Sam. They might piss off again. How about if I take them to Beasley Hall? You follow me. Where do I put them?"

"The old unused barn in the back. Rory's there patching up where they chewed through the rotted wood. Crawford has no sense."

"Well, no hound sense. We'd know not to put them in there."

Within twenty minutes the three had unloaded the hounds at Crawford Howard's barn.

Struggling with ready-mix concrete, Rory tried to get it to the right consistency to slap over the chewed place. "Pretty hopeless in this cold."

"Yeah. Got any riprap?" She named a large type of stone most quarries carried.

Sam piped up. "We do. Leftover from when Crawford put in the culverts."

"My suggestion," said Sister, "and it's only a suggestion—you gentlemen do as you like—would be to take heavy-duty page wire, run it along the sides, curve in the bottom of the page wire, and put down riprap at the edges until you can properly pour concrete or sucrete."

"It's going to be a bitch to dig through this frost to get the wire down in the ground." Sam did not relish this task.

"Yeah, it is; and bending it forward is no picnic either. Crawford might not want to spend the money on page wire and concrete. He's going to build a new kennel, right?" Sister inquired.

"Right," Rory answered.

"You can't have these hounds running all over the country. Apart from the bad will it creates, some will get killed. They don't know where they are yet. This is going to be hard as hell to patch up until the temperature is in the high forties at least. I think you're going to have to spend the money on cinder blocks against the wall and some kind of grid like Equistall for the floor. You've got to secure these hounds."

Crawford had walked in behind them.

Sister turned when she heard the bootsteps. "Happy New Year, Crawford."

"She brought back three couple of hounds that were at Iffy Demetrios's," Sam quickly apprised his boss.

"Iffy is, well, Iffy." Sister shrugged. "I'll be getting on home. If I see any more, I'll pick them up."

It pained him, but Crawford was man enough to utter "Thank you." He then puffed out his chest. "They won't get out again."

"Dumfreishire blood?" Sister asked sharply, knowing from their looks that the hounds had that type of Scottish blood. Although originally hunted in Scotland, the Dumfreishire was classified as an English hound.

"Right." Crawford nodded.

"Handsome." She left them to their labors and thought how foolish Crawford was thinking he could handle this type of hound.

The Dumfreishire, a large handsome hound, would be less high-strung than an American hound, but the good-looking black and tans would rapidly discover that Crawford knew nothing. They'd hunt on their own, discounting him. Also, their nose, not quite as good as that of the American hound, would frustrate him.

The English hound developed in a land of abundant moisture and rich soils. The red clay of central Virginia, occasionally enlivened by Davis loam, put the picturesque English hound at a disadvantage. Crawford would blame the hound, not himself.

On those perfect scenting days, this pack would hunt with brio. The other little thing Crawford would discover the hard way is that English hounds, as a rule, don't have the cry that American, crossbred, or Penn-Marydels do. Again, given where they were developed, they didn't need it to the degree that the New World needs a big booming sound, for much of the English countryside is open. One can see the hounds working.

They were big, they were beautiful. That part would swell his ego. Maybe he should just mount up and parade them around until he could find a real huntsman.

As she passed the beginnings of the stone St. Swithun's Chapel she had ample time to consider the unholy mess Crawford was creating for himself—and for her, too.

"Happy New Year." She sighed.

As she drove through the imposing gates, two huge bronze boars guarding the entrance had icicles dangling from their snouts. Their bristly chests glistened with ice rivulets. She turned west.

A quarter mile down the road she noted Donny Sweigart's treads from last night's supposed deer hunt.

Curious, she pulled as far off the road as she could given the conditions, hit her flashers, and got out. She wanted to see if there was a carcass or deer offal in the snow. She looked down the slight embankment, then over the expanse of snowy meadow. A copse of trees and shrubs stood out against the white. Something bright caught her eye.

She slid down the embankment. Tracks were partly covered with snow, but she could make out boot marks. She followed them toward the copse. Once there she saw a glob of congealed blood, fist sized, bright red.

There were no signs of struggle, no feathers either. If Donny had set out a trap she'd see it. No trap.

It was eerie, a hunk of frozen blood. She returned to her truck wondering what the hell was going on.

CHAPTER 10

Ben Sidell slouched in the passenger seat of Sister's red GMC early Monday morning, January 2, St. Basil's Day. "Take me to Paradise."

"If I were young, I would," she sassed back.

He laughed as he unrolled the map on the dash.

These expensive, lovely maps had been donated to the Jefferson Hunt by Francis McGovern, a buoyant member more on the road than home to hunt.

"Apart from the home fixtures, how old are the fixtures adjacent to Paradise?"

"Mill Ruins, Mud Fence, Orchard Hill, Chapel Cross are original fixtures going back to the beginning of the hunt. Course they're older than 1887, but once the hunt was founded their landowners were part of the fun. What's happened in certain parts of the county, especially the east because it's closer to town, is large estates, over time, have been broken up. Newcomers don't understand foxhunting or they plain don't like it, and we lose, say, fifty acres, which make the one thousand acres we use to hunt unhuntable for practical purposes because we can't get around the fifty acres. Even if we do figure out a way around, hounds can't read. They go through the No Trespassing area and you get an enraged phone call, Sheriff."

"In time some of the comeheres change their minds."

"Some." She nodded. "But there are other people who just don't get it and never will. They want to live in the country, but they aren't of the country. Pretty much they look down their noses at us."

"Do they look down at people like Tedi and Edward Bancroft?"

The Bancrofts had been wealthy since the Industrial Revolution, the family wise in nurturing that wealth.

"The comeheres don't even know they're not in the loop. If they see Tedi and Edward at a big party they think they've made it. Know what I mean?"

"I think so," said Ben. Originally from Ohio, he had been hired three years earlier to be sheriff of the county.

"It boils down to this: the arrogant ones only talk to other arrogant ones. They're ignorant of their social status. They think because they've built a McMansion on twenty acres, they're elite—if you can stand that word. They haven't a clue that they're close to the bottom of the barrel. A poor but warm person from an old family has much higher status than they do."

He smiled wryly. "You're at the top of the heap."

"Not in wealth but in other respects, yes. No point in false modesty. And the reality is, if you're of it, you don't dwell on it. I mean by that, you take it for granted. Maybe the first lesson new people need to learn is to treat people with respect regardless of their bank balances."

"Yep."

She slowed. "Okay, here's Chapel Cross. Orchard Hill and the other fixtures all fan out from this crossroads, an old tertiary road in highway department terms. Everything you see, I'll drive slowly, is our territory right up to the Blue Ridge. The top of the mountains divides us from Glenmore Hunt in Augusta County."

"Why don't you go up the mountains?"

"Would you?" She laughed. "For one thing, it's hard going. For another thing, there's boar up there, and I fear them like death. Lastly, there are folks in those hollows who come to town maybe once a year. They are famous for the purity of their country waters."

He knew about the distilleries in the hollows but not their location. Most moonshine busts were made when a trucker was pulled over and moonshine was discovered in the rig's closed bed.

Also, no prudent sheriff in any county would send a lone deputy to seek out the stills.

"Let me go back for a minute. Some of the new people really are good. They take to hunting, they value wildlife, they are good stewards of the land, and we're lucky to have them. We're lucky, too, because they're usually more liberal, politically, than we are and they challenge us, force us to question. I believe that's a good thing. If all you do is converse with people who think just like you do, you don't learn much." She slowed again, pointing to a lone brick fireplace. "Used to be the gatehouse to Paradise."

The gatehouse pillars, brick with a shield of arms near the capped top, still stood.

"Are you going to tell me the Yankees burned it?"

"No." She laughed a deep appreciative laugh. "Not this one. Way back before you were born, electrical wire was wrapped in silk. Anyway, a short burnt it to a cinder. The big pile with towering Corinthian columns is at the end of this road. It was incredible. It survived 1865, but each year it fell further and further into disrepair." She paused. "Thanks to Margaret's efforts, we'll be back hunting here. You'll see it Saturday. Decayed as it is, there's magic to Paradise. God, what it must have been in its heyday."

"Why did Margaret help?"

"Walter and Jason asked her to do it, and she likes to see the hunt. She's just not a hunter. Golf is her game." Sister paused. "Just one of those things. Binky and Alfred had another major disagreement—not face-to-face, of course, but through their lawyers—so the lawyers suggested no hunting because of the liability. Alfred's always been warm to hunting, and, really, Margaret worked on her father. Once lawyers get in anything it's a mess."

"Yeah," Ben agreed.

"In a way this is still paradise. There's a forlorn majesty to the ruin." Sister felt the pull of the place.

"Where are we, about four miles north from Chapel Cross?"

"Right. Good judge of distance. If we turned around, passed through Chapel Cross, we'd reach Tattenhall Station. From Chapel Cross, Little Dalby and Beveridge Hundred are on the south and west side of the road. Orchard Hill and Mud Fence are on the south and east side. Tattenhall Station is straight south. Paradise is five thousand acres, and it covers both sides of the old road north of Chapel Cross. Beyond Paradise it's billy-goat land owned by Franklin Foster in northern Virginia. At long last, he's given us permission to hunt there. Walter and I drove up to Fairfax to see him last summer. With the leaves off the trees and snow on the ground, you get a good sense of how the land rolls. All crisscrossed by creeks. It's good soil. Some of the grades might scare you on a tractor, though." She laughed.

"I just heard that Jason Woods made an offer on this land."

"Good God." Sister's silver brows shot upward. "He'll have his work cut out for him. Binky and Alfred won't agree to sell." She added, "Offer must be less than a day old. I usually hear about those things. It's hard to keep a secret in this county."

"I think it's a place of secrets."

She considered this. "Maybe you're right. The little secrets leak out. The big ones—well, some escape like evils from Pandora's box. And others we'll never know. I'm thinking about Nola Bancroft buried near the covered bridge for all those years."

Tedi and Edward's oldest daughter had been murdered and buried at the site where the bridge was being built. Decades later her skeletal hand, huge sapphire still on the third finger, had broken through the surface, ultimately pointing to her killer.

"That was one of my first big cases on the job." He glanced at the hunt club map again. "That's when I learned to listen to you."

"Go on." She smiled.

"Forgive the pun, but you know where all the bodies are buried."

"Some. Not all."

"The brothers live simply?" Ben inquired.

"In dependencies, buildings that used to house workers like the farm manager. Smaller ones housed slaves. They live at opposite ends of the farm, so they don't have to pass and repass too much, as we say. Oh, one other thing, Arthur maintains all the machinery."

"Mechanical ability runs in the family," he noted.

"Right." She nodded. "What Margaret does is mechanical in a way."

"Do you think Arthur keeps a still on the property? I've heard rumors to that effect."

Sister, not one to tell on people, replied, "Arthur wouldn't be that stupid. There are so many hollows with clear running streams as you get right up next to the mountains, he'd do it there. Arthur wouldn't jeopardize Paradise."

Ben considered this. "Good point."

She dropped into a lower gear as the road narrowed, beginning the switchback climb up the eastern slope of the mountain. "Seen enough?"

"Sure."

She turned around, sliding. She'd learned to drive in snow before four-wheel drive. "Ben, there are many ways to circumvent the law. For instance, if someone wants to poach bear on my land, they can take their license plates off, shoot the bear, say up by Hangman's Ridge, and even if I stop them what do I have? No I.D."

"I know. You foiling Arthur's line, are you?" The corner of his mouth turned up as he used the hunting term.

"No. There are, however, greater sins than making moonshine. Do I think he makes it? Of course. Do I know where? No. Nor do I want to know. Ignorance is protection. If I don't know, then I'm not in a position of covering up, right? I don't cotton to lying for someone."

"I understand." And he did.

"You know, Ben, there are a lot of things I don't understand. Seems to me you spend just as much energy breaking the law as you do making an honest living. You know we have thousands of years of evidence to prove the wisdom of the Ten Commandments. They're broken every minute."

"Yep." He turned his head to the right as they passed the pillars and lone fireplace near them again.

"Then there are things you learn on your own."

"Such as." He was interested.

"Anyone who refuses love is a fool. Every now and then the gods give us the chance to open our hearts."

He placed his forefinger on the sensitive skin just above his upper lip, a habit when thinking. "I hear you."

She laughed. "The worst that can happen is you'll have a great story to tell when you're my age. The best that can happen is you achieve paradise."

CHAPTER 11

Jefferson Hunt took out hounds on Tuesdays, Thursdays, and Saturdays, weather permitting. This Tuesday, January 3, the weather was permitting but the footing tried the patience of all the giving saints. However, the fixture card read Tattenhall Station, 9:00 a.m., and Tattenhall Station it would be.

Hunts varied their meeting times to adjust to the light and the temperature. Cubbing days would begin at 7:00 a.m. or 7:30 a.m. As fall gained strength, Sister moved the time to 8:00 a.m.

For cubbing most hunts did not print a fixture card. A fixture card was a handy list of times, dates, and places, called fixtures, usually printed on heavy stock paper, the print perhaps in the hunt's colors. Traditionally, a fixture card should fit into a jacket pocket.

Some hunts dispensed with tradition, issuing fixture cards

in varying sizes and even on lightweight paper, which meant the card couldn't hold up to the rigors of a season.

In the family scrapbook, Sister could read fixture cards used by her grandparents.

A stickler for tradition, Sister, the fifth master since 1887, had printed Jefferson Hunt fixture cards exactly like those from 1887.

The Franklins' printing business had dies from that time.

Fixture cards were usually received by mail before Opening Hunt. They could also be personally handed to a member by the master. This was considered a proper invitation to hunt.

Sans fixture card, a person rode as the guest of a member. The member's social obligation was to call and inform the master.

Someone who landed in Sister's hunt territory without knowing a member could write or call to ask permission to cap on a particular day. A cap was the amount of money a visitor paid to hunt that day. It can be collected by a field secretary or dropped in the offered field master's cap. Recently people had begun to e-mail to request permission. Strictly speaking, this was not a 100 percent correct way to ask the master.

Sister would inquire if they were a member of a recognized hunt. It not, had they capped at other hunts or ridden with farmer packs?

The point of these queries was to gather information so as not to overface the rider. The last thing any master wanted was for people to risk injury or to scare the bejabbers out of themselves.

If callers truly were neophytes, Sister suggested they go out with the hilltoppers. If their schedule was flexible, she'd suggest a day when territory was more forgiving.

Riding was necessary for foxhunting, but not sufficient. A foxhunter needed to know the fundamental law: hounds always have right-of-way.

The old siding lot at Tattenhall Station originally existed for mules and the baggage carts they pulled. As the mules disappeared cars began to park there. In the early 1960s, railroads abandoned unprofitable spur lines. This fate befell Tattenhall Station. The tidy, dark mustard board-and-batten buildings that housed the switchmen, the fireboys, various laborers, and the all-important telegraph operator looked picturesque covered with snow.

Their condition was a tribute to Norfolk & Southern's solid construction.

The few residents of the pretty little community around the old spur line faithfully plowed out the parking lot, still called the siding.

Nine rigs and the party wagon came out on Tuesday.

Ronnie Haslip and Henry Xavier rode up behind Sister. Charlotte Norton, Bunny Taliaferro, Dr. Jason Woods, Tedi, and Edward trudged through the snows. Bobby Franklin followed with Garvey Stokes and Lorraine Rasmussen in tow.

However, after an hour, Shaker and the hounds doing the best they could under clear skies, Shaker called it a day. No point in frustrating the hounds.

The worst the field could complain about—if they were in the habit of complaining, which, praise Jesus, they were not—was that they enjoyed a bracing winter's ride among good company.

Back at the trailers, Ronnie Haslip, a childhood friend of Ray Jr. and treasurer of Jefferson Hunt, surprised everyone. He had hired one of the silver-quilted food trucks, Jack's Snacks, that visit construction sites to stop by.

Hot coffee, hot tea, hot soup, hot dogs, and hamburgers warmed everyone.

"Ronnie, that is the classiest thing any member has ever done." Xavier held up a Styrofoam cup to toast him.

The others joined in.

Ronnie, shoulder to shoulder with Sister, asked, "Does Gray want my job?"

"No; do you want out of it come May?"

May 1 was the general meeting date on which master or masters were elected, along with administrative officers.

"No."

"Are you baiting me?" She smiled at Ronnie, two inches shorter than herself, whose turn-out was always impeccable.

"A little." He grinned, for he loved gossip, any manner of personal information. "Isn't this his first day at Garvey's?"

"It is," she laughed. "You'll notice Garvey is here, so he doesn't have to deal with it."

Jason, who had devoured an entire bowl of chili and was glowing from the warmth, joined the conversation, "I'll probably have to prescribe tranquilizers for Iffy this afternoon."

Ronnie's eyebrows raised. "She's always been high maintenance."

Jason thought a moment. "Even people who aren't high maintenance can become that way if they're sick or injured."

Sister agreed. "People need extra reinforcement."

"Attitude." Ronnie pronounced judgment. "Attitude is everything."

"Medicine helps," Jason wryly smiled.

Betty walked over. "Ronnie, spectacular idea!"

"Thank you."

She turned to Sister for a moment. "The weatherman predicts the temperature will climb into the high fifties tomorrow. All this will start to melt, then freeze over every night. But he said it will be a short January thaw."

"I know." Sister frowned. "If it's really bad, I'll cancel Thursday's hunt, but I'm not going to worry about it until seven Thursday morning."

She put changes to the day's hunting on the Huntline two hours before the time posted on the fixture card.

"This will take a long time to melt." Jason looked around at the dazzling snow.

Ronnie noticed Xavier on the other side of the small knot of people. "His lordship commands my presence."

"You're awful."

"Speaking of high maintenance." He winked at Betty as he excused himself.

"Jason, I heard you've made an offer on Paradise?" Sister asked. Ben hadn't said this was privileged information, so she felt free to bring it up.

"Put down the earnest money last night." Triumph illuminated his face.

"Paradise? DuCharme's Paradise?" Betty couldn't believe her ears.

"The same." Jason's lad cap added a jaunty air to his presence.

"How did you ever get those two nitwits to come to the table?" Betty blurted it out.

"Well, one came to the operating table. He credits me with saving his life." Jason tried to sound humble.

"That may explain Alfred's cooperation, but what about Binky?" Betty's curiosity flipped into the red zone.

"Milly worked on him. No contingencies in the offer. No financing. She knows they'll never see an offer like this again. They can't afford to run a place that big. Don't think Margaret, when it passes to her, can afford it, either. The far fields are going down. The houses they live in aren't in great shape, either. This is an answered prayer for the DuCharmes."

Betty reached for a hot dog and hot coffee. She wasn't sure it was an answered prayer. However, she simply asked, "Have you signed a contract?"

"Two weeks from now. Both parties wanted their lawyers to read it. Cut and dried, but we'll go through the lawyer song and dance." He paused, eyes down, then up quickly. "Both said Margaret had to agree. I made the offer New Year's evening, and I haven't talked to her yet."

"Five thousand acres," Sister said in wonderment.

"Plans?" Betty knew she was being nosy.

"I'm going to work from old photographs and restore Paradise."

"Those stone barns are beautiful. The slate on the roofs held up." Sister lusted after stone.

"What shell remains is better than I'd hoped, even though it looks like a war relic." He laughed. "I know I can restore the outside of Paradise. The interior will be the challenge."

"What a fabulous project." Sister meant that, but she was equally glad she wouldn't be doing it. She wondered exactly what was in that contract, noting he didn't utter the dreaded word "development."

"Meant to ask you"—Betty touched the blackthorn crop he carried on informal days—"where'd you get that?"

"A present from Iffy." He paused. "She can be very thoughtful, but she gives me too much credit. She wanted to be well." He paused again for effect, then smiled. "Do you two ladies believe the story about the treasure at Paradise? From the War of 1812. I've heard more than one version."

"I do." Betty flatly stated. "It's there."

"I'd like to." Sister smiled.

"Which version do you all subscribe to?"

The two women looked at one another, then Betty spoke. "We always heard that Sophie Marques, a maternal I don't know how many greats-grandmother, raided a pay wagon for the British somewhere on the Bladenberg Pike. Anyway, she came here rich as a queen and bought all the land we know as Paradise. Before Sophie it was virgin timber. She created every pasture you see, sited every barn and outbuilding."

Sister interjected, "She built a little house on it, a two over two. She lived in it while she created Paradise. What she didn't spend she buried."

"Why?" He shrugged.

"Didn't trust banks. She'd seen too many collapse," Sister responded.

"You're telling me that the ancestor of those two yokels was a highwaywoman?" Thus he revealed his disdain for Binky and Alfred, who weren't exactly yokels.

"Well . . . yes." Betty hedged a moment. "The story goes that she worked throughout Maryland during the war as a spy. A pretty woman, she used her wiles to extract information from British officers. After serving her country for no pay she made one big haul in 1814 and had the wisdom to repair to Virginia."

"Make a great movie." He laughed.

"I expect there's a good story about every old place in Virginia." Betty took it for granted.

Jason's cell rang. "Excuse me." He walked to his trailer. Amid the hubbub of conversation he could not be heard, but Sister noted the expression on his face.

He finished the conversation, closed the phone. "Iffy." He sighed. "She's feeling shaky. Says Gray is making her sick." He paused. "I don't know if one's emotional state can trigger cancer. I doubt it, but I do know we all do better if we're stable."

"Can she truly recover from lung cancer? Excuse me. I realize a doctor can't discuss a patient. I apologize," Betty asked.

He waved it off. "Her tumor is gone. Starved, to put it in layman's terms. The danger for Iffy is if the tumor was able to seed itself. Despite all our advances, we don't always know that. It's one of the reasons I continue to run tests on Iffy. But she has an excellent chance for survival. Her work now has to be with a physical therapist. The treatments debilitated her more than most people. But let's face it; they're unpleasant for anyone." He waited a moment. "Speaking of time, I could begin walking out hounds in February. That gives me time to adjust my schedule. Will that work for you?"

"Yes." Sister's shoulders stiffened.

"Make me a whipper-in, and you'll see Paradise." He beamed.

She didn't quite know whether this was an offer or a bribe. "Jason, I see paradise each time I hunt," she said good-naturedly.

CHAPTER 12

The large silver commercial horse van pulled into Roughneck Farm at three in the afternoon.

Matador, who had passed his vetting with flying colors, stepped off the ramp, stopped, and took in his surroundings. Ears forward, eyes bright, beautifully conformed, he lowered his head when Sister held out her hand to him. She brushed his muzzle, then stroked his ears.

"Boss, he's a beaut," Shaker exclaimed.

"For his price he ought to be." Sister smiled, but she, too, found the flea-bitten gray dazzling, flea-bitten referring to the brown flecks in the gray coat.

Horsin' Around, one of the many good commercial haulers in the country, covering coast to coast, knew Sister and the farm.

"How'd he load, Hank?" she asked the driver.

"No problem. He's a real nice horse."

The staff horses in their various paddocks and pastures viewed the newcomer with curiosity.

Lafayette called out to him, "*Pretty is as pretty does.*"

Matador turned his head toward the other gray in the barn, snorted, but said nothing. He figured he'd show them.

Keepsake, half thoroughbred and half quarter horse, a friendly guy, simply said, "*Good shoulder.*"

"*Good shoulder is one thing. He'd better damn well take care of our master.*" Rickyroo stared at the charismatic animal.

Aztec, youngest of Sister's hunt horses, said, "*Sister Jane has been riding horses since she was four. I expect she knows a good one when she sees him.*" He paused for effect. "*After all, she picked us, didn't she?*"

Sister handed the cashier's check to Hank with a fifty-dollar tip. She took the clipboard and signed the paperwork. "January 4. Already four days into the new year."

"Time flies." Hank took back the clipboard and thanked Sister for the tip.

Shaker was leading the new fellow into the barn as Hank pulled out.

Sam, in Gray's Land Cruiser, came down the drive. He bounded into the barn. "Had to see 'im."

"Well?" Sister raised an eyebrow.

Sam walked around him, stroked his neck, then stood behind as Shaker led him to his stall. "I liked him when I rode him. He really is your kind of horse. Bold."

"Your word is dipped in platinum." Sister dropped her arm around his shoulder.

Shaker closed the bottom half of the stall door. He leaned over the top half as Matador checked his surroundings.

"Well, I'm not hunting him until the footing improves. We'll exercise him, but I do want to give him every chance to get settled and show his best."

"How about some hot coffee, or what about hot chocolate?" Sister invited Sam into the house.

"Thanks, but I'm heading home. I'm going to work on the kitchen cabinets. Went in at six this morning. Rory and I are working all hours to get the hounds settled along with the other chores."

As they walked outside to the car, Sister discreetly dug into her pocket for money. She'd gone to the bank earlier. "What are you doing with Gray's pride and joy?"

"He wanted me to pick up distressed oak. He's driving my wheels." Sam smiled. "Hope the car lives long enough to get him home."

As he slipped behind the wheel of the expensive SUV, Sister stuck five hundred dollars in the front of his coat. "There's more coming."

"For what?" Sam fished in his pocket to hand it back. She gently held his wrist. "Part of your finder's fee. I appreciate you telling me about the horse, and, of course, I appreciate you keeping your brother from other women."

He sighed. "If I don't take the money you'll send it to me as a check."

"You got that right."

He grinned. "Gray doesn't know other women exist."

"Oh la!" She rolled her eyes.

"While we're on the subject, I'll work for food. I'll muck stalls, groom—I'll recite poetry even, if there's a woman out there who'd have me."

"Funny, isn't it, Sam? Time was when you trailed clouds of women. None of them did you much good."

He quickly interjected, "I didn't do them much good, either."

"Six of one, half dozen of the other. There's a lid for every pot. Look at Shaker."

"Lucky man."

"Be patient."

As Sam drove off, Sister hurried back into the stable to admire Matador. "Well, let's bring these other actors inside."

As she and Shaker led in the other horses they talked about Thursday's draw, who to take. The sun touched the horizon. They were glad to be with the horses and one another.

This was not the case at Aluminum Manufacturers. Iffy, buried in paperwork for Farmers Trust, grimaced each time Gray passed her door.

Each time Gray asked her for information, she gloried in retarding his efforts.

She'd erupt, sulk, and use her cane to stomp around, eventually complying with Gray's request.

She left the office at five. Damned if she'd work late.

No sooner had she passed through her back door when the phone rang. "Hello. Garvey, what do you want?"

"Hate to call you at home, but Sonny called after you left."

"It was five. Quitting time." She glowered.

"I'm fine with that. But why I'm calling you at home is because someone must have told the state president of the bank that we were performing an internal audit. He told Sonny to hold approval until Gray finished the audit."

"Bullshit." She exploded. "Sonny is president of Farmers Trust for our region. He has the power to make the loan."

"Sonny's madder than hell. Look, we've got to speed up this audit."

"Why can't Sonny face down the Big Prez in Henrico County?"

"You know, Iffy, once banks started merging, once computers replaced people who actually knew their community, it all changed. If the economy were up, I expect Sonny wouldn't have heard a word. But interest rates are rising; the Dow is falling. You know the rest of the story. The banks are nervous."

"I'll talk to Sonny. No, let me just take him what I've done so far. We're rock solid. I resent this."

"I do, too." Garvey thought a minute. "Let me handle Sonny. If you worked with Gray, how quickly could you two finish the audit?"

"I can't work with Gray. I'm your treasurer. If I work with him that could be construed as a conflict of interest. There goes the enhanced line of credit."

Garvey exhaled a long sigh. "Of course, it would. I don't know where my head is."

"Have you spoken to Gray?"

"Yes. He suggested I hire Freddie Thomas, another independent, to work with him. Even with Freddie they'll be pushing to get it done by next week." He sighed, irritated and worried. "The devil is in the details."

"Always is. Is Gray still there?"

"Just left. He said his mind is tired. He's going to be coming in at seven-thirty, and he'll work until five."

"Who ratted to the big president?"

"No idea." He thought it funny that she said "ratted."

"Why would someone call the president of Farmers Trust about us?"

"Our audit isn't a deep dark secret. I doubt anyone called. Sonny probably mentioned it to his staff or at a meeting in Richmond. I doubt he expected this complication."

"Rotten timing." She took a breath, then exhaled. "There will be small discrepancies, Garvey. I mean *small.* It's a bitch to get it to the penny. If you'd kept Gray out of this, forgotten the audit idea, you'd have had the loan the first day of business this year, I swear. I could have finished up the paperwork in a hurry before Sonny could blow his nose." She paused again. "Turn in our last tax return. It will give Sonny and company something to read. When Gray finishes, they can compare the two. I don't want this to drag out any more than you do. Of course, we haven't done last year's income tax returns. No one has. To be safe, I'll turn in the prior three years' returns. That's a start."

"Thanks, Iffy."

On the drive home, Gray's teeth rattled. The shocks in Sam's rattletrap were that bad. The checking of invoices against services and goods received must be thoroughly done.

Iffy approved invoices for payment. Although he'd just begun this task, he noted that Aluminum Manufacturing had poor internal control. He suspected as much. He observed that any purchase or service over ten thousand dollars carried Garvey's initials. Iffy could approve anything under that sum.

Iffy prepared the checks and signed them.

A quick study, he felt that by tomorrow's end he would have some sense of regular monthly payments and services.

All businesses exhibited a pattern.

He was reviewing this when he pulled into the drive, now hard-packed snow. Sam wasn't home, which surprised him.

He was even more surprised when Ben Sidell called him. Sam had been shot coming home from the lumberyard and had veered off the road, totaling the Land Cruiser. But Sam was alive.

CHAPTER 13

There should be a reality show, thought Gray, where interior decorators compete to see who can put together a hospital room that doesn't make one gag. Bad enough to be injured or sick. Worse to be flopped in a bed, an ungainly TV jutting out overhead.

Gray sat beside his brother. Odd to be once again at Sam's side, but this time Sam wasn't suffering from the DTs, screaming his head off. Sister, called by Walter about the same time Ben Sidell had called Gray, had hurried down to the hospital.

Sister sat beside Gray while Walter stood at the end of the bed.

Sam had been conscious during the entire ordeal. At the sight of his brother, the first words out of his mouth were "I didn't touch a drop."

Walter simply nodded slightly when Sister glanced at her

joint-master. "He was lucky. The bullet passed through his shoulder. It entered from the front, passed through the back just under his scapula, nicked his rib, and broke it. Lower, and the damn thing would've blown out his heart."

"Did you see who shot you?" Gray reached for his brother's hand.

"No. I came around the curve at Soldier Road, just before Roger's Corner. Next thing I knew, I heard a pop, something hit me, and the windshield crinkled into a thousand tiny pieces." He blinked in rapid succession for a few seconds. "It took a minute for me to know I'd been shot. It kind of delayed the pain, I mean."

"Thank God for safety glass, or you'd be cut up." Sister cared deeply for Sam.

"Hope it was the last of the deer hunters. Thought I'd put most of my enemies behind me." He smiled ruefully. He sat up, winced, dropped back. "Car's trashed. I . . ."

Gray butted in. "I don't care about the car."

Walter smiled. "That's what insurance companies are for."

Gray murmured, "Well, brother, what else is tore up?"

"Knee."

Walter spoke reassuringly, "The patella's fine, bruised. We can drain the fluid off. Sam wasn't eager to allow any procedures done to his perfect body," Walter remarked with humor. "But Sam, your knee will swell even more. Let's take care of it. The needle feels like a big hornet sting, but it doesn't last long."

"It'll go down." Sam was defiant.

"Sam, trust me. Drain the knee now. I can understand you feel you've had enough for one night, but the knee will hurt worse than your broken rib."

"Do like he says." Gray squeezed Sam's hand.

"Birds in your hand," Sam said sharply.

"Sorry." Gray released the pressure.

"What?" Walter didn't understand.

"When we were kids, Peter Wheeler used to tell us when we'd hold the reins too tightly, 'Little birds in your hands. Don't squeeze them to death.' "

"I can ride with a bum knee. Plenty of people do."

"Yes, you can." Walter smiled at Sam. "Running will hurt. And if you jump, landing will be a bitch. Sooner or later, Sam, you'll need to have the knee scoped. It's probably a torn ACL."

"It can wait."

"It can, but since you have your brother here and Sister, come on—let's drain the knee."

Sam sank deeper into the pillow. He didn't want to look like a chicken. Truth was he hurt, he was shaken, and he hated needles. On the other hand, get it over with, because Walter wasn't going to give up.

"All right," Sam grimly agreed.

"Be back in a minute." Walter walked out to the nurses' station, had them call Margaret DuCharme, and apprised her of the situation.

Within five minutes she arrived, along with a thin nurse who carried a porcelain kidney-shaped bowl. A long, long needle was in the bowl with a towel over it. She also carried a small packet of ice in a padded circle that would conform to the knee.

"Can you sit up and dangle your legs over the side of the bed?" Margaret asked. "I'll put a chair under your feet, if you need it."

Gray helped Sam sit upright.

The bullet's path stung, his rib ached, and his knee throbbed. He closed his eyes.

"I've seen worse," Margaret said reassuringly.

"Dr. DuCharme, I don't want to cuss," Sam said, which made her laugh.

"I don't either. This won't be the worst pain you've ever felt, Sam, but you will feel it. I'm going to stick this needle in and draw off the fluid. Then we'll pack this ice band around your knee. You'll be surprised at how quickly you'll feel relief. Ready?"

Sister stood to the side, placing her hand on Sam's shoulder. Not squeamish, she was nonetheless glad that long needle wasn't being plunged into her knee.

Sam stiffened.

As Walter and Margaret promised, it was over in a minute.

Both doctors looked at the clear light yellowish fluid. Some blood was in it, which they know was consistent with a torn ligament.

The nurse wiggled the ice bracelet up to his knee. "There you go."

"That's it?" Sam's cheeks sported a gray tinge.

"That's it," Margaret smiled. "I'll check on you tomorrow. You're tough as nails, Sam Lorillard. Always were."

"Family trait," Gray said as he and Walter helped Sam swivel back to rest on the pillow.

"Sam, I know you don't like drugs, but that wound is going to throb. Your knee shouldn't hurt as much as it did before draining. Let me give you a mild sedative. You need a good night's sleep." Walter's deep voice soothed.

"No. No drugs." Sam pressed his lips together.

"Sam, you aren't going to get hooked. We monitor those things," Walter reassured him.

"With all due respect, Walter, my body chemistry . . . well, let's just say if there's any kind of downer, booze, or narcotic, I crave it. I fought too hard to get where I am. I'd rather deal with the pain."

"Can he take aspirin?" Sister asked.

"Yes." Walter admired Sam's desire to stay straight, although he felt he could control the situation.

As Margaret reached the door Jason Woods walked in. There was a moment, a slight tension, as they acknowledged one another. Margaret left and Jason entered.

"Sam, heard you escaped an invitation to heaven," he joked.

"Might have been the other place." The exhaustion had begun to show on Sam.

"Very possible." Jason smiled, then spoke to Gray. "He has friends here, Gray. He'll be all right. Why don't you go home?"

"No, I'll spend the night."

"We'd like to keep him for at least two days, but I expect we'll be lucky if we can keep him for one." Walter resigned himself to Sam's determination.

Sister kissed Sam on the cheek as he nodded off. She kissed Gray. "Can I bring anything back for you?"

"No thanks." Gray kissed her again. "We'll both be up and out of here come morning. I'll be fine. You go on home. I'll call Crawford about this so that's taken care of."

She walked outside with the two doctors.

"What a crazy damn thing," Jason murmured.

"Yes." Walter motioned for Sister to wait a moment as Jason returned to his rounds.

Walter leaned against the wall. "Sam got any old enemies left?"

"I don't know, I expect."

"The path of the bullet doesn't lead me to believe it was a stray shot. Someone waited by the road and fired right when he came round."

"He was in Gray's car. Maybe they wanted to kill Gray." Sister felt a ripple of fear pass through her as she leveled her eyes on Walter's.

"Jesus."

"We need Him now."

CHAPTER 14

"You look like the dogs got at you under the porch." Iffy, carrying a file folder while using one cane, walked into Gray's temporary office.

"Spent the night in the hospital."

"Are you all right?"

"Fine. Tired." Gray noticed her quizzical expression. "Sam was in a car accident." He held back the small detail that Sam had been shot. He was tired and didn't feel like indulging in speculation with people who weren't close.

"Oh, no; he didn't fall off the wagon?" Iffy exclaimed without thinking.

Gray shrugged. "Skidded off the road. He's home. Banged up, but"—Gray motioned for her to sit, which she declined—"all right." He half-smiled. "He couldn't get out of that hospital fast enough."

"I'm sorry." She handed the folder to him. "Hanson Office Supplies. First quarter." She paused. "Sometimes I keep things in my office instead of putting them in the central files. Going up and down steps is hard sometimes. Oh, is Freddie coming in?"

"At three every afternoon. We're lucky to get her. Her business is booming; but she likes Garvey and understands the situation."

"M-m-m." Iffy tossed her head. "I wouldn't want to be self-employed. Too Iffy." She smiled at her joke.

Gray smiled, too, then said, "The company doesn't pay any bills by automatic draft, does it?"

"No. We receive an invoice for every service or bill, and I cut the checks once a month."

"All right, then." He nodded, and she left.

The morning's hunt pleased Sister and Shaker. They took out more young entry than usual. In the beginning of cubbing they'd put two couple of youngsters in with the pack. Keeping the number of young entry small allowed them to study them. By now, January 5, Thursday, enough of the youngsters had settled in that they could take more than two couple. However, it usually took a season, sometimes two, before a young hound fully came into her or his own.

Often an older hound would be retired or pass away and a young hound would step into that hound's position, a bit like a first baseman retiring and a rookie taking over. But even if the young ones were learning quickly, a large number of them in the pack in their first year often meant excessive excitement, overrunning the line.

This Thursday they'd taken three couple, six young entry from the "A" litter." Perhaps next Tuesday they'd take four couple. Since the field was usually large on Saturdays, Sister avoided a large number of first-year hounds. She didn't want to overwhelm youngsters with too many people.

The snow had sunk down to the consistency of hard vanilla sauce. The footing gave everyone flutters. Horses slipped, although it didn't bother the horses as much as it bothered the people. Most people instructed their blacksmith to put borium on the shoes. A few people used screw-in caulks, a bit like small spikes on baseball shoes. While they could be tremendously useful on a day like today, they could also be dangerous. If a horse overreached or inadvertently clipped himself, he'd tear into flesh. Worse, if an owner forgot to unscrew the caulks, the ride home could turn into disaster for the horse. And unscrewing the ice-cold caulks, when hands were frozen was not a congenial task.

Sister stuck to borium, a powder applied to spots on the shoe rim. Slightly raised and rough, it helped the animal get purchase. Besides which, borium created much less damage if her horse stepped on himself. She'd rather slip and slide than risk injury to her horse.

Despite the skating, they ran two foxes. The saucy creatures were fully aware that the footing gave them a great advantage. The hounds fared better, thanks to their claws, but they couldn't keep up with the lighter foxes on a day like today.

Uncle Yancy, a venerable fox with peculiar habits, one of which was watching TV while sitting in Shaker's window, sauntered in full view. As it was, he was all the way over on the Lorillard place. This surprised Sister, Shaker, Betty, and Sybil because Uncle Yancy usually kept within a small radius of Roughneck Farm, occasionally taking over a den at After All Farm.

Uncle Yancy was experiencing domestic problems with

Aunt Netty. She said old age was making him dotty and querulous. He said she was an old harridan and her brush looked like a rat's tail.

So Uncle Yancy was sleeping on the sofa, as it were. He explored the Lorillard place and was impressed with the brothers' accomplishments. But it was too far east for him.

When hounds caught his scent, their third fox of the morning, Uncle Yancy headed west to Tedi and Edward's After All Farm, which was where hounds had met for the first cast. He skated a few times, but it was fun. Uncle Yancy liked the cold air in his nostrils.

He hastened all the way to the pattypan forge, five miles as the crow flies, which St. Just was doing. The crow tracked Yancy the entire way, but both animals knew nothing would come of it. Still, it afforded St. Just a thrill to see the old red fox loping along. He hurled down insults.

When Uncle Yancy dropped into the pattypan den he kicked himself. He had discounted it as a homesite because he'd be within two miles of Aunt Netty. Once inside he changed his mind. He'd avoid her as best he could, but he wasn't going to pass up the chance to live in this exotic labyrinth.

Hounds marked the spot.

Dragon sailed through the window. Cora, Diane, and Asa followed.

"You won't blast Uncle Yancy out of here any more than you did Target," Cora complained.

"I know. I'm looking for an arm or a leg. Or old bones. Remember the blood last time?" Dragon answered.

"Shaker will think you're dawdling." Asa turned to jump back out the window.

"If I show up with a human leg he'll think otherwise. And a bone

is a bone. Doesn't matter what animal it comes from." Dragon lifted the fur on his shoulders.

"Ass." Asa jumped out.

"Take that, too," Dragon called after him.

Cora didn't feel like wasting time on Dragon, so she, too, jumped out.

Dragon looked at his sister. *"A quick check."*

She turned to leave, but her curiosity got the better of her. She put her nose down. Seconds later at the actual forge she came up on another large glop of congealed blood, the cold giving it an odd glisten.

"Here."

Outside Shaker called them.

Dragon hurried over. He trotted along the side of the old bellows. *"This is weird."*

Diana joined him. Another frozen gelatinous lump, palm sized, had been dropped on the other side of the forge. Diana was baffled by this. Given the cold, not much scent came off this substance, either.

"Come on, Diana. Come on, Dragon."

Dragon ran back to the blood, inhaled deeply. What little scent he could pick up with his long nasal passage made him sneeze. *"Human blood, but something's wrong with it."*

Both hounds then jumped out of the window in tandem. If they could return on a non-hunting day, maybe they could find more. But they left the kennels only for hunting or for hound walk. It was a sorry hound that ran off during hound walk. He'd lose his privileges or be coupled to another hound, berated by that hound for being a damned fool and being out of step besides.

Later, as Sister and Betty cleaned tack they heard the sound of a six-cylinder Wrangler. A lime-green Jeep pulled into the stable lot. Three young women crawled out, swinging their legs over the high bottom lip of the doorway.

"Sister!" Tootie, Val, and Felicity ran inside the stable.

After hugs and kisses, Sister and Betty listened to their stories of Christmas vacation, dreary dates, even more dreary family reunions, and how cold the dorms were when they arrived back at Custis Hall. How tough Bunny Taliaferro, the riding instuctor, was. Christmas vacation made her meaner.

"How cold?" Sister enjoyed the hyperbole.

"My toothbrush froze." Val tossed her blonde ponytail.

"In her mouth," Tootie added with a sly smile.

"My," Betty simply commented.

"I'm surprised it's still not stuck to your mouth, Val. Your Wrangler can't be that warm," Sister teased.

"But it is. Daddy bought me the hardtop. We can lift it off, but we have to disengage the wires to the windshield wiper on the back. Isn't it cool? Isn't it the coolest car you have ever seen?"

"It is. Looks like fun." Sister loved being around these kids.

"You need one. Red." Felicity imagined the master tooling around the back roads.

"Black," Tootie said.

"I knew you'd say that." Val laughed.

"Really, black with a blue and gold pinstripe. How cool is that?" Tootie folded her arms over her chest.

"Pretty cool." Sister imagined the sight.

"You're ahead of Jennifer. She still doesn't have a car," Betty said. "Wants a Pontiac Solstice."

"Me, too. Howie wants one in that titanium color." Felicity found a way to drag her boyfriend into the conversation.

"Howie will have a long wait," Val replied.

Felicity ignored Val's remark.

"How many great hunts did we miss? Tootie e-mailed us your reports. I wish we'd been here." And before Sister could open her mouth, Val bubbled over. "But we can hunt Saturday. Bunny said so. I can't wait! It's horrible not being around horses. I love Mom and Dad, but my horse is here. I can't live without Moneybags."

Moneybags was a handsome gelding.

"Who's the new gray?" Tootie noticed the compelling thoroughbred.

"Matador. Sixteen hands, but a big enough barrel he'll take up my leg. Chaser." She used the abbreviation for steeplechase horse.

"Wow." Felicity walked out of the tackroom to Matador's stall. She returned smiling.

"Are you girls going right back to the dorm?" Sister asked.

"No. We want to hang with you," Val announced.

"I'm glad to hear that. If you help me for just an hour I promise I'll feed you well."

"Don't pass up the apple crisp." Betty smiled. "Made it this morning and brought it to the tailgate. There's lots left."

Once the tack was cleaned, Sister checked on the hounds and put Raleigh and Rooster in the house. The girls followed her to the spot where Sam had careened off the road.

Betty, too, followed.

Sister briefly recounted the events.

A dirt road, now snow packed, fed into Soldier Road on the opposite side of the road from where Sam had crashed. All three vehicles parked there.

"Girls, what I want you to do is walk three abreast in this field. Pay special attention to bushes and trees. And tell me if you see tracks: animals, human. Betty and I will walk up here on the road." She turned to Betty. "Why don't you walk against traffic, and I'll walk with it? Shouldn't be much, but I've got on this red scarf. Anyway, I expect Ben's crew found whatever there was to find."

They walked slowly. Only two drivers passed, one being Roger, the owner of Roger's Corner, the last convenience store heading west before one climbed the Blue Ridge to drop into the Shenandoah Valley below.

After a half hour, the cold beginning to seep into their feet even with heavy socks and Thinsulate boots, Tootie called out, "Found something."

The rest made their way to her.

Random pricker bushes dotted the snow. Deer tracks, crow tracks, and raccoon tracks were evident, all heading toward Broad Creek. The human tracks were scuffed so no sole tread would be apparent, and the size was indistinguishable.

"Damn." Sister whispered as she noticed that. "Smart, too."

CHAPTER 15

Odd dates and facts rolled around Sister's mind.

She often conceived of her mind as a closet, which when opened would reveal the usual apparel but also a few dead moths, the remains of long-perished spiders, and tiny little skeletons of whatever Golly had secreted there long ago.

Yesterday had been the day of St. Simeon Stylites, born 390 and died 459. Apart from his piety, gentle preaching, and self-abnegation on top of the pillar that had given rise to his name, Stylites, he must have stunk to high heaven. Perhaps that was his plan. After all, the Olympians enjoyed the fragrance of offerings slaughtered or burnt in their honor. Perhaps Simeon's Christian God liked human unwashed scent.

Sister doubted this. Simeon had had doubts, too, but they were of a higher order.

Today, January 6, belonged to St. Peter of Canterbury, birth date unknown, who died in 607 after an eventful life. On a mission to Gaul, disunited then (and perhaps still), poor Peter drowned in the English Channel. When found, he was unceremoniously buried by pagan locals. But a mysterious light danced over his grave at night, which made them reconsider Christ's message.

Sister would have welcomed a mysterious light—any light to shed on the disquiet she felt. She'd driven to town at first light to meet with Ben Sidell, already in his office.

After informing him of the scuffed foot marks, she asked, "Any luck with other Land Cruiser owners?" She gratefully drank from the mug of hot tea she'd brought along.

He shook his head "No," then added, "Brad Johnson was deer hunting here around that time, but he was on the other side of the road. Not much, but you gather these little bits of information. Eventually some kind of picture emerges."

"I'm trying to convince myself the shot was an accident. If only Brad had been on the west side of the road."

"I hope so, too, but I'll keep on it—just in case."

"Hunting Saturday?"

He nodded, "Yes."

After classes, Tootie, Val, and Felicity carefully put out their kit for tomorrow's hunt. Valerie as class president had a room to herself in the corner of the oldest and therefore most prestigious dorm. Tootie and Felicity, each carrying 4.0 grade averages, also lived on the same hall.

Custis Hall's founder and succeeding headmistresses judiciously used earned status to motivate the girls. This part of the school had been built in 1812, along with the only other structure at that time, the administrative building, which had been used for classes as well back then.

Since 1812 Custis Hall had entertained building programs consistent with the rise and fall of capital cycles. The newest dorms, very attractive and with every modern convenience, had been built in 2000. The three seniors would slit their wrists before living in the newest dorm.

Old One, as their dorm was called, had been remodeled sporadically. Modern insulation, electricity, and plumbing had been installed. But each room still had a fireplace, and the girls had to take proper care of it or lose the privilege of living in Old One.

Val's room had served every senior class president since 1812. Many had gone on to become the wives of senators, generals, admirals, and captains of industry. A few made their independent way in the arts. Fewer still started their own businesses, although more graduates had moved into the business world after the 1970s. Still, Custis Hall girls, after college, married well if they married.

As Val's room was the largest, both Tootie and Felicity sat there shining their boots.

"I can never get this stuff out of my fingers," Tootie grumbled.

"Me, neither." Felicity, slender and observant, vigorously rubbed in the black paste.

Val's boots gleamed under her mahogany valet, where she'd hung her frock coat, her white shirt, her ironed stock tie. She pinned her stock pin through the buttonhole of her black frock coat so she wouldn't lose it in the hustle of leaving in the early morning. Her canary vest was over the shirt, the coat over the vest. Her britches were draped over the bar constructed for that purpose. In the tray of the valet she'd placed two long thin strips of rawhide, one penknife, one pack of matches, and a cotton handkerchief. She'd already put her Virginia hunting license in her vest pocket. Her velvet hard hat, tails up, sat next to her boots but in a special hat case wherein she kept two pairs of gloves, one white and knitted, one deerskin with a cashmere lining. Inside the hat case were small packs of handwarmers and extra hairnets.

"Val, how'd you get everything done? You're usually behind," Felicity inquired.

"MinPin." She named a freshman by nickname.

"Wish I had a slave." Tootie didn't especially like the cloying freshman.

"I could be really obnoxious," Val warned.

"Free blacks could own slaves, too, Val." Tootie fired away because she knew what Val was thinking. Tootie was also black. "I know my history."

"Not my strong suit, is it? But hey, I'm good at calculus."

"You're good at anything if you want to be." Felicity made peace. "That's what makes me wonder where Howie will go to school. His grades are okay, but you know."

"We know," Tootie and Val said in unison.

Blushing, Felicity remarked, "He's such a good quarterback. He's been scouted by a lot of schools."

"Princeton isn't one of them," Val flatly said. "We're all going to Princeton."

"We haven't got our acceptances yet," Tootie reminded her.

"We will. You know we will."

"Well, if not, we have our back-up schools, but I don't think

Howie could get into Bucknell or some of our others." Felicity bent lower over her boots.

"So? You see him on big weekends unless he winds up in Kansas. Then you can see him at Christmas." Val picked up a small hard-bristled whisk brush to brush Tootie's coat.

Little clouds of fine dust whirled up and made Val choke.

"Here?" Tootie stood up, reaching for her coat.

"I can do it. You'll get bootblack on the coat. What'd you get into? This coat is a mess."

"Remember when we got muddy, last hunt before vacation? I brushed it off but not so good." Tootie apologized.

"That was fun staying with Sister after the dorms closed. I didn't really want to go home," Val said. "Glad I did." She laughed.

"You didn't know your dad was getting you the Wrangler for Christmas?" Felicity didn't envy her the car. She had no envy in her.

"No." Val looked down as students walked across the oldest quad. "Wonder if she'll really go to Ole Miss?"

They knew she must be watching Pamela Rene, an African-American student from great wealth.

Pamela didn't like Tootie because Tootie was beautiful and popular. Pamela was neither, but she was smart.

"She won't go," Felicity predicted.

"Hell you say." Val used the old expression.

"One dollar." Felicity held out her hand.

She kept the kitty, which was filling up rapidly. One dollar for every swear word uttered by any of them. The plan was to use the money at the end of the semester for a party.

"She'll go." Tootie's alto sounded firm.

Both white girls stared at her. "Why?"

"To defy her mother; to prove she can do it."

"You mean survive in the Deep South?" Valerie caught on.

"Right. Her mother, the drama queen, thinks she'll be walking into the arms of the Ku Klux Klan."

"Thought they were strongest in Indiana. I swear I read that somewhere," Felicity added. "Or maybe Howie told me. His favorite subject is current affairs."

Tootie stood up, putting her boots on the floors to allow the polish to set before buffing. She walked to the window to watch Pamela. "Guess she'll be hunting tomorrow."

"She's a good rider," Val grumbled. "It's the rest of it."

"She's lost weight. How does anyone lose weight over Christmas vacation?" Felicity, thin, wondered.

"Her mother wired her mouth shut."

Val arched one eyebrow, a neat trick.

Tootie and Felicity burst out laughing.

"Felice, my darlin'," Tootie grinned, "You'll be okay if you and Howie are at separate schools."

"He's hoping for a football scholarship to Wake Forest. And they've offered him a tutoring program. I wouldn't mind Wake."

"Princeton!" Val fiercely said, her heart set on being a tiger.

"Are you in love or something?" Tootie sat back down beside Felicity.

A long silence followed. "I don't want to live without him. I guess I am."

"I am going to throw up!" Val swatted Felicity on the shoulder with the whisk brush. "You can't fall in love. We're too young. I mean, that's like prison."

"Val," Felicity blazed, "in the last century most people our age were married. It's natural to fall in love when you're young."

"Bullshit." Val, a beautiful six-foot one-inch blonde, tossed her long hair.

"She's right." Tootie defended Felicity. "We're the strange ones, out of step with biology."

"Since when are you a biology major?" Val would have none of it.

"You've never even felt a twinge for someone?" Felicity asked quietly.

"Only you." Val smarted off.

"Val, you can be such an ass sometimes." Tootie didn't say this with hostility.

"One dollar."

"God, Felicity, you're relentless!" Tootie handed over her dollar. "Val, you owe two."

"I know." Val opened her bureau drawer and pulled out two crisp dollar bills. "You're going to be a banker, I know it."

"Maybe." Felicity did, though, have a head for business, and she liked it.

"And you'll run for public office after law school." Tootie started buffing her boots.

"I will," Val agreed. "And I'll put off getting married until my middle thirties. Make every male voter believe he could be the one."

Tootie appreciated this shrewdness in Val, "Sometimes I think I'll marry, and other times I think never."

"When you meet the right one, everything falls into place." Felicity glowed.

"You're seventeen. Lust—okay, I can understand that, but love? Come on, Felicity, get over it." Val really couldn't understand this.

"Let's change the subject." Felicity sighed.

Before they could do that, Pamela Rene popped her head through the open door, but she had the manners to knock first on the door frame. "Hi."

"Hi," the three said.

"I lost my stock pin. Can I borrow one?"

"Sure." Tootie, who kept extras, reached into her coat, which Val had finished brushing. "Here you go."

"I'll give it back after tomorrow."

"Keep it." Tootie worked hard not to allow her feelings about Pamela to surface.

"I'll order everyone a backup from Horse Country," Pamela offered. "Be here next week."

"Good idea. Got the catalogue?" Val asked.

"Yeah."

"Can I see it later?"

"You can see it now." Pamela, also a resident of coveted Old One, turned on her heel and walked down the polished wooden floor to her decorated room. She returned with the glossy catalogue. The four girls strained to view it, but Tootie gave up and buffed her boots now that the polish had set.

"Retail's pretty amazing." Pamela also liked business, but from a different angle than Felicity.

"I wish Marion would take on apprentices," Felicity laughed, mentioning the owner of Horse Country. "I'd work for clothes."

"Me, too," Val agreed.

They commented on various delightful offerings and deplored their relative poverty, which was funny considering they were rich kids. But they were still kids and, with the exception of Val, were kept on a fairly strict allowance. Val's parents often overdid; she liked that in material terms, but it embarrassed her with her peers.

The funny thing about Pamela's parents was that they kept her on a short money leash, but then her father would send the corporate jet for her. Of the four girls, Pamela's home life was the unhappiest. Her mother, Thaddea Bolendar, had been a highly paid model in the 1970s. She'd made the cover of *Vogue* more than once, and she never ceased to remind her daughter, a few pounds overweight, that she wasn't perfect and she'd never make *Vogue.*

Val reveled in unconditional love, which gave her tremendous confidence. She was a happy young woman, if occasionally overconfident.

Felicity's parents also provided support, but they were exacting about her grades. They expected her to succeed, and this expectation was inferred, not expressed. She had lived up to it so far.

Tootie's parents loved her dearly, gave her a sharp moral compass, and had taught her discipline. Young though she was, she was the most organized and focused of the girls. Her father, who measured all things by money, pressured her to become an investment banker. Her mother mostly expected that she would have a dazzling career in whatever she chose and would marry an appropriate man. That meant rich. Both parents would prefer he be African-American, but the real cutoff was money.

They sat there, chattering away, talking about their studies, their friends, their beloved horses.

"Tomorrow's hunt is going to be the best. I just know it," Val enthused.

"The grays are mating. Reds should be, too," said Tootie, who loved nature far more than banking.

"Bet it's one of those hunts we never forget." Pamela, too, was enthusiastic, a rare occurrence. She was glad to be sitting with the other three. She wanted to be part of the group but lacked that easiness and warmth that make others comfortable. At least the chip on her shoulder was shrinking.

"I remember every single one." Tootie was so serious the others looked at her.

"Really?" Val recalled highlights, not every detail.

"Tomorrow will be a good one. We'll all remember," Pamela again predicted.

CHAPTER 16

The freezing and thawing, and a few days of mid-forties temperatures, made parking at Orchard Hill unwise. The nights stayed cold. The farm road leading in was too narrow to handle the volume of trailers, and there was no way to park in the fields, which would be frozen at first cast but possibly a muck hole when hounds returned.

Two hours before casting hounds, Sister put a message on the huntline number that everyone should park at Chapel Cross. The membership knew to check in. They were glad they did, because the area around the tiny church had been plowed.

Masters must be mindful of landowners, sextons, and other kindly people who call in useful information. Each year the hunt club made a nice donation to Chapel Cross, and she herself always gave the sexton one hundred dollars at Christmas. It helped that she liked everyone there, so it never seemed a chore to make the rounds.

Adolfo Vega, the sexton, was grateful for the cash and for the straw and manure that the members carried to his mulch pile. Adolfo prided himself on the gardens around the white clapboard church. He credited the manure for some of the result.

Any members not properly cleaning up after their horses faced a stiff fine, accompanied by a reprimand from the master. The reprimand was worse than the seventy-five dollars. Sister bided no disturbing of landowners who were friends of hunting.

Walter arrived an hour early to direct parking so no one would get stuck. The parking lot, not huge, called for maneuvering. Clemson, his older tried-and-true hunter, stayed on the trailer, happily munching from his hay bag while Walter, in his Wellies, got everyone squared away.

Sister and Shaker liked to park the party wagon slightly distant from the rest of the trailers. The hounds, obedient but curious, could be tempted to investigate someone's tack room if the door was open once they were out of the party wagon. Trinity evidenced a streak of kleptomania. In the bustle to mount up, someone usually forgot to latch a trailer door.

Today, the party wagon parked behind the chapel in front of the tidy churchyard, snow banked up against gray tombstones. Adolfo, knowing Sister's habits, carefully plowed out a circle on the north side, sheltered from the winds because of a double line of blue spruce trees. Little snow had melted, although it was packed down, so Adolfo, without realizing it, had plowed off the gravel path back there over dormant grass and had plowed over a den entrance. Foxes prudently dig more than one way in or out of a den. Even so, the medium-sized red dog fox who lived there was irate at having to clean out the snow to clear his entrance.

Shaker parked right over the entrance. Given the shade back there, he didn't see it.

When the hounds bounded out of the party wagon, Ardent wiggled under the trailer.

"Fox."

Before the others could join him, Shaker, thinking the older hound was having a silly moment, called him away. And Ardent, who deserved his appellation, crawled out. No point in getting into trouble before the hunt even began.

It mystified the hound that Shaker couldn't smell the den; it was potent, even with the sun barely nudging the horizon.

Noting his mournful face, Cora predicted, *"Don't fret, Ardent. By the time we come back here he'll smell it, and you'll be golden."*

"I forget how bad their noses are." Ardent fell in with the others as they walked down the gravel road, heading south and east to Orchard Hill.

The brisk air tingled in nostrils, on cheeks. Those who had slipped toe warmers into their boots had reason to be grateful. The mercury hung at thirty-one degrees but would surely rise to the mid-forties. The day, overcast, promised good hunting.

The fields and farm roads would require vigilance, for the surface would loosen with the rise in temperature, but underneath the soil would stay tight. Streaks of snow where the sun couldn't reach looked like icing. In other places the snow had drifted so much it hadn't melted down. But the general lay of the land was packed-down snow, with some bald patches due to earlier winds, all covered with heavy sparkling frost.

Puffs of condensation escaped horses' nostrils, peoples' mouths, and hounds' mouths. A bit of steam lifted off horses' hindquarters, but not much, not yet.

Sister loved mornings like this. Canada geese, many of which stayed throughout the winter, flew overhead, honking flight directions, their V formation later imitated by fighter pilots. Rabbit tracks were encased in the frozen snow and mud along with raccoon and possum tracks. Deer tracks crisscrossed meadows.

She felt a warm wind current as they approached the turn into Orchard Hill. Just as quickly she passed through it. Today, January 7, was the feast day of Raymund of Pennafort, who lived to near one hundred, going to his heavenly reward in 1275. Raymund, from Catalonia, had become a Dominican: a dog of God—or watchdog of God, if one prefers. The two words *dominus* and *canis* had merged together. Raymund believed in reconciling heretics, Jews and Moors.

With husband and son both named Raymond, Sister had always thought January 7 was a lucky day. The embracing temperament certainly applied to her husband in a more earthy fashion, but it truly applied to her son emotionally. His impulse had been to include, to find what was good about a person, to build bridges.

Those thoughts flitted across her mind until finally they reached a narrow covert, snaking along a tiny creek that fed into a much larger one. Ice crystals stood out in pretty clumps along the farm road.

"Lieu in there," Shaker called. Then he blew "Draw the covert," one long note followed by two short sharp ones.

Hounds dashed into the covert. Colder in there than out on

the field, they nonetheless had the advantage of being sheltered from the light breeze swooping down from the northwest.

Trudy worked alongside Cora, her hero. Not as fast as the older strike hound, Trudy absorbed all of Cora's knowledge. She wasn't slow, but Cora could pull ahead of all the hounds in the pack save Dragon, her nemesis. Rabbit scent curled up. The bitter odor of dried berries and bent-over pokeweed also was apparent.

The sun, now clear of the horizon, cast long scarlet shadows. The hounds worked through the narrow covert to where the little creek fed into the big one.

"To the left," Shaker called out, and the whole pack wheeled as one, working the left side of the fast-moving creek.

Tootie, Val, Felicity, and Pamela rode at the back of first flight. The custom for centuries had been for children, young people, and grooms to ride in the rear. On days when fields were quite small, Sister invited the girls forward. On the children's hunt, adults followed children.

The reasons for this were sound. Young people could observe those in front who had earned their colors. Those members knew the territory, respected hounds, and nine times out of ten were strong riders. Watching how they approached a tricky fence, negotiated a drop, dealt with an obstacle whose approach had been poached, churned up like cake frosting, taught the youngsters. Being nimble, they could more easily dismount and mount up than many older members. If someone dropped a crop or needed a hand, the young were expected to supply it. Also, if there was damage to a fence or to anything else, they weren't expected to repair it, but they were expected to remember. The person doing the damage was to report it immediately to the field master, even during a hunt, so long as they didn't disturb hounds. But the young provided a backup in case the offending rider did not. In their defense, sometimes so many people hit a fence that no one was a culprit. Still, all should 'fess up.

The other thing about having young people ride in the rear was that everyone in front had also performed these services, watched the experienced riders, prayed for the moment when they, too, would be one of them: the hunt's colors proudly worn on their collars, hunt bottoms sewn on their frock coats.

Hunting was a chain stretching back thousands of years. Tootie, Val, Felicity, and Pamela profited from the wisdom of the ages.

Tootie, fond of history, particularly responded. She never felt alone when she hunted. Ghosts rode with her.

Walking behind her hounds, still searching, Sister noted she'd seen no deer hunters. This was the last day of deer season, which could be as frightening as the first. Harvest had been good this season, many hunters reaching their bag limits. Anyone out today was most likely from the city. Not one orange cap or jacket flashed human presence.

A hunter needed a good memory for the seventy-three firearm regulations in the state of Virginia. Adding to the burden was the fact that each county also had specific regulations.

Hunting generated income. First, the state raked it in from the licenses, and then if the sheriff or animal control officer cited a hunter for a violation, there was that tasty fine, which was dumped into the county coffers. Without hunters of all stripes, states would go bankrupt.

Usually Sister could focus on the hounds, but when the going was slow, her mind wandered a bit.

She woke up, though, as Dasher opened, followed by Diana and Tinsel. They had picked up a line along the large creek bed.

Betty, on the right side of the large creek, loped along on Magellan and cleared a large tree trunk, keeping hounds well in sight.

Sybil, on the left, paralleled an old cart road, its ruts frozen. She passed a stack of pallets used during apple picking. A packing shed in serviceable condition sat near the pallets. The apple orchard covered the lands to the west, rising upward for fifty acres on the west side of the creek.

The fox kept straight as an arrow, but he was well ahead of hounds. He'd been courting, and having been unsuccessful in his designs had turned north, which meant he headed back toward Chapel Cross, where the tertiary gravel roads formed a perfect cross.

The field galloped through the western orchards and passed into the wide hay field with the one-hundred-thirty-year-old sugar maple of epic proportions in the middle.

The fox veered further north, picking up speed. The field, sweating now, cheeks flushed, cleared coops, rail fences, and a line of brambles entwining a disintegrating three-board fence. On they ran, hounds in full cry, ground beginning to soften in spots, for they'd been out an hour.

The fields, frost shining gold as the sun rose ever upward, rolled onward. The Blue Ridge Mountains provided a spectacular backdrop, the ice on deciduous trees and on pines flaming in the climbing sunlight.

"What the hell!" Dreamboat cursed as an eight-point buck shot right past him.

However, hounds smelled no hunters.

As they ran on and on, scent intensifying along with their

cry, Sister and the field noticed deer moving past them or cutting at angles. No deer ran away from the direction of the hounds. If anything, they were running to the hounds. Four miles past Chapel Cross, galloping flat out, they thundered into Paradise.

Bobby Franklin, leading the hilltoppers, pulled up on a high hill for a moment. He'd fallen behind because the old gates, rusting on the hinges, had taken some doing to open. The youngsters in the back of the hilltoppers dismounted to open the gates. This was done in twos so no one would be alone at a gate, everyone rushing off, their horse eager to join them.

Bobby heard Shaker's horn, piercing. He saw his wife flying across an open meadow with Sybil on the left. The hounds, tightly together, dashed over the meadow. Shaker next hove into view. He was followed by Sister on Rickyroo, his long stride eating up the ground. Behind Sister the field strung out, some already succumbing to the pace. The four Custis Hall girls were passing those who faltered or were pulling up, which was their right to do.

Just before Bobby squeezed his horse, a big fellow, something told him to wait.

More deer appeared, then a black and tan hound, followed by another and another. They looked like black jellybeans tossed over icing. To their credit, they weren't chasing the deer. A few had their noses down, but others had come up on the line that Dasher, Cora, Diana, and the others were following. The black and tans had been running backward on the line.

Within a minute they smashed smack into the pack.

"Pay them no mind!" Cora ordered.

"Cur dogs!" Dragon yelled to the young ones.

"Be damned if I'm a cur dog, sir." A black and tan snarled at Dragon, who snarled back.

Shaker, coming up hard, tucked his horn into his coat between the first and second buttons. Clear and loud, he commanded, "Ware riot!"

"Don't worry," Diana said, her nose down.

"Who are they?" Young Delight, baffled, yelped.

"Deerhounds. Pay them no mind," Ardent counseled.

One black and tan, reversing herself to join the Jefferson hounds and run in the right direction, replied, *"We're foxhounds. We're out here with a human who is a perfect fool."*

Dana, littermate to Delight, was about to reply, but the scent grew stronger. She stretched out, pushing off with her powerful loins supplying smooth power.

One by one, the black and tans reversed to fall into the tricolor pack. All the voices sang a crescendo of happiness that echoed off the mountains.

Sister now came up. Without faltering, she pushed Rickyroo on. "Jesus H. Christ on a raft."

"Yeah, but isn't the sound great?" Rickyroo flicked his ears back, then forward.

She laughed out loud because she loved him, because the pace was searing, the sound divine, the situation unique.

Just as Bobby moved out again, Jason Woods, perfectly turned out, galloped toward Betty. Hounds had turned toward him, so he pulled up, reversing with them.

Jason's Kilowatt, though beautiful, was no match for Magellan, who pulled alongside, then sped by him. Jason labored to keep up.

Crawford appeared, hanging onto Czpaka for dear life. Marty, a better rider than her husband, rode on his right as a whipper-in, a position she had no burning desire to fulfill.

Crawford blew into his reed horn. A thin note escaped.

Within seconds the doubled pack blasted right by him, as did Shaker, then Sister, then the field.

Sputtering, Crawford turned, only to find himself between first flight and the hilltoppers. As he tried to blow again, Bobby rode by him and hollered, "Don't!"

"Who the hell are you to tell me how to handle my pack?"

"You look fool enough, Crawford. Don't sound like a sick hen and make it worse."

Furious, Crawford threw the reed horn onto the ground.

He had no choice but to fall behind Bobby, since he couldn't catch up to first flight, now flying at Mach speed.

A fence row ahead, sagging, had a gap where one rail had long since fallen off. Hounds soared over, followed by Shaker forty yards later, then Sister, then the field.

Hounds screamed.

The fox, safely ahead, heard the music. This pack could wake the dead.

He cut sharply right, dipped into a wide ravine, popped back up, and skedaddled to the ruins of Paradise, its Corinthian columns majestic under gray, cottony clouds.

He slowed, flicked his impressive tail, and sauntered into his main entrance under the marble steps.

Four minutes later, all the hounds, jubilant, announced they had put their fox to ground.

Betty rode over but didn't take HoJo when Shaker dismounted to praise hounds and blow "Gone to ground."

Walter had ridden up to hold the reins, having been told to do so by Sister.

Given the cacophony and the strange hounds, Betty stayed outside the circle of hounds, as did Sybil on the other side.

Jason, breathing hard, rode up.

Betty said not one word.

Finally, Crawford rode up, Bobby hiding his laughter behind his gloved hand.

Crawford glared at his hounds, glared at Jason, and was about to bark at his own wife until he noticed she had a hound with her. Marty was the only one who did her job.

Sister smiled as her hounds watched Shaker for a sign.

The only ripple of discontent came from Dragon, who raised his hackles at a large, handsome dog hound.

"Dragon," Shaker quietly called his name.

Dragon turned his face from the offending hound and walked over to his huntsman.

"Come along." The hounds clustered around Shaker, but so did the black and tans.

"Where's your horn?" Jason asked.

"Threw it away." Red-faced, Crawford spat, now at the edge of the combined pack.

"Well, you'd better call your hounds out." Jason stated the obvious.

"I know that!" Crawford, enraged, slunk down in his saddle, then bellowed, "Come on."

Not one hound turned his or her head.

Crawford dismounted, so Czpaka walked over to Walter, HoJo, and Clemson. Crawford grabbed a hound roughly by the collar.

Sister, lifting her feet out of her stirrup irons, swung her right leg over, dismounting effortlessly.

"Don't touch a hound like that!"

Crawford wheeled. "It's my goddamn hound and I'll do as I please."

"You don't deserve these hounds."

"She's got that right." A beautiful black and tan bitch agreed.

Sister walked right up to Crawford as Shaker, still as a mouse, had all the hounds around him. "If you so much as touch one of my hounds, I will knock the stuffing right out of you!"

Crawford, vanity wounded and ego aflame, moved toward her. "Don't tell me what to do, you old bitch!" He pushed little Diddy out of the way with his knee.

"Ouch," Diddy cried.

Sister stepped forward with her left leg, her hands fast. She followed with a hard left, then a hard right, her whole weight in the punches.

Blood spurted from Crawford's mouth. He spit out teeth as he staggered.

He rose and threw a wild punch.

Sister ducked and came up, swinging both fists as hard as she could into his gut.

He doubled over, then sank to his knees.

Walter, mesmerized by the sight, walked toward them, three horses in tow.

Shaker, pack still with him, moved toward her.

Both men were encumbered.

Jason leaped off his horse and ran between the two antagonists. "Crawford, we'd better leave."

"I'll sue your sorry ass," Crawford cursed as he spurted blood.

"You just do that." Sister was ready to belt him again.

Walter reached her and placed his hand on her right shoulder.

Crawford, helped up by Jason, cried, "Furthermore, you're trying to lure my hounds away from me."

"Smoking opium," Cora said as all hounds laughed.

"I'll sue you. I'll see you bankrupt," Crawford threatened.

Jason, loud enough for those close to hear, sensibly said, "Crawford, what do you think will happen when you testify that you were beaten up by a woman in her seventies?"

This had the desired effect.

Marty prudently turned her horse. "Come along, hounds."

"We want to stay with them," a large fellow replied.

Jason handed Czpaka to Crawford and held his hands together so the bloodied man could mount up. Czpaka, sense of humor intact, took a step as Crawford tried to put his right leg over the saddle. Jason had to run alongside propping up Crawford until he was finally in the saddle.

No sooner was Crawford mounted then down the main drive to Paradise, churning old snow and mud as she roared, came Margaret DuCharme. She skidded to a halt and got out, slamming the door of her little Forester.

Margaret pointed her finger at Jason and Crawford. "What are you doing on my land?"

Crawford looked down at her. "It's not your land."

Jason groaned, then turned on the charm, smiling broadly at Margaret. "We'd like to know the foxes, human and otherwise."

Voice controlled, ice cold and loud enough for the entire field to hear, Margaret replied, "I will see you both dead before I let my parents sell Paradise."

"Alfred wants to sell." Crawford, rattled, had just let the cat out of the bag: he knew too much.

"We'll see about that."

Walter, Clemson and HoJo with him, walked over to Margaret. "It was one of the best runs of the season." He smiled. "Thank you for allowing Jefferson Hunt on Paradise. Can I help you with anything?"

She liked Walter and replied quietly, "Thanks, Walter. Get these trespassers out of here, please, before I really lose it."

"His hounds will follow ours. We'll get them and him out." Walter said this so Shaker could hear, too.

She half-whispered, "I'll see Jason in hell. I really will."

"You buy Jason's ticket. I'll buy Crawford's." Sister regained her composure.

Two egotistical men, pride wounded in different areas, seethed on their horses.

Marty, hound tagging along, rode up to Margaret. "I am truly sorry."

"Marty, I can't understand how someone as lovely and sensitive as yourself could marry such a . . ." Words failed her. Margaret threw up her hands, and Marty knew this wasn't the time to defend Crawford, no matter how much she loved him.

Useless as tits on a boar hog, Crawford and Jason couldn't extricate their hounds from the Jefferson Hunt hounds.

Another motor was heard in the distance: a big, booming diesel.

Sam Lorillard, in the passenger seat, eyes wide open, involuntarily smacked his forehead with his hand as Rory stopped the truck and trailer.

Sam emerged stiffly. Rory cut the throbbing motor and walked around to the back. He opened the trailer door.

They couldn't get the black and tans to load.

Sister, on foot, Rickyroo's reins now in hand, called out to Shaker, "Help them, or this will get even worse." She then directed Betty and Sybil: "You, too, if you don't mind."

Diddy leaped onto the new trailer.

"Diddy, out," Shaker gently chided the eager little girl. "Hold up," he instructed his hounds, who quizzically looked at him and at Sister, then Betty, then Sybil.

"Kennel up." Sam called the black and tans to him as Sybil and Betty quietly, with no fanfare, moved at the edges of the hounds who didn't break.

Sister breathed a prayer of relief the black and tans didn't bolt but loaded up.

"Told you this would be a good hunt," Pamela bragged.

"Not over yet," Val replied.

Watching this was Ben Sidell. Nonni, his gentle teacher, took it all in as she stood next to Bobby's big draft cross.

"Ben, I'm old enough to know when hounds won't hunt for a man. Those hounds will never hunt for Crawford—not even if he feeds them calves' liver daily," Bobby drawled.

Sam, soaking up the tension, clambered back into the truck as soon as the black and tans were loaded.

The big trailer also carried the horses. Crawford, Jason, and Marty dismounted and walked their horses onto the trailer.

It was against state law to ride in the trailer, but under the circumstances, Jason urged them to do so. They'd get out of Paradise more quickly, and the ride back to his SUV wasn't that far.

"I'll get you for this!" Crawford shouted to Sister as Rory slammed and bolted the door.

Sister didn't reply.

Shaker, back up on HoJo, apologized: "I'm sorry I couldn't get to you fast enough, Boss."

"Maybe we both belong in the ring." She half smiled, referring to their boxing prowess.

"Hell of a combination." He smiled broadly.

"Was, wasn't it?" She couldn't help but feel pride, even though she knew that worm Crawford would churn up mud.

Hounds moved off. At the edge of Paradise people could hear the big diesel truck straining.

It was nearly noon when they arrived back at Chapel Cross. This time the whole pack wedged under the trailer.

Shaker bent over, then got down on his hands and knees, mud on his white breeches. "Holy smoke!"

"Now what?" Sister swung her leg over Rickyroo.

"There's a den right under the trailer."

"Shaker, you've denned your fox. How about giving tongue?" She bent over laughing.

Sheepishly, he stood back up and called hounds out from under the trailers. "Ardent, you were right."

"Golden." Cora beamed at her friend.

Reluctantly, one by one, hounds gave up their quarry, who was unconcerned in his cozy quarters.

The field gathered round for the spectacle.

At the tailgate, everyone buzzed with the unusual events of the day.

Finally, at one, Sister drove back, Betty as her passenger.

"Wait until I tell Gray. Poor baby, he's at the office, and Garvey's there, too. Oh, they missed a show!"

"The audit sounds difficult. I couldn't do that tedious work."

"Since Sam's accident, Gray's been staying home with Sam, who can't dress himself without help. Of course, even if he were with me, he couldn't say anything. Gray is a very principled man, and really, most accountants are. I do know Garvey needs Gray's report for the Farmers Trust."

"Red tape. Pure and simple."

They drove along, wondering what to do about Crawford, wondering how Sam could stand it, and feeling sorry for a nice pack of hounds who were being ruined.

A minivan, going much too fast, began to pass them.

"Iffy. What's with her? And why isn't she at Aluminum Manufacturers? This may be Saturday, but it's all hands on deck at Garvey's."

Sister turned her head slightly as the dark blue metallic van flew by. "Is everyone nuts today?" She focused on the road again. "You know, if there is an irregularity at Aluminum Manufacturers, she's the first one on the griddle."

"I'm sure she knows that," Betty replied.

"Wonder if she knew Crawford would be over here today. Her land backs up to his at that ridge."

Betty interrupted, "I don't think being a neighbor gave her the inside track."

"You're right. Then I wonder if Alfred knew. Someone had to know. I mean—would Crawford really be dumb enough to cast hounds here?"

"Big ego." Betty, too, wondered. "Or he was set up to fail?"

They looked at each other, saying in unison, "Jason."

"Makes no sense." Sister shook her head.

CHAPTER 17

While Iffy blew through Chapel Cross, having worked that Saturday morning in a race to get papers back to Farmers Trust, Gray used her absence to approach Garvey. Iffy said she'd come back after lunch, so he watched the clock.

Having placed a large folder and a bank deposit bag on Garvey's desk, he sat opposite the younger man. "Garvey, Freddie, and I worked through the night. She's been terrific."

Garvey's stomach tightened. "You do look a little rough."

"Been a hell of a week." He stood up, opening the folder and placing four stacks of invoices before Garvey. "Look at these."

Dutifully, Garvey inspected the invoices. "They look okay to me."

"They're computer generated."

Garvey studied them afresh. "Isn't everything?"

"No. These invoices are identical except for the print. Each business has a different print color. For instance, Hanson Office Supplies is blue, Rickman's Sanitary Service is black, L&L Commercial Cleaners is red, and Dalton Rubber Supply is green."

Confused, Garvey bent his head over the invoices. "I'm missing something, Gray."

"It's uncommon to find identical invoices setting apart the print color. Freddie went online to see if these businesses existed. I called a colleague in Richmond at nine this morning. He's never heard of them. Freddie and I flipped through the Richmond phone book to be safe, and we checked to see if in the last five years any of these companies could have been bought out by a larger company. Sometimes they'll use up the old paper. Not often, though."

"Where's Freddie now?"

"She went to work straight from here to catch up."

"Gray, you're telling me these are bogus."

"I am. You don't initial or countersign checks this small. Iffy signs them. You'll also notice that these invoices are addressed to P.O. boxes. There's no telephone number on the invoice, no street address, no e-mail address. While each of these companies has a different P.O. box, they are all located at the main post office in Richmond."

A sickly look passed over Garvey's pleasant features. "Two thousand to Rickman's Sanitary Service, seven hundred and fifty for office supplies."

"Every month. Freddie also ran a computer search to see how many vendors of like services or supplies had the same zip code. No matchups. We have the cancelled checks." He zipped open the standard bank deposit bag used by businesses. "All are signed by your treasurer, and all are endorsed by a rubber stamp that says 'for deposit only.'" Gray pulled out a few checks for Garvey's inspection.

"My God." Garvey slumped in his chair. "Iffy."

"She goes to Richmond the third Thursday of each month. She picks up the checks and she deposits them in her own account. Obviously, we can't seize her personal records until you charge her."

His face flushed. "She deserves the right to explain herself. She's been with me for years."

"What she deserves is arrest. All these fake invoices are dated on the same day of the month, and they are all deposited on the same day of the month, the third Thursday. Garvey, it's an old scheme, and it's tried and true as long as the person doing it knows when to get out. It's called disbursements fraud. It's always an inside job, usually committed by a chief financial officer. If you don't have her arrested the minute she walks back in this door, I can tell you exactly what will happen."

"What?" Garvey whispered.

"She will say she needs to talk to an attorney. She'll leave, and my guess is she can access the money very quickly. She'll leave the country."

"I can't believe it." Garvey dropped his head into his hands.

"I'm sorry. I truly am."

"How much did she steal from me?"

"Freddie and I want to go over the cashed checks again. We also want to see if there aren't other things we may have missed simply through exhaustion."

Garvey lifted his head, raised his eyes, "Gray, how much?"

"Two million."

"Oh, my God." Garvey picked up the phone and dialed. "May I speak to Sheriff Ben Sidell?"

CHAPTER 18

"You take it too seriously." Jason shrugged off Walter's anger at his whipping-in, if it could be called that, to Crawford Howard.

"Yes, I do. Seriously enough to drive over here after the hunt on my day off. You don't know what you've done."

Jason's dark eyebrows lifted. "I rode with an undisciplined pack of hounds, Crawford got his lip split open by Sister, and Margaret threatened my life. So what?" He laughed, albeit hollowly.

"You rode with an outlaw pack. You can't ride with the Jefferson Hunt again or with any other hunt associated with the Master of Foxhounds Association of America."

"Bullshit."

"The MFHA was founded in 1907 to avoid exactly what happened. And you'd better believe they'll enforce it. If, for example, you try to ride with Keswick, and if word got back to the MFHA that the masters allowed you to do so, they would risk losing their recognition, which is like losing your medical license. I'm telling you, Jason, you don't know what you've done."

Jason pushed his back against the chair. "Well who is going to report me? Sister? You?"

"She'll wait for you to come to your senses today. If you do, she will explain to the president of the MFHA that you were unaware of the rule and you will never ride with Crawford again. If you don't call today she will report you, or I will. We have no choice."

Jason slammed down his coffee cup. "It was supposed to be fun. I've all but bought Paradise."

Fortunately, the cup was heavy.

"You don't own it yet." Walter stated the obvious.

He'd driven to Jason's spacious brick house downtown. Jason had bought it as an investment, declaring he'd sell it as soon as he found the country property he wanted.

The fireplace in the kitchen had Delft tiles around it. Jason had paid a decorator who mixed antiques with modern pieces, to lovely effect.

"I don't need Sister's help or your help. I'll call the MFHA myself."

"That will make matters worse," Walter grimly predicted. "Apologize to Sister, then let us handle it."

"I suppose she's mad at me?"

"We're all mad at you. And let me tell you why you'll need her help. It's a small world, and most foxhunters recognize why we can't countenance outlaw packs. You're going to be on everybody's shit list, not just Jefferson Hunt's."

"Countenance? You sound like a preacher."

"A Virginian, at least," Walter half smiled. "We grow up on the King James version." He leaned across the rectangular table. "Look, I'm upset that you rode out with Crawford, who means us no good. But I'm your colleague, you know. The hospital is a small world—like foxhunting. I'd like things on an even keel."

Jason listened, holding his cup with both hands. "Tell that to Margaret."

"She has every right to be angry with you. You need to apologize to her, to Binky and Millie and Alfred."

His dark eyebrows raised, then lowered. "I will. I'll smooth the waters. But you know, if they don't sign that contract next week, I'll buy another property. They'll never ever get a deal like mine. Seven million dollars. No financing."

Walter, though the sum was impressive, wasn't impressed. "The DuCharmes have owned Paradise for just about two hundred years. You aren't from here, Jason. It's hard for you to realize the pull of blood and time. It truly outweighs money."

Jason's voice dripped sarcasm. "Two old men without a pot to piss in. They live off Margaret and cutting timber every five years. They have to agree to my terms, which are very generous." When Walter didn't respond out of good manners, Jason, exasperated, announced, "I offered them seven million dollars for a bunch of Corinthian columns."

Walter glanced down at his cup, then up at Jason. "And five thousand acres, much of it in good Davis loam. The timber program is good. You sell Alfred short. He's managed the farm wisely, and Binky has had the sense to stay out of his way and run his little gas station. They may be pathetic, battling old men to you, but they aren't stupid. And Margaret is smarter than both of them put together."

Jason flared up. "I saved Alfred."

"You have a remarkable record as a doctor. I respect that. Your patients, cured or in remission, are walking advertisements. But this is different. If you don't apologize to Sister Jane, you're cooked. If you don't back off from Crawford, you're cooked. Am I clear?"

Silence followed. The stainless steel wall clock ticked loudly.

"If I back off from Crawford, I'm cooked." At last, a genuine emotion, worry, played on Jason's face.

"You're in the tank?" Walter used the old political expression, meaning you've been bought off in one respect or another.

"Yes."

"How deep?"

"He's my silent partner in purchasing Paradise."

"I can't imagine Crawford wants to see you restore Paradise to its former glory. So you are going to develop Paradise?" Walter clamped his mouth shut. "You lied."

As Jason had bandied about some of his plans for Paradise, Walter knew he'd made a big to-do about respecting the past, allowing no development, and other such pious statements.

"Not exactly."

"Oh, is this like Clinton saying a blow job isn't really sex?"

Jason's face darkened. "We'd wait a year. We'd develop one thousand acres as an equestrian paradise. It would be impeccably done."

"And you'd both make double-digit millions—and you get to live in Paradise as well."

"Oh," Jason corrected him, missing Walter's sly comment. "We'd generate jobs and revenue for the county."

"No doubt. That does put you over a barrel. Do you want to hunt with an outlaw pack, or do you want to make even more money than you already do?"

"I'll bring Crawford around to registering his pack."

"Good luck. He's publicly derided the MFHA. Crawford's not one to reverse a public position."

"If it's in his extreme self-interest, I'll bet he will."

"Like I said, good luck," Walter admonished. "I know you don't want to get on the bad side of Crawford. I understand, but you don't want Sister angry at you. She can take you down."

"She knows how to throw a punch," Jason nodded. Then he leaned nearly halfway across the table. "Is it true her husband was your father?"

"Yes."

"That doesn't upset her?"

"No."

"Does it upset you?"

"For my father, it did. But Big Ray was one of those men who walked into a room and women's heads swiveled around. Whatever he had, if we could have bottled it, we'd be worth billions." He exhaled. "Things just happened around Big Ray. 'Course they happened around Sister, too." He shrugged. "Ancient history. I love her. I've always loved Sister. When I was a kid I wanted to ride like her. Working with her is one of the joys of my life. I just wish I knew what she forgot."

"Plenty of good foxhunters out there."

"She's beyond good."

"Look, I'll concede that Crawford doesn't know shit. Those hounds running all over proves that, but it's not rocket science."

"Exactly." Now Walter leaned forward. "It's an art woven into primeval instinct. She has it. Sister has horse sense, hound sense, game sense, and that something extra. You can't teach it. You can't buy it. I'm learning hounds and game, but I also know that what she has I'll never have. What I have is a sharp political sense. I'm useful to her for that. And I love hunting. I'd lose my mind without hunting."

"Suppose I would, too. That's why I want to whip-in. I don't want to be in the field watching everyone's ass over a jump."

"Some of those asses are mighty fine."

Jason leered. "Well, yes."

"Jason, we'd all like to whip-in to this pack. To whip-in at Jefferson Hunt is to be taken seriously by other foxhunters. None of us are immune to that kind of attention. I can't do it, but I wish I could."

"Why?"

"I'm not that good a rider, and I don't have much hound sense, although I like the hounds. But I have people sense."

"I can ride," Jason boasted.

"What about the rest of it? She's right to make you walk-out. And I don't know if she'll keep that offer after what you did yesterday."

Jason shifted in his seat. "If I bow to Sister, I lose Crawford. I have to find another way." He exhaled. "Or accept that I'll not be hunting with you."

"Jason, I wish I knew what the middle way might be. Until you, I, or someone else can think of it, you've got to calm the waters. You'd better apologize to Sister."

Jason's cell phone rang. He flipped open the cover to see the caller's number displayed. "Damn. Excuse me." He pressed the talk button. "Hello."

Iffy bellowed, "Jason, where are you?"

"I'm in a meeting." He didn't mention that he wasn't in his office.

"A meeting with whom?"

"Walter."

"Get out of it. I have to see you."

"Don't worry about the insurance paperwork." He sounded soothing.

"It's three-thirty. I have to see you. Not in your office," she persisted.

"All right, but let me call you right back. This is an important meeting." A note of irritation crept into his voice.

She slammed down her phone.

Walter noticed the expression on Jason's face. "I'd better be going."

The shorter man folded his cell phone up. "She needs a psychiatrist. Iffy."

"I wouldn't know." Walter thought it best to stay out of this discussion.

"Her health is improving; her personality is not." Jason, exasperated, shoved the phone aside.

Walter rose. "If you don't call Sister by tomorrow, I'll call Dennis Foster at the MFHA Monday. I don't want to do that."

Dennis Foster was the director of the MFHA. As a lieutenant colonel, retired, in the U.S. Army, he could be forceful when he needed to be. Jason would find this out in a hurry if he didn't mend fences.

"I'll do it. Will you do me a favor?"

"What?"

"Don't mention that Crawford and I are partners in the Paradise deal. Look, it's possible we won't develop it. If I can put my ducks in a row, I might be able to buy him out."

"He's not one to pass up a big profit."

"If there's prestige involved, he might."

Walter cocked his head slightly. "What kind of prestige?"

"Master of Jefferson Hunt."

"Jason, that will be a cold day in hell."

"Stranger things have happened."

Jason was right about that.

CHAPTER 19

Hunt days were outlined in bright green on Sister's month-at-a-glance calendar on the kitchen wall. A smaller version was tacked onto her bathroom wall. Today's fixture, Little Dalby, owned by the Widemans, interested her. During summer and fall, hunt club members reopened old trails and built jumps. The property, in limbo for years, had suffered neglect. The lawyers in charge of the old Viault estate lived in New York City. They had thought they were protecting the property by throwing off Jefferson Hunt. The reverse had happened, because it was the hunt club that had kept the hundreds of acres cleared, hayed, and tidied up during those last years of Mr. Viault's life. It was Jefferson Hunt's thank-you to a family that had been a vibrant part of foxhunting.

Pricker bushes, pokeweed, chickweed, and broomsage choked the once luxurious pastures. Outbuildings listed. A hole had been punched in the roof of the main house during a hurricane. The lovely little church, St. John of the Cross, had suffered comparatively little damage, although a great horned owl was now in residence.

Sister wondered whether the owl had converted to Christianity. She suspected not, given that the owl is sacred to Athena. Then, too, Christians talked too much about lambs and sheep and not enough about owls.

Last night Sister had called Anselma Wideman to make sure Crawford wouldn't be hunting and to find out whether he had hunted the territory at all. The "all clear" pleased her. She wondered how long it would take Anselma and Harvey to realize this arrangement wouldn't work.

After she'd checked in with Anselma, she and Gray hung on the phone like teenagers. Since Sam's accident, he'd stayed home to help his brother. Usually from Friday night through Sunday night Gray spent the weekends at Roughneck Farm. Sister found she missed him. Apart from sharing a bed with him, she missed his picks and pans as he read choice passages from the morning's paper.

Gray operated under a code of ethics as strict as that for physicians. He couldn't discuss a client's affairs, but she could tell from his voice that something was amiss. She figured the tension was because Farmers Trust had thrown a monkey wrench into the process of extending credit. But last night, she could hear in his tone that something was wrong, something more significant than Farmers Trust. Of course, she knew nothing about Garvey's call to Ben Sidell. Nor did she know that the deputy sent to pick up Iffy couldn't find her. She had flown the coop.

Gray promised to spend next weekend with her. Sam swore

he could fend for himself. He told Gray to go; he was tired of being with a lovesick moose. Sister liked hearing that.

Right now she liked hearing little Diddy opening at St. John of the Cross. After drawing through a still unrehabilitated pasture for twenty minutes, Shaker finally jumped the coop into the woods. Sister noticed hound sterns waving. Diddy marched right up to the heavy front door, the cross on the graceful steeple covered in snow, and she sang out.

Since Diddy was a second-year entry, Diana trotted over to double-check.

"Good!" The beautiful anchor hound seconded Diddy's excellent work.

With that, the pack put their noses down, inhaled deeply, and opened in joyous chorus.

They threaded through the woods, the low limbs of spruces, bearing the snow's weight, touching the ground. As hounds moved through they'd brush under the spruces; snow would cascade down in a shower of tiny sparkles.

Sister stayed on the farm road. No point plunging into the woods as long as she could keep near hounds. They were moving west. The folds in the land grew tighter. As she burst out of the woods the sun touched the top of the Blue Ridge Mountains, turning the snow crimson.

Scattered clouds began to glow underneath.

She turned to look behind. Tedi, Edward, Walter, Val, Tootie, Felicity, and Bunny Taliaferro constituted the field. The cold weather and last layer of snow had kept others at home. Then, too, the holiday season had ended, so folks redoubled their efforts at work. There were all those Christmas bills to pay.

The hounds suddenly shut up. Sister stopped on the

meadow's rise, the mild wind stinging in the cold, to behold them casting themselves.

Asa, wise, walked into the wind. Thirty yards later he picked up the scent, faint though it was, for the wind had blown it off the actual fox's line and the scent dissipated as it lifted.

"Hop on it. Fading fast," he commanded.

Not one hound would ever question Asa. They collapsed on the line and opened again, pushing ever westward.

Ahead, Sister saw Betty with Outlaw, her favorite mount, a tough little quarter horse, battling snowdrifts like a destroyer in heavy seas. To her left, Sybil was jumping a stout stone fence, some center stones having tumbled down over the years. Sybil kept alongside the hounds but far enough away not to bring their heads up or cause them to question her presence. The whole pack turned as one and cut sharply left, heading southwest now, to disappear into second growth forest.

Sister squeezed Keepsake, her thoroughbred/quarter horse cross, the perfect mount for this terrain and these conditions. He found his spot, soared over the stone fence, and then stretched out as they flew along the deer path in the forest only to burst out onto another meadow, broomsage spiking up through the snow.

They galloped down to a swift-running creek, where hounds threw up, meaning they lost the line, throwing up their heads. Unfortunately, so did Felicity. As hounds cast for the line she dismounted, ran behind a bush, and tossed her breakfast.

She came back, bright as a penny, and hopped up on Parson.

Tootie reached over to feel her forehead. "No fever," she whispered.

"I ate too many doughnuts on the way over," Felicity whispered back.

"Me too." Val put her gloved hand on her stomach, the white string glove contrasting sharply with the black melton coat.

"You going to heave?" Tootie whispered.

"No." Val shook her head as Bunny turned to glare at them for whispering during a check.

Cora moved further away from the pack, but she could find nothing.

Dasher stared down the steep bank of the creek, then launched himself. Airborne for a moment, he hit the water with a splash, swam with the current, and reached the far bank fifty yards downstream. He clambered out, put his nose to ground and worked back. He passed the pack on the other side and kept working. After five minutes, he had found nothing.

"Come on, Dasher. Good work, boy." Shaker called the hound back.

The big fellow hurtled off the opposite bank and swam again, the current carrying him downstream. He emerged, shook himself, and trotted back to the others, working in vain.

"Helicopter." Dasher laughed.

"Yeah." Trident agreed that the fox must have stepped into a helicopter to be lifted right up.

Nothing remained. Not the tiniest scrap of scent.

"I hate this!" Cora, filled with drive, kept searching.

"Come along." Shaker called them together. "Good work. I'm proud of you. We'll hunt back."

As they turned to hunt on the south side of the fixture, moving in an arc toward the trailers two miles distant, Sister heard a siren.

As the crow flies, they were little more than three miles southwest of Chapel Cross. By road it would take fifteen minutes, but the sound carried.

Sister wondered if one of the DuCharmes had finally met his Maker.

No, but one of the DuCharmes was deeply troubled.

Ben Sidell stepped out of his squad car. Margaret, in shearling coat, came out of the small dependency in which she lived.

"I'm so glad to see you. You made good time."

"I was going against morning traffic." He noted the rich seal-brown color of her hair falling over the shoulders of her coat.

"Look at this." She walked to her Subaru Forester and opened the door.

Ben touched nothing but carefully noted Iffy's wheelchair on its side, blood spattered over the backrest.

CHAPTER 20

Although his partner accused him of clutter, Uncle Yancy hotly denied this. Target collected possessions just sitting under a rosebush. Uncle Yancy believed his treasures had been carefully selected, not just picked up in collector's mania.

True, he built little caches into which he stored the odd mouse part, chicken wing, or rabbit. He used to push corn, even fat millet heads, into his cache piles. Lately, though, he kept the grains in his den. For one thing, he couldn't always find his caches under snow. He could hear mice two feet under snow. They'd burrow through if snows hadn't packed down hard. There was plenty of oxygen for them. He'd hear those tiny claws, and he could pounce. But caches made no noise, so he'd learned to keep a grain bank account.

Since he had taken over the pattypan forge, storage space was ample. He'd lined his main sleeping quarters with grasses.

He'd bedded down his storage chambers, although not as deep. Some foxes didn't mind sleeping with frost in their dens. He did. That's why he insulated his sleeping quarters.

The quiet pleased him. The only thing that didn't please him was returning to find a glob of blood near his den. Human footprints clearly stood out in the snow. The blood carried an odd odor, so he didn't touch it.

He'd returned from desultory hunting that morning. The two-mile trot down to the main house at After All had invigorated him. He'd intended to hunt, but Tedi had left out corn oil–soaked kibble behind her stable. He'd stuffed himself.

Sister would refill the special feed buckets Thursday night. One was tied to a tree perhaps a quarter of a mile from pattypan.

At eleven, his restorative sleep was interrupted by Aunt Netty.

"Wake up, you lazy ass." She pushed him with her dainty paw. *"Filthy, as always. Frozen blood by the den entrance. You are disgusting."*

He opened one eye. *"My precious."*

"Don't precious me. I'd heard you took over pattypan. Knew you wouldn't stay over there at the old Lorillard place. Boring over there. Besides"—she paused, half closing her eyes to savor her imagined triumph—*"too far from me."*

Uncle Yancy, no fool, smiled. *"You're right."*

"It's beautiful here. I always wanted to live at pattypan, but the minks—well . . ." She shook her head disapprovingly.

Minks, little weasels, possessed ferocity in inverse proportion to their size. They had run out the foxes who'd lived at pattypan years ago and then had bred more minks. Squabbles increased with the population. The younger minks left, heading west. Many now lived on Hangman's Ridge, but they usually kept out of view. Others pushed on to Mill Ruins, where vigorous mouth battles with other animals, especially squirrels, were daily dramas. The older minks at pattypan flourished until they challenged Athena. Like most arguments, silly though it was, it illustrated the incompatibility of both parties. Furious, Athena systematically killed them until there wasn't one old mink left.

Their celebrated courage couldn't help them when death came from the skies. Fearing the younger minks might return, other burrowing animals still did not take over pattypan.

Uncle Yancy had hit it at the perfect time. Everyone else had settled in a den, young foxes usually establishing themselves in early November in central Virginia.

"I'm not far from a feed bucket, which is nice in bad weather." He hoped she wasn't going to get pushy.

"See that you don't get fat."

"I've never been fat."

"You've never been old. We're getting on, Yancy. Which brings me to my point. I'm not breeding this year. Not just because of my age, but something tells me it will be a hard spring and summer. We must be wise about these things."

Uncle Yancy, like most males, deferred to the female. They just knew. He asked, "*What about the younger girls? Charlene, Grace, Inky, Georgia?*"

"Georgia will wait another year. For one thing, she's not far from her mother, so if Inky should produce a litter, Georgia will help. I haven't spoken to Inky. Charlene, in her prime, will chance it. As for Grace, haven't talked to her either."

"What about the deer and the squirrels? Have you talked to them?"

"Some will, some won't; most are cutting back. Bitsy isn't." She grimaced.

Uncle Yancy's jaw dropped. *"Bitsy's never laid an egg in her life."*

"That's just it. She says she wants to do it, and furthermore she's ensconced in Sister's barn, so there's plenty to eat. Can you stand it, husband? More screech owls. As it is she wakes the dead." She sniffed. *"Athena can't even talk her out of it."*

"Earplugs," he laughed.

"Not me. I want to hear the huntsman's horn." She settled into the sweet grass. *"This really is beautiful. I could make this even better. Why don't you go out and clean up that blood if you aren't going to eat it?"*

Uncle Yancy's heart skipped a beat. How was he going to get out of this? *"When it comes to decorating, I lack your talent, but"*—he heaved a huge mock sigh—*"I'd bring in a shiny can and you'd be upset. Or I'd snore."*

"U-m-m," she hummed. *"Before I get comfortable I brought you a housewarming present."*

He stewed while she scooted out of the main entrance, returning with a lacquered mechanical pencil. *"Here."*

He pushed the deep burnt-orange pencil. *"It's gorgeous."*

"Long hunt last night. Restless. Anyway, I wound up at the old Lorillard place. The graveyard enticed me. Lot of Lorillards there from way back, centuries back—and, you know, there was a fresh grave, covered in snow. I could smell the fresh earth underneath. We had that bit of a thaw. God knows, you can't dig up frozen ground, so whoever dug the grave knew that much. Well, I started digging because I thought it might be a cache. Something we could use. But no, too deep. I did find this. Under the snow, on top of the packed earth."

"Expensive."

"Yes."

"How deep do you think the cache is?"

"Three feet perhaps. The frost came back hard, so I could just get a whiff of meat."

"Could have been the mountain lion. They're around. They leave a big mound, and they mark boundaries with their caches."

"I told you, the earth was packed. Not like a cache. Humans pack down that way." Aunt Netty, seated, was cross that he didn't instantly agree with her.

"No Lorillards died." Uncle Yancy, like all the foxes, knew the events of humans in their hunting territory.

"Hadn't thought of that."

"Netty, this isn't a good thing. It's clever, too."

"Well, it's none of our affair." Drowsy, she closed her eyes.

He viewed his partner, instantly asleep. *"Damn. Double damn,"* he said under his breath.

Another fox of sorts considered the facts before her. Sister now knew Iffy was missing. The radio and television newscasters had asked anyone who had seen her to report it. The newscasters didn't speculate on why she might be missing. That would come in the ensuing days.

She sat at Big Ray's partner's desk in the warm den and speculated plenty.

Finally, she called Ben Sidell. A yellow legal pad filled with scribbled notes testified to her attempts to put the pieces together.

"Sister, how are you?"

"Fine. Ben, here I am again coming out of left field. Allow me to make a suggestion. Exhume Angel Crump."

"Who's Angel Crump?"

"She was Garvey's assistant since the earth began. She died

last year, age eighty-four, of a heart attack. Garvey walked into her office and found her slumped over her desk."

"Why do you want her exhumed?"

"She hated Iffy. In the best of circumstances they would have clashed—personality differences—but I have to wonder if Angel harbored suspicions. Maybe the animosity was based in fact."

"Garvey hasn't mentioned this."

"Ask him if Angel ever accused Iffy of wrongdoing. And mind you, I don't know what's going on down there. Gray can't tell me, but I hear the strain in his voice. Iffy's missing. I'm not a genius, but I can put two and two together."

"I appreciate your idea. Let me talk to Garvey first. If Angel did come to him with suspicions, then I'll put the machinery in motion. As you know, if relatives oppose an exhumation it can take some time for the legal process to sort it out."

"I know. And it's just a hunch but perhaps Angel's death proved quite convenient."

She hung up the phone, cupped her chin in her hand, fiddled on the legal pad.

Golly batted at the pencil. She liked commandeering the desk because the dogs couldn't get on it and because she could see everything Sister was doing.

Raleigh and Rooster stretched out on the leather couch. Rooster's head rested on Raleigh's flank. They were dead to the world.

"January 11. You know, Golly, no saint today? That's particulary interesting. Odd." She'd checked her *Oxford Dictionary of Saints.*

"I'll take the day, then." Golly stopped the pencil with both paws, held it to bite the eraser.

"Golly," Sister laughed.

"There are cat saints." Golly managed an indignant stare as Sister wiggled the pencil from her grasp. *"Who do you think kept the mice out of Little Lord Jesus' crib? A cat."*

Sister listened to these determined meows, then burst out laughing.

CHAPTER 21

Riding down from their stable, Tedi and Edward heard the mighty rumble of the Chevy Duramax 6600 before they reached their covered bridge.

Sister and Shaker, double-checking the hound list by the trailer, also heard it.

"He wouldn't." Sister held the clipboard to her chest as large snowflakes began to fall. Even though Jason had apologized profusely, she thought he'd allow some time to pass for emotions to cool.

"Only one engine sounds like that." Shaker was as surprised as Sister.

The small field assembled this Thursday morning turned their heads. The girls from Custis Hall, Bunny Taliaferro, Henry Xavier, Ronnie Haslip, Lorraine Rasmussen, and Bobby Franklin glanced at one another.

Betty Franklin walked around the trailer as her husband tightened his horse's girth. "Do you hear what I hear?"

"I do." Bobby frowned, a snowflake falling on his nose.

"The man must be out of his mind."

"Arrogant." Bobby clipped down his words. "But he did express his regrets. Sister made sure we all knew that."

Sybil, who had ridden down ahead of her parents in order to help with hounds, leaned down to Sister. "Would you like Dad to throw him off?"

"No. Landowners can't refuse a hunt member the right to hunt their land with the hunt. A landowner can refuse the hunt but not an individual. This isn't to say it doesn't happen, but it's counter to proper practice. It's the master's responsibility to send a member home. The problem really gets ugly if you have a weak master."

"Why can't a landowner refuse permission?" Sybil, intent on being a good whipper-in, didn't pay too much attention to MFHA policies not related to actual hunting.

"Because that member's dues built jumps on the landowner's land. And because every time someone gets into a spat it would affect who hunts where. Eventually you'd see fields of two people until one of them pissed off the other." Sister pulled off her old gloves, cut off at the fingertips, to put on white string riding gloves. "Let's say you and I had a fight. A big one. One would assume you wouldn't come on my farm to hunt. You'd steer clear of that fixture because it makes life easier for everyone. But some people like being the center of attention. That kind of person would show up." She shrugged as Jason's rig came into view.

Sister mounted Aztec, ready to go and eager to prove to Rickyroo how good he was. He would tell all back at the barn. As the youngest hunter in the barn Aztec endured a lot of ribbing.

All the horses were keen to see how Matador would pan out. He was in work but had yet to hunt, since Sister didn't want to hunt a new horse on bad ground. This pleased Lafayette, Keepsake, Rickyroo, and Aztec because it showed how much she trusted them.

Tedi and Edward clattered through the covered bridge and rode over to Sister.

Tedi raised an eyebrow.

Edward, a gentleman, quietly said, "Would you like me to go over there with you?"

"All clear," she replied. "As you know, he apologized to me. I'll give him credit for that." Looking up into her old friend's gray eyes, she shrugged. "You know how I think."

He smiled. "I do."

Tedi smiled as well, keeping her peace.

Sister gathered the small group to her. "Good morning."

"Good morning, Master," came the reply, the same as it had been for centuries.

"As we have such a small field today, I would like to invite the Custis Hall girls to ride up front. Also, they are being allowed to come out weekdays with us if they each write a paper for their environmental studies class. Perhaps if they have questions after the hunt, you would answer them."

Tootie on Iota, Val on Moneybags, and Felicity on Parson all glowed. To ride behind the master was a singular honor.

Walter rode next to Jason in the rear.

It was truly dawning on Jason that he hadn't just offended Sister and Shaker; he'd pissed off the whole club.

Dragon, impatient, drifted toward Nola's and Peppermint's graves.

"Dragon," Betty reprimanded him in a low tone.

"Bother," he sassed, but he did rejoin the pack.

Sister and Shaker discussed the first cast the night before a hunt and reviewed it in the morning, often changing it when they reached the fixture, since winds and temperature might change.

The temperature had bounced up four degrees to thirty-four degrees Fahrenheit. After All was subject to the same north-west winds as Roughneck Farm. As the day wore on, the mercury might rise or fall, depending on whether a front was scudding in from the northwest, bringing a taste of Canada with it. While Sister checked thermometers and the Weather Channel, ultimately she relied on her bones.

Cora ignored Dragon, pushing by his side in the pale gray light.

At the stone wall around the graveyard, Dragon stopped. The pack put their noses down even though Shaker had yet to cast them.

The huntsman wisely worked with his hounds instead of insisting they stick to his program, which was to move into the woods and hunt east.

Tight pawprints were visible, now beginning to be covered by the lazy flakes falling on Nola's grave.

Doughboy, a second-year entry who had been a little slower to catch on than his littermates, leaped over the low wall, nose to the pawprints.

At Nola's grave, he said, *"Charlene."*

In an instant, all the hounds opened, jumping into the little graveyard, then out the other side. Apart from being exciting for the humans, finding the line was a confidence builder for tricolor Doughboy.

Betty stayed parallel on the eastern side of the creek.

Sybil had faded off to the left, though she was still in sight on the undulating snow-covered pasture.

Charlene, shopping, had been walking along the creek heading back to her den when she heard the pack. Given the conditions, she didn't dally hitting full speed.

The hounds moved faster as Charlene's scent grew stronger.

Only the fox understands scent. Humans try to intellectualize it. They conduct experiments with barometers, moisture in the air, time of day, season, and moon phase. Hounds smell it and know what to do with it, but only the fox knows the good days, the bad days, and the in-between days.

This was a good day, so Charlene hurried on, her distinctive odor lifting up slightly.

Charlene, only a half mile from her den, ran up a fallen tree trunk, then dropped down. Lichens, running cedar, and other plants useful in foiling scent were covered with snow. She had to rely on speed today as well as using whatever obstacles presented themselves. Being forty-five pounds lighter than the hounds worked to her advantage.

She sped through the woods, the wide bridle path serving her well. Hearing hounds come closer, Charlene darted to a gopher hole, paused for a split second, then flew onward.

Trident reached the gopher hole just as the disturbed but slothful animal popped his head out.

"Beg pardon." Trident sat down on his haunches.

"Leave him," Diana ordered the second-year entry. *"Just an old gopher."*

As the hounds moved away from him the gopher remarked, *"I am not old. I just look old, and I've got rodent teeth. I can make a hole in you if I want to!"*

Delia, older, solid as a rock, was bringing up the rear just as the gopher revealed his long teeth. *"Terrified,"* she laughed as she zoomed by him.

"Hateful canines." The gopher watched the humans fly by, then added, *"Another useless species."*

As Charlene ran the snow turned into sleet. Although the temperature rose four more degrees, the rain felt colder than the snow.

Sister was glad she'd put rubber reins on Aztec's bridle. Strictly speaking, since she used a snaffle bit, she should have had lace reins but those rules had been formulated for hunting over the English countryside. The Virginia countryside was much wilder than most of England, the weather much more harsh, with great temperature swings between summer and winter. Some allowances needed to be made, and Sister, a stickler for tradition, knew when to make them.

The hanging tails on her hunt cap sprayed sleet.

Charlene scrambled over a snow-dappled stone fence. She dropped down as the land sank into a long wide plateau, six feet above the feeder creek into Broad Creek, aptly named. She ducked into her den under a mighty walnut tree.

Hounds put her to ground, but they didn't bay in triumph, for Dragon raised his head and moved off toward the creek just as Shaker leaped over the stone fence.

"Coyote!" Dragon bellowed for them to follow the scorching, heavy scent.

Hounds flew straight as an arrow, launching off the bank down into Broad Creek.

Sister trotted downstream to look for a better crossing. A narrow deer trail snaked down the bank at a forty-five-degree angle. It would be slippery, but it was still better than jumping down five feet into a rock-bottomed creek.

Tootie, behind Sister, sat back as she'd seen the old foxhunters do. This was no time for a pretty position. She moved her leg forward of the girth for extra insurance.

Once in the fast-moving water, Aztec picked his way over the large stones. He scrambled out on the opposite side, where ice crystals coated the bank. The deer trail climbing at a forty-five-degree angle was manageable. With care, master and horse achieved the top.

One by one the riders climbed up over the bank, but each horse brought down a bit of earth until the last rider, Lorraine, with Bobby leading her, struggled through the worst footing.

When she had made it, Bobby whispered, "Well done."

Lorraine was learning. The encouragement brought a big smile to her face.

The straight-running coyote took no evasive action but just turned on more speed. While a fox is preferable, coyote is legitimate game.

A warm wind current, a rising tunnel of air, caressed Sister's face. Five big strides, and she was once again in crisp air. Now even she could catch snippets of scent: oily, heavy, lacking the sharp musky fox odor, which when one grows accustomed to it is almost pleasant.

A simple coop lay ahead, the base half covered by snow blown against it.

Aztec thought about it for one moment, heard, "Go on," and did just that. He trusted Sister. She trusted him.

Hounds, running hard, barreled through abandoned pastures and across rutted farm roads, ever straight, ever eastwards. The pastures, snow covered, rolled on. As the whole pack moved farther along, the land became better tended.

After a half hour of slipping here and there, sleet stinging, Sister and the field galloped onto the old Lorillard land.

Hounds headed right for the family plot, which, like most graveyards predating the Revolution, was squared off and protected by a two-foot stone fence, each stone dry-set by hand in the 1750s. Occasionally patched, the stone bore testimony to endurance and beauty even as the graveyard contents announced the fleetingness of life.

Hounds, bearing down on the graveyard, could not see over the fence. Shaker saw it first, then Sister and the field.

Uncle Yancy and a large dog coyote were snarling at one another.

Shaker blew the horn. The coyote still threatened Yancy, but the fox, knowing there was no time to make a run for it, climbed the pin oak in the graveyard.

Folks swear that only gray foxes climb, but reds can do it. Sister had seen it before and wasn't surprised to see it now. But she was surprised to see the coyote pause for a moment and dig down again, then decide he'd better run on.

Coyotes usually run only as fast as needed. This one underestimated Dragon's speed. Dragon came alongside, snarled, and bumped him. That fast the coyote turned, sank his fangs into the hound, and leaped sideways to avoid Cora, who was a split second behind Dragon. He then put on the afterburners. The pack had been running hard for a half hour. Besides, they'd been out for another forty-five minutes above that. Fresh, the coyote had the advantage, but the Jefferson Hunt hounds possessed unquenchable drive. They snapped close to his heels. He charged up a slope, crossed a meadow where soil was poor, dropped down the embankment on the eastern side, and disappeared into a large jagged rock outcropping. The pack gathered in front of the narrow opening between two huge boulders.

Shaker dismounted, blew "Gone to ground," and quickly remounted.

He wanted to pull the pack out of there because all manner of larger predators found the rocks with fissures and small caves very attractive.

Tootie, Val, and Felicity, burning hot, welcomed the ice bits on their cheeks. Their core body heat hadn't begun to cool.

Uncle Yancy posed in the pin oak on a lower branch, which was nevertheless too high for hounds to yank him down by his lovely brush, quite in contrast to Aunt Netty's pathetic little tail.

"Close call," he cheerfully called down as the pack came near.

"What are you doing all the way over here?" Asa wondered.

"Netty brought me a beautiful pencil, so I came to see if there's more. Dead human, pretty fresh in a shallow grave. That's why the coyote was digging here. Well, 'I was here first,' I says to him, and he says, 'Bug off, Pipsqueak.' If you all hadn't come along when you did, I might have got the worst of that fight."

Dragon, bleeding all over the snow, limped along.

Shaker stopped before reaching the graveyard and called back to Sister. "We'd better put him in Sam's woodshed. I'll come back for him. Don't want him to walk all the way back to the trailers."

"Shaker, maybe there's a better way." She motioned to Betty, who rode in closer. "Betty, call Sam on your cell phone. See if he'll leave for a minute and load up Dragon in his truck."

"He can't lift him." Betty reached inside her coat for her phone.

"Right." Sister nodded, for she'd momentarily forgotten Sam's wound. "Call Gray. Maybe he can slip away. If not, we'll have to ride back, then drive back. I hate to leave him for long."

"Okay." Betty punched in Gray's number as Sister gave it to her.

As Betty filled in Gray, the field watched Uncle Yancy, about one hundred yards away, talk to the hounds who sat underneath the tree.

"This place is full of dead humans. Why would the coyote dig one up?" Diddy asked.

Ardent sometimes forgot how young the last "D" litter was. *"They bury six feet down so we can't smell the body. This grave has to be less than that. Peculiar. Humans are fastidious about planting their dead."*

"Go on over there. Even with the snow and sleet, you'll get a whiff," Uncle Yancy suggested.

"No. You'll back down and run off," Dasher said.

"Ha! What do you take me for?" Uncle Yancy replied.

Diddy and Ardent walked over as Shaker rode up, followed by Sister.

"He's right. I can get a whiff." Diddy closed her eyes for a moment.

"Coyote helped. He clawed out six inches or more. Ground's not as cold here; the graveyard is sheltered from the wind. It's a lovely spot."

Shaker dismounted and walked to the pin oak. "Uncle Yancy, you should know better than to pick a fight with a coyote."

"I was here first." Uncle Yancy refused to recognize Shaker's point.

Betty raised her voice so Sister could hear, for she had walked to the other side of the graveyard just in case hounds took a notion. "He'll be here in twenty minutes, tops."

"Thank heavens," Sister sighed. The sleet was now mixed in with more ice bits.

Shaker reached Diddy and Ardent. The pack followed. He stared at the small hole in the ground. He couldn't smell what they smelled, but he could see where the snow had been pulled away, where the ground was freshly disturbed. He scuffed that area with the toe of his boot. "Sister, something's in here."

The weather was worsening steadily. Sister asked Tedi to take the field. She handed Aztec's reins to Tootie to lead back.

"Shaker, I'll stay with Dragon. Let's put him in the woodshed out of the weather. You load up and get on home before the roads really get ugly. Gray can drive Dragon and me to Marty Shulman at the vet clinic. We'll get Dragon stitched up and fill him with antibiotics."

Ice rattled against the worn tombstones like clear BBs.

"All right." He knew her plan was wise.

"Betty, call Ben Sidell. Tell him he needs to come out here."

"I could stay with you. Val can lead Outlaw back."

"You need to be with the hounds. You and Sybil. Go on, now."

Jason rode up and touched his cap with his crop. "Ma'am, I would be privileged to stay. If you find some thread and a needle, I can stitch him up."

"Thank you, Jason, but really I'll be fine, and Gray's on his way. Save your skills for humans," she replied.

"All right, then." He turned to fall in alongside Walter, who had mounted up after checking Dragon.

Although they were human doctors, if Dragon needed emergency surgery or stitching, Walter or Jason could do it. In a pinch, a vet could put together a human, too.

As the field rode away, Sister noticed how well turned out they were. Hunched against the weather, all were correct in their attire, their tack. They had such pride in being part of the Jefferson Hunt, and she had such pride in them.

She put her hand on Dragon's head. "That's a deep ugly wound, but it's a long way from your heart. Thank God for Walter; he stanched some of the bleeding. Come on, big fella."

"It hurts, but I can do it. If you'd put your nose over that hole, you'd smell the carcass." He then remembered the odor wouldn't register with her.

"Wish you'd killed that damn coyote. Marauders, every last one of them."

"Wish I'd killed him, too." Dragon, head down in the biting weather, agreed.

Once inside the woodshed, Sister sat on a low line of stacked hardwood logs. Dragon rested by her feet. Leaning over, she rubbed his ears, a comfort to a dog. She stroked under his neck, praising him for closing so quickly on his quarry.

"He miscalculated." Dragon, despite his pain, touted his skill. *"I'm fast. Really fast."*

Both animals, grateful for the shelter, listened to the rattle of ice on the rooftop, to the wind picking up.

Sister checked her pocket watch. The hounds and field should have crossed into After All by now. If Tedi picked up a trot where the footing was good, they'd be at the trailers in another fifteen minutes. She reminded herself to give Tootie a small present for taking Aztec back. Leading a horse through rough territory, which some of this was, took talent on the part of the human, cooperation on the part of the horse.

Dragon shivered.

"Getting to you, buddy." Sister took off her coat, draping it on the hound. She sat down in the dirt beside him to hold the coat closer on him. "You'll make it, Dragon; you'll make it."

"I love you." He half closed his eyes.

Both heard the welcome note of the eight-cylinder Land Cruiser engine.

Sister stepped outside, waving to Gray, who drove off the driveway to reach her.

"Janie, you'll catch your death of cold."

"No, I won't. Honey, he'll bleed on the backseat."

"Put it down. Garvey gave me a blanket he kept in his office for when he sleeps over. I'll buy him a new one." He smiled as he strode into the woodpile, knelt down, and gently lifted the seventy-pound hound into the Land Cruiser.

Dragon immediately felt the warmth from the car heater as Gray closed the door.

The windshield wipers clicked against the ice as Gray drove on good roads to Crozet Veterinary Clinic.

"Think he'll make it?"

"He will. The wound is deep; he's lost blood. I don't want him to go into shock. I checked his gums when I put my coat around him. But Marty can handle it. He's dealt with worse cases than this." She filled Gray in on the coyote, on Uncle Yancy in the tree, and on the possibility that the graveyard had been disturbed by more than a coyote.

"After Betty called me," said Gray, "I called Sam. He'll be there when Ben arrives."

"He can't drive, can he?"

"He shouldn't, but my little brother will manage. Crawford may allow Rory to go with him, but if he doesn't, you know Sam."

Once they were inside the scrubbed clinic, Marty Shulman

checked Dragon, put him under anesthesia, and thoroughly cleaned the wound.

Sister would need to pick him up tomorrow, but Dragon would be good as new once the wound healed. He'd be out for the season, which would hurt Dragon more than his wound. Yes, he was arrogant and could be hardheaded, but the hound breathed fire like a dragon. He lived to hunt, and his nose and voice were outstanding.

Driving west back toward Roughneck Farm, Gray sighed deeply. "Funny, we haven't been apart that long. I didn't realize how much I look forward to our weekends together until now. You spoil me."

"I do," she agreed lightheartedly.

"This last year has been one of the happiest years of my life."

"Mine, too."

"I can't wait for Friday."

"How about if I make that pork roast you like so much? Your mother's recipe?"

He smiled. "How about if I bring you a gardenia bush in full bloom?"

She turned to stare at him. "That's major."

They pulled into the farm as Shaker walked out of the kennels. Gray stopped. "Get in the car, Shaker; the ice is coming down too hard." Shaker hopped into the back, where the seats were laid flat, and sat with his legs straight out.

"How's the boy?"

"Being sewn up as we speak. Pick him up tomorrow."

"You should have seen it." Shaker leaned forward.

"Sister told me it was dramatic."

"And funny. On the way back, Uncle Yancy followed us. He

hung back with Bobby and Lorraine. No fool. Going home is a lot easier for him if he can follow in our footsteps, since this will probably turn worse. And the wind was in his face. Hounds couldn't get a whiff. Amazing creatures."

"Did Bobby notice where Uncle Yancy left them?"

"The big sycamore at the second creek crossing."

"Changed dens." Sister liked knowing where her foxes lived.

"Gray, honey, I need to see to Aztec. I'll have to leave you."

"Girls did everything. Cleaned your tack, too. Cleaned up after Felicity," Shaker remarked.

"What did she do?"

"Threw up coffee."

"I'm going to call Charlotte. Felicity might have a bug. This is the second time she's thrown up."

"Well, don't be so fast. She took a bet from Val that she couldn't chug the thermos full of coffee. Val bet her ten dollars. She said it's much harder to chug a hot drink than a cold drink. So Felicity took the bet. She held it down for about fifteen minutes. Dumb kids." He laughed.

"Felicity is in charge of the kitty. Guess she's trying to fatten it up. I'd think Val's profanity would be doing that," Sister said.

"I never hear Val swear. She's a lady." Gray was surprised.

"Among her peers she swears like a trooper." Sister filled him in. "So Val, Tootie, and Felicity each put in a dollar if they swear. At the end of the semester, they're going to throw themselves a party."

"Good idea." Gray nodded.

"Need any help in the kennel?"

"No, Boss. All done. Lorraine's got the fire going. She said she's making navy bean soup." He winked. "By the time that's done she won't be able to drive home. These roads aren't going to get better."

"Lucky devil." Gray laughed. "Wish I could say the same, but I need to get home and see if Ben is there."

"Something's not right." Shaker rubbed his hands together. His joints hurt on a day like today.

"Damn kids. They knock over the tombstones. I guess this time they've dug up someone, or tried to. What's the matter with them?"

"Last year two kids dug up a lady buried back in the 1930s because they'd heard she was buried with her jewelry on." Shaker found it gruesome but titillating. "What they found wasn't jewelry but the sheriff, who came up on them at the right moment. Remember?"

"I do." Gray paused. "Did you notice which grave had been disturbed?"

"Not exactly disturbed. Coyote dug a hole. But the earth was packed down. Recent. Too recent." Shaker wondered what was going on at the old Lorillard place. He put his hand on Sister's shoulder. "Good hunt."

"It was pretty good. I'm high on the second-year entry. They've got it now."

"So do you." Shaker patted her, then opened the door, stepping into a stiff wind.

Gray drove to the house. "I'll drop you at your door. Shaker forgot to tell me which grave was messed up."

"Jemima Lorillard, 1761 to 1847. A good long life."

"One of the white Lorillards. You know, I think we may be the only family where the white Lorillards are buried with the free black Lorillards as well as the slave Lorillards. It's quite a history, our family."

"Most people think Jemima is a black name. It was quite popular in England and here in the eighteenth and early nineteenth centuries. Pretty name, really." She stopped. "Gray, I know you can't tell me details. But let me tell you what I think, since you're sitting in the middle of it down there at Aluminum M." She shortened Aluminum Manufacturing to "M."

"Okay." Gray said only that.

"Iffy is missing. I expect she's been milking money out of the company for years. I suggested to Ben that he get an order to exhume Angel Crump's body."

"What?" Gray's eyebrows darted up. "That will upset Garvey as much as everything else."

"Well, let me go on here. Angel thought little of Iffy. Iffy hated Angel. I expect Angel caught on. At any rate, Iffy's disappeared."

"Looks like she got away with it."

"That's just it, Gray. What if she didn't get away with it?"

CHAPTER 22

A wall calendar, new, large pages as yet uncurled on the bottom, hung in the coroner's office. Lyle Aziz, MD, liked his work but wished for more pay, a common desire among state employees. However, as a teaching physician in the pathology department down in Richmond at the Medical College of Virginia, he made enough to support his family. Better yet, he would never return to Egypt.

One of the dangers of people coming to the United States to study was that they might not return to their former countries, especially if those countries seethed with internal dissent. As a Christian Lyle never felt secure. But he missed the ways of his country, the warmth of everyday encounters, the raucous gossip. He realized that living in the American South he was as close as he could get to these qualities among peoples of European descent, colder peoples than his own.

"She is in such good condition," he enthused over the state of Iffy's body.

Only a pathologist would make such a statement. Anyone else viewing human remains unceremoniously buried in a shallow grave for four days would feel otherwise. Thanks to the cold and the three feet of dirt she had been under, Iffy still had her nose. Her extremities, swollen and discolored, blood pooled there, contained all her digits. Patches of decay showed in spots, and gases filled her, but she could have been much worse. No flies in the winter. She remained intact, if not a cover girl.

A single shot to the head had sent Iffy to the hereafter.

Ben always carried a small jar of Vicks VapoRub in his jacket. As Iffy thawed he made use of it.

"Looks simple enough."

Lyle, gloves on, carefully inspected the wounds. The gun had been placed at her right temple. The bullet exited on the other side of her head. "True, but my father used to say, 'Suspect a trap where the sand is smoothest.' "

Tattoo markers dotted the left side of Iffy's chest where radiation had been administered, square blocks within. Any physician or cancer patient would recognize the markers.

"I'll leave her in your capable hands," said Ben.

"Even though she's missing part of her skull where the bullet exited, how do you know she wasn't slowly poisoned? She could have shot herself in despair over her sickness. You never know until the evidence is in. Every autopsy is a detective story." Lyle's black eyes met Ben's. "Were these more primitive times, if I didn't have a state lab at my disposal, slow though it is, I'd go with cause of death is gunshot. Not self-inflicted. No powder burns. Her arms are short. She couldn't have held the gun far enough away to produce this wound. If you're going to do yourself in, you put the muzzle smack up to your temple or your mouth. She was murdered."

"I figure Saturday night, early Sunday morning." Ben was a good judge of a corpse's condition and the time it took to reach that condition relative to season. "Thirty-six. Suffering from lung cancer."

Lyle nodded then said, "Well, I'll start in. If I find anything unusual, I'll call you."

"Thanks for coming in. I know this isn't your regular day."

"I teach only Tuesdays and Thursdays. Friday's no problem. I'll get right to work."

Three hours later, Ben's cell phone beeped. "Sheriff Sidell? Lyle here."

"Yes." An expectant note rang in Ben's voice.

"Iffy Demetrios did not have lung cancer. When I found no tumors, to be certain I sectioned out quite a bit of both lungs. This isn't to say there might not be a cancer cell that the lab will pick up, but you said she had lung cancer. I found no evidence of disease in her lungs."

A long, long pause followed. "Lyle, that's the most interesting thing I've heard in this new year."

Within fifteen minutes, Ben stood in front of Jason Woods. As it was his office day, Jason had graciously agreed to see the sheriff immediately.

"You treated Iphigenia Demetrios for lung cancer. Correct?"

"I did. She was responding beautifully. We caught it early."

"May I see her records?"

Jason balked for a moment, then said, "Under normal circumstances one must ask the patient or next of kin."

"These aren't normal circumstance." Ben's voice conveyed authority.

"Of course." Jason buzzed his secretary, who brought in a color-coded file. "Let's start with the x-rays." Without being asked, Jason walked to a wide metal file cabinet and pulled open a drawer much like those used in graphic arts businesses. Flipping through large manila envelopes, he pulled out Iffy's and then put it up on the light box. "Note the small but discernible mass right here, lower portion."

"Yes. I see it."

"This was the first x-ray. Naturally, I ran a battery of tests, although I've seen enough of these to feel I can recognize a malignant tumor. Still, one must be prepared for the anomaly." He pulled out another x-ray. "Here is the lung after her last series of treatments."

"Which were?"

"The first protocol involved radiation and chemo. The side effects troubled her. Once started, you must finish the exact number of treatments. She did. In view of her adverse reaction, I gave her more time to regain strength. Three months later she submitted again to radiation and chemo. I do the treatments here, which makes it much easier for the patient. This is the result." He pointed to the area where the tumor had originally been diagnosed. It had vanished.

"Remarkable."

"Like I initially said, early detection was critical. However, each day we make progress. As you may know, this is the third most common form of cancer. I'm proud of my success rate, and apart from aggressive treatment I think putting a patient on the chemo IV here in more pleasant surroundings raises a patient's spirits. I'm involved with them. My nurses offer support. It makes a huge difference."

"What are the odds of the lung cancer returning?"

"Well"—Jason stroked his chin—"the rule of thumb is if it doesn't recur in five years, you're home free. My feeling is the cancer may not return to the original site. It can migrate. Sometimes a tumor will send out seeds, if you will. The patient celebrates the five-year mark, yet three years after that the cancer manifests itself in a new site. We know when a patient comes in that if the cancer has metastasized into the lymph nodes that's usually the end of the journey. What we don't know is why some tumors create other cancers in other parts of the body and some don't. Maybe I shouldn't say this, but I don't know if we can conquer cancer, say in the way we have conquered TB. But we may advance to where cancer is a chronic condition that can be managed. A patient can enjoy a good life."

"Did you think Iffy was cured?"

"Yes, of the tumor." A troubled pause followed. "She had other complications."

"Oh?" Ben found medicine fascinating.

"Her platelets were higher than they should have been. That raised my suspicions that some cancer cells had established themselves elsewhere, but her tests were clean." He pointed to her bulging chart. "After her first round of chemo and radiation, she experienced trouble walking. Occasionally, radiation creates neurological side effects. Sometimes the side effect doesn't go away when the patient recovers. It's rare, but it does happen." He paused. "Granted, in time her legs might have become stronger, but that's one of the reasons I kept running tests on her. She wasn't bouncing back as fast as I'd hoped. If she was on her feet too long she'd become fatigued."

"What about drugs? They can cause odd responses in some people."

"Illegal, you mean?"

"Yes."

"Clean." He rustled through her folder, plucked out a sheet, and showed Ben Iffy's latest blood tests, pointing to the bar graphs on the page from the lab. "Clean as a whistle."

"What about alcohol?"

"She drank socially, but here"—Jason pointed to that test result—"within the boundary. Iffy was a challenge."

"Could some of her behavior have been psychologically motivated? Some kind of neurosis?"

Jason shook his head, a light smile on his lips. "That's not my field, Sheriff. Was she insane? No. Was she moody, erratic, cantankerous? All the time."

"Some of that could be a result of her medications, you think?"

"When she was undergoing chemo and radiation, yes. After she recovered, no."

"One last question. You've been very good to give me your time. Did you like Iffy?"

A broad smile covered Jason's face. "I did. Even when she was at her most uncooperative, I really did."

"Ah." A shadow crossed Ben's strong face. "I'm sorry to tell you, Jason, your patient is dead."

Confusion, doubt, suspicion registered in Jason's face. "What happened to her?" He sat down abruptly. "After all she'd been through."

"She was shot."

"Good God."

"I'm sorry. I hope you understand that I'll ask more questions over time. I may even have to requisition your records, but I am sorry. You saw her through a great deal."

"You know"—Jason's voice was misty—"nasty as she could

get, there was a kind side to Iffy. She would talk to other patients during chemo. She'd bring fruit and candy. She complained ad infinitum to the rest of us, but with other cancer sufferers, she was marvelous. Why would anyone kill her? I can't understand it."

"My job is to find out."

"I'll help you any way I can."

"You already have." Ben left. For the time being, he'd keep Lyle Aziz's revelation to himself. Best to wait for the lab reports from Richmond.

Driving to Aluminum Manufacturers, he wondered how Garvey would take the news. After all, he was missing two million dollars. The culprit most likely had been shot in the head.

He wanted to talk to Sister Jane, too. She used all her senses in a situation like this. Most people used only their eyes and ears.

As he turned into the parking lot he remembered it was Friday the thirteenth.

CHAPTER 23

Winter's gray skies depressed many people but not fox-hunters. Low fleecy clouds, ranging in color from pearl gray to gunmetal gray, cast their darkening shadows on the snow.

Sister sat quietly on Lafayette as the huge tree, over three hundred years old, on Hangman's Ridge waved its branches in the breeze as if beckoning.

The fixture card, printed on heavyweight good paper, had been sent out before Opening Hunt, the first weekend in November. The Jefferson Hunt tried to stay close to St. Hubert's Day, November 3, for their opening. Crawford had left the club a few days before Christmas. Today they would have hunted from Beasley Hall, Crawford's estate. That had to be changed. The easiest thing to do would be to hunt from the kennels. Since foxes flourished around Roughneck Farm, After All Farm heading east, and Foxglove Farm heading north, it should be fine.

Like most masters, Sister loathed changing a fixture once it was in writing. She thought scheduling one of the hardest tasks a master had to perform. She hadn't much liked doing it as a wife and mother, either. Those Friday nights when Big Ray, RayRay, and she had sat at the kitchen table, individual calendars open, the large hanging family calendar off the wall to be altered had given her fits. She'd worn out one big white India-rubber eraser each Friday night.

She missed hunting at Beasley Hall. Crawford had spared no expense in opening territory. Coops, zigzag fences, tree trunks lashed together, even a beautiful river stone jump bore testimony to his largesse. Crawford had directed the workers, although at the time he'd known nothing about siting a jump. Sister had used all her tact to make sure the jumps had a decent approach.

Foxhunters, accustomed to leaps of faith, didn't worry about sight lines or ground lines, but they sure worried about footing.

This Saturday, January 14, Crawford would be hunting his pack at Beasley Hall. She wondered what the foxes would do.

Despite her years at the helm of the Jefferson Hunt, she wanted to show good sport for members and guests, and was a bit nervous before each hunt.

This Saturday she had riders from Casanova Hunt. This pleased her, as it was one of those four-star hunts.

She also had Vicki Van Mater riding Jaz and Joe Kasputys on Webster from Middleburg Hunt. This, another glamour hunt, had hard-riding members.

Having a check on top of Hangman's Ridge gave her the

shivers. The wind always blew there even in summer. Winter's wind, however light, cut. The ghosts of murderers, mountebanks, and hard-luck men whispered along this long wide plain, high above the cultivated fields, the one huge wildflower field, and way beyond to Soldier Road, snaking east and west.

Hounds worked the large ridge, then moved down into the underbrush, tight even in winter. The horses used the deer paths on the north side, the old farm road on the south. The remnants of the colonial road, originally the road up to the Potomac, a hundred miles and then some, occasionally would be cleared. That ran in a big S down the north side out to Soldier Road.

Hounds moved that way; Sister walked behind them and Shaker. A sudden burst of wind sent a moan from the giant oak. Her spine tingled.

Did dead souls meet? Would Iffy join these men and spin her tale of woe? She wasn't surprised that Iffy had been secreted over Jemima Lorillard. What surprised her had been that not one penny of the filched money had been found in her bank account, nothing in her house.

Ben had come by Friday night. She fed him fried chicken, greens, and cornbread. Halfway through the impromptu supper, Gray had arrived, worn down by events but bearing the gardenia bush in bloom as promised.

Ben rode out this Saturday. He needed the hunting to clear his mind, and it was his weekend off. In fact, the field, at sixty-seven, proved cumbersome on such a cold day. The ones in the rear, continually pushed up by the Custis Hall girls, grumbled, but if they didn't keep up, then Bobby Franklin would sweep them up and they'd need to stay with hilltoppers instead of first flight.

Lafayette stopped, pricked his ears.

Uncle Yancy shot straight in front of him, followed by Inky, the black fox vixen, and Comet, her saucy brother. A collective intake of breath from the field followed by everyone with their derbies, top hats, and hunting caps off pointing in three different directions added to the confusion.

When the hounds blew through the bracken back out onto the ridge, they split into three different prongs. How could anyone fault them, for the scents were equally hot? Had one line been fresher than the other, the huntsman could have hoped his whipper-in on the side where the pack split could send them back. Today, Shaker faced an unenviable dilemma. As he reached the ridge again, up from the north-side deer path, he caught a glimpse of three brushes disappearing in three different directions.

During January or February, a huntsman would rather chase a dog fox than a vixen if one could choose. But Shaker couldn't choose. Cora led the group on Uncle Yancy. Dasher roared after Inky, taking many young entry with him. To everyone's surprise and Sister's delight, little Diddy, showing her mettle for the first time as a strike hound, blew after Comet.

Shaker paused under the moaning tree, then plunged down the south side, using the farm road. He stuck behind Diddy. First off, he delighted in seeing this development. Second, he wanted to get the pack onto Comet. He didn't want to run Inky. Not only was she a vixen, but her den was too close. Too short a go. Also, today was January 14. It was possible she was pregnant. He never liked running a pregnant vixen, even early in a pregnancy.

Luckily, Betty, on Magellan, was further to his right. She

could push back Dasher and the young entry. Dasher, a biddable hound, might wonder why he was being called off a hot line, but he trusted the huntsman and he trusted Betty.

Sybil, on his left and out of sight, was still learning the intricacies of whipping-in. A brilliant rider, she was developing nicely. However, hounds would test her long before they'd test Betty or Shaker. Then, too, if they heard a reprimand from Sister riding up behind them almost like a tail whip, which Jefferson Hunt did not use, those hounds would do as told.

As it was, Sybil rode like a demon to get in front of Cora, a hound of speed and intelligence.

Cora turned her head. Why was Sybil, on her big bay thoroughbred, Bombardier, riding like hell to get in front of her? She was right as rain. She was on Uncle Yancy.

"Leave it," Sybil called.

Cora refused. The human was wrong.

Then the crack of Sybil's whip like rifle fire brought her head up. She slowed. Her concentration broke, and she heard Shaker's horn blow "Gone Away" from the farm road. She was in the middle of the wildflower field, white with snow.

"Go to him," Sybil ordered.

"What's going on?" Dreamboat, second-year entry, asked.

"Too many foxes, but I picked the one who had furthest to run. Dammit!" Cora cursed.

Tinsel suggested, *"We could go on."*

"Better not. Better trust Shaker." Cora reluctantly turned right, heading back toward the farm road, a line of pines breaking the increasing wind.

"Good hounds," Sybil called after them.

"Good, yes, but I picked the fox, the best fox for the day. Why, we could have run all the way to pattypan!" Cora grumbled to herself as

she loped across the field to rejoin the center splinter of the pack. *"What is Uncle Yancy doing over here anyway? He's all over the place."*

"Ha!" Uncle Yancy stopped right in the middle of the wildflower field when the pack turned.

Sybil, trotting behind the hounds, turned to face him. "You're one lucky devil."

"Not with my wife, I'm not." He grinned raffishly. *"Had to get away from Netty. Here I am."*

Sybil laughed when he barked at her. That flooding sensation of speaking with another species filled her with awe. In a sense, the two creatures understood each other.

Bombardier understood every word and whinnied, *"Long hike to escape your wife."*

"Hells bells, I gave her pattypan. I came back to my old den."

Uncle Yancy's old den, originally shared with Aunt Netty, was on the west side of Roughneck Farm, about a half mile from the apple orchard where Georgia, Inky's daughter, now lived.

That was the last den where he and Aunt Netty had cohabited.

"Maybe you should become a bachelor," Bombardier grinned, his big teeth quite a contrast to Uncle Yancy's sharp fangs.

"You're a gelding; what do you know?" Uncle Yancy taunted the bay.

"I have imagination." Bombardier humped his back, kicking out playfully.

Sybil, enraptured by Uncle Yancy, had slowed to a walk. The buck brought her to her senses. She squeezed Bombardier's flanks, and the two moved along faster.

Cora, speed serving her well, had already reached the main body of the pack. The others, not far behind her, joined in.

Cora came alongside of Diddy. *"Well done."*

Wild-eyed with excitement, Diddy yelped, *"I can do it!"*

"You can do it when I retire." Cora pulled ahead, but she said this with warmth.

One thing, she'd never relinquish her position of strike hound to Dragon. If only the coyote had severed his jugular. She'd think about training Diddy. Somewhere down the line they'd both have to deal with Dragon.

Dasher, pushed back by Betty, now joined the pack, too. Inky had popped into her den just as Betty rode near the northernmost splinter of the pack.

He stuck his head in Inky's den to prove what he'd done. Betty told him he was really wonderful but he'd better yank his head out of that den and get to Shaker.

Once the two groups had joined the chase after Comet, Shaker blew the long note followed by three short ones. They were all on.

The sixty-seven riders, amazed at their good fortune, contended with the packed snow, the patches of ice, and the splotches of frozen mud churned up during the short thaw earlier in the week.

Faces flushed, they were breathing hard, and sweat soaked their backs even though the temperature was barely nudging forty degrees. Comet raced straight down the farm road in full view. He had a head start and trusted his fleet paws as well as his cunning.

His special treat for them today was to run for the trailers. He ran in the back door of one big rig and out the tack room door, swinging open. Two minutes later the pack did the same, except that they jammed in the tack room door, and that slowed them down.

He ran into Joe Kasputys' rig, heard Caesar, the German shepherd, bark from the truck cab, and quickly bolted out of that trailer. When the hounds hurtled into the trailer it rocked back and forth. This plucked Caesar's last nerve.

Next Comet ran around the kennels, which sent every hound not hunting that day into a frenzy. The cacophony was deafening and confusing because it took some time for Shaker to recognize where the pack was once the hounds were on the other side of the kennel.

He managed to pick his way around it and realized the pack was blowing through the orchard. A few unpicked apples rested under the snow. One couldn't race through there. The horses carefully walked through, emerging back out on the farm road.

However, a few hounds stopped by Georgia's den. This also cost time. Georgia, relaxing, became irritated when two hounds dug at her main entrance.

Betty had to push them on.

Back together again, the pack now leaped over some old hedges, neatly trimmed. They crisscrossed the farm road three times, jumping those same hedges, as did the field.

Comet, in his glory, thought to run through the wildflower field but decided against it in case there were drifts. Much as he wanted to show himself to the humans and rub his superiority in their faces, he prudently blasted down the farm road, just nipped through the corner of the apple orchard again, then snaked through the trailers, causing pandemonium once more as hounds rattled through shining aluminum trailers, older steel ones, and one big old horse van, rarely seen among foxhunters these days.

After this display of agility, he made a beeline for Sister's house.

Golly, not a cold-weather girl, had been out for her constitutional. The racket intrigued her, so she sat on the back stoop to watch the show. Her cat door, not far, reassured her she could escape if need be.

Comet, seeing the snotty cat, ran straight for her. *"I'm going to get you."*

"Oh, balls, Comet." Golly turned and ducked into her door, the flap closing as the magnetic strips touched each other.

Comet easily fit through the same door.

Facing Golly in the mud room, he heard Raleigh and Rooster come to life on the other side of the kitchen door.

Golly, frozen in astonishment, puffed up to twice her size. She danced sideways.

"You look like a broody hen," Comet laughed.

"I'll scratch your eyes out."

"No, you won't. You'll pop through that second cat door there and tell those idiot dogs how smart I am. And how generous. I could bite you in two."

"You wouldn't dare." Golly hissed a spectacular shower of droplets.

He stepped toward her.

She backed right up to the door as Raleigh tried to poke his head through the cat door.

"Raleigh, you dolt. I need to get through."

Raleigh withdrew his head. Golly turned and shot through the door, then hit Raleigh on the nose as hard as she could.

He screamed as bright red blood drops appeared on his moist black nose. *"Harpy!"*

"You were in my way. Comet out there could have bitten me, although I would have hit him, too."

Comet, flamboyant stinker, stuck his head through the door. *"Domesticated twits."*

Rooster lunged for him, but Comet just stepped back.

"You're lucky I'm on the other side of this door. I'd tear you limb from limb," the harrier threatened.

"Dream on, fatty." Comet then sat back down to groom his tail while the entire pack hit the door like a tricolor avalanche. Couldn't get in, of course. This pleased the gray fox immensely. Sister wouldn't open the door. He was as safe as if he'd been in his own den, a half mile away.

Shaker, flummoxed, a rare occurrence, lifted both feet out of the stirrups, vaulting off HoJo, who, curious, stepped up after Shaker to get closer.

Shaker looked to Sister.

"Blow 'gone to ground.'" She laughed.

He lifted the horn to his lips, the happy notes filling the air along with the cries of the pack, Raleigh and Rooster's howls, and the voices of the entire kennel.

Golly hollered at the top of her considerable lungs, *"I denned the fox!"*

This shut up Rooster for a second. *"You did."*

"Oh, Christ, Rooster, there will be no living with her now," Raleigh moaned.

"Now? There's never been any living with her."

"I am the Queen of All I Survey." Golly sashayed to the cat door and stuck her head out. *"You're the asshole."*

Lightning fast, Comet lunged for her. She reeled backward, falling over herself.

He now stuck his head through the cat door. *"I'm the boss. You're the applesauce."*

As the house pets endured Comet's doggerel, Sister said, "Let's pick them up, Shaker. I don't believe we've ever had a day like this. Best to stop while ahead."

"Want to go into the house? Through the front door," Shaker laughed. "I'll hold Lafayette."

"No. I don't hear crashing about. I expect he is availing himself of the dog food in the mud room. I'll let him out later if he doesn't leave of his own free will."

With some effort, as the hounds were terribly thrilled with this new type of den, Shaker, Betty, and Sybil managed to walk them to the kennels.

No sooner were they all in than Comet slipped out through the outside cat door to sit on the stoop. Leaving was the furthest thing from his mind.

"Tally ho," Tootie whispered, taking off her hat.

As she was back at the Custis Hall trailer, Val, Felicity, and Pamela turned, also removing their caps.

Vicki Van Mater noticed and took off her cap. Joe Kasputys followed suit.

The babble of human voices subsided. Everyone turned. Even the hounds in the kennel runs who could see that side of the house watched in amazement.

Finally, Sister, having dismounted, stepped forward. She removed her cap, bowed, and swept her cap before her with an actor's grand flourish. "I salute you, Comet."

Smiling, he walked down the steps, took in this tribute, then walked around the house and vanished as only a fox can do.

The humans cheered.

Walter, buoyant, raised both arms over his head. "Well, we've cheered the fox. How about three cheers for the hounds!"

After three lusty cheers, the people wiped down their

horses and removed their bridles. Some took off the saddles; others loosened the girths but allowed the saddles to stay on the horses' backs. As the horses cooled down, their riders threw blankets over them.

The hunt breakfast was potluck. People gingerly negotiated the snow, dishes in hand.

No one could miss Comet's scent when they hung their coats in the mud room.

Raleigh and Rooster, let out, tried to pick up the wily fellow's trail. No luck.

Golly, meanwhile, told everyone within earshot of her valor.

Excitement bubbled over along with the coffeepot.

Few mentioned Iffy. She hadn't been a part of the club, although Sorrel, Walter's steady, expressed her sympathy to Jason on losing Iffy.

"Thank you," he replied. "She turned the corner." He drank a hot toddy, then spoke again. "One of the things about our profession"—he nodded toward Walter—"is you must accept death."

"I suppose, but Walter hates to lose a patient."

"I do too, but Sorrel, there's a time to live and a time to die." Then he smiled. "You know what's worse than death? The paperwork!"

Tootie patted her britches pocket. The lockback knife Sister had given her was there. She hadn't expected anything for leading back Aztec on Thursday and was delighted with the beautiful knife.

A foxhunter should always have a pocket knife in a coat or britches pocket.

The girls talked with one another. Pamela felt more of the group these days, although she could still get on their nerves, especially Val's. She did, however, give each of them a steel-tipped stock pin from Horse Country, as promised.

Sister pulled Walter to the side. "Haven't had a minute to talk to you."

"What a day."

"Was, wasn't it?" She touched glasses with him.

Tedi came up. "I feel twenty-one again."

"Me too." Sister laughed. "Today is Felix of Nola's feast day. I remember because of Nola."

"How do you remember these things? What did Felix do?" Walter grinned.

"Survived torture and persecution in the third century AD, going on to perform conversions and miracles. Died 260 AD."

"Every day is a miracle." Tedi beamed.

"Today certainly was." Walter noticed Sorrel motioning to him. "Excuse me."

The phone rang. Val, next to it, picked it up and cupped her head over the receiver. "Sister," she called over the din. "Sam."

Sister pushed through the crowd, listened, then hung up the phone as Gray walked over to her. She started laughing. "Crawford has hounds out all over the country. Sam asks if we see any, would we pick them up." She asked for silence, then added, "You can take them to the barn in the back."

"Damned if I'll help Crawford," a member groused.

"Hounds first," Sister simply replied.

Margaret DuCharme slipped in the back door. Her eyes watered a bit from Comet's signature odor. She found Ben. Sister had invited her and told her that no one thought for a second she had anything to do with Iffy's disappearance. However, it was damned inconvenient that Iffy's wheelchair had been in her SUV. With Iffy dead it became quite upsetting.

Sister had asked her to come for Ben. She'd noticed their connection at the New Year's party. And she really did want Margaret to know she was above suspicion. No one was pointing the finger at her.

They were pointing it at Golly, who had soared onto the table, grabbed a succulent slice of ham, and jumped off, racing upstairs with her prize.

"That damned cat!" Sister couldn't get through the crowd to smack Golly's bottom.

Ben's cell phone rang as he was talking with Margaret. He flipped it open and recognized the number. "Excuse me, Margaret." He listened, said little, then flipped the phone back. "We have permission from Angel's great-niece in Richmond. That saves time."

"Permission for what?" Margaret asked.

"To exhume Angel Crump."

CHAPTER 24

Angel Crump was in much worse shape than Iffy Demetrios, but then she'd had a year and a half to molder. Embalming, limited as it was by social consent, and being interred in a casket preserved some tissues. The bones, intact, might yield something.

Lyle Aziz snipped what he could. Given that it was January 16, he hoped the results wouldn't be eight weeks in coming. Not much happened in the dead of winter except for car wrecks, someone crashing through ice and drowning. The murder rate dropped down; the violent outbursts of summer's sticky heat abated. The state lab ought to be able to get back to him faster than in July.

Still no results from Iffy's remains. As for Angel, how many ways could someone kill another without arousing suspicion?

When the victim—if she was a victim—was in her eighties, the possibilities increased. People expected older people to die, not considering wrongdoing when it occurred.

Angel had been slumped over her desk as though asleep when Garvey walked in with papers for her. He'd assumed her passing was natural. Why kill Angel Crump?

As Lyle worked away he was glad those were not his concerns. He did his job and expected everyone else to do theirs.

Ben Sidell was trying to do his. As Lyle bent over what was left of dear old Angel, Ben faced a furious Crawford Howard.

"Why would I kill her?" Crawford exploded as he sat in his sumptuous stable office, with cherrywood paneling, no less.

Ben stood before him, since Crawford rudely did not ask him to sit. Sam worked outside, bandages itching. He and Rory were grooming Czpaka in the crossties closest to the office just in case they might hear something. They heard that sentence.

Ben, voice lower, replied, "You aren't under suspicion."

Crawford shifted in his leather chair. "Iffy was an unreliable neighbor."

"How so?"

"She'd say one thing one day and another the next."

"Could you give me an example?"

Without hesitation, Crawford launched in. "Last fall I asked if I could ride over the low hills that separate us and ride the perimeter of her farm." He explained as if talking to a child. "To sweeten the request I had Mostly Maples plant a ten-foot sugar maple in her front yard. She called, thanked me and mentioned she liked Southern hawthorns. Waynesboro Nurseries planted two for her. She finally agreed. A week later, Sam and I rode over late one afternoon, and she flew out on her broom. Apoplectic." He drew in his breath. He shrugged. "The woman had a mental condition."

"She said she had lung cancer."

"Doesn't matter, does it? The result is the same."

"Perhaps it matters in how we respond to someone like that."

"Bullshit. She got away with murder. I know other people who have cancer and they don't use it the way Iffy used hers. She was a useless person."

"Better off dead?"

Crawford raised an eyebrow. "Yes, but"—he raised his voice—"that doesn't mean I shot her. Traced the bullet yet?"

"No."

"Hot gun." Crawford raised his eyebrows. Stolen guns and knockoff models of expensive guns, sold cheap out of the backs of cars, were usually untraceable.

"If it is from a registered gun, we'll track it down, but you're right." These were golden words to Crawford, so Ben smiled when he said, "It's easy to procure a used clean gun."

Crawford puffed out his chest a bit. "You guys want us to believe you can solve murders with technology. I say it's still an easy crime to commit and walk free."

Ben waited a beat. "If someone is very intelligent or very lucky, it's easier than I would like it to be."

"Anything else?"

"No. Thank you for your time."

"Might want to talk to Sam. She hated him."

"Thanks." Ben left the office, crossed the center aisle, and stood quietly while Czpaka closed his eyes in pleasure.

Sam massaged the warm-blood's long neck while Rory curried along his back. "Heard you all had some kind of hunt Saturday."

Ben grinned. "How Shaker, Betty, and Sybil got that pack together, I'll never know, and Sam, what a good run it was, too."

"Starts in the breeding shed just like for horses," Sam responded.

"Ah, yes, of course." Ben then said to Rory, "You're getting good at that."

The dark curly-haired fellow nodded. "Sam's teaching me a lot."

"Mind if I ask you a few questions, Sam? We can go in private if you like."

"Rory's my buddy." Sam indicated that Ben should start in.

"Crawford said Iffy hated you."

"Not always." Sam chose his words carefully. "She was sharp with me, but that was Iffy's way. Got bad at the end."

"What do you mean?"

"Didn't matter what I said or did; she'd jump down my throat. When the hounds dug out, Sister picked up three couple, but about two hours later, one lone fellow showed up at her door. I go to pick up the hound and she comes out waving a steak knife at me."

"Why do you think she hated you?"

Sam thought a long time. He looked at Rory, then back at the sheriff. "Alcoholic. I asked her to go to AA with me once."

Ben replied. "No one else has mentioned this about Iffy."

Rory spoke up. "Said she suffered from her treatments. Maybe she did, but she was a drunk."

"It takes one to know one." Sam supported Rory's assessment. "Whatever medication she was on, she was still a drunk."

"She hid it well," Ben remarked.

"Not so well," Rory piped up.

"If you know the signs, she couldn't hide it. She was a functioning alcoholic. Most are. Less than five percent of alcoholics end up like Rory and me, on the street drinking sterno. She went to work, held her job. I guess she did a good job, but she was an alcoholic. She did her drinking at home. Maybe she hid a bottle in her car. Don't know. There are people who get through the day. When the sun sets they hit the bottle. Every day."

"Women hide it better than men," Rory opined.

"Hide everything better than men," Sam agreed.

"And you don't think anyone else picked up on this?" Ben asked.

"She preyed on people's sympathy. She'd totter around with her canes, or she'd slump in her wheelchair."

Ben asked, "Are you saying she could walk just fine?"

"Unless she was loaded."

"Do you think she could have faked her illness?" Ben said quietly.

This didn't surprise Sam or Rory, which in itself surprised Ben.

"It's possible. She was very smart."

"I checked her medical records. The tumor is obvious." Ben frowned for a second.

"Doesn't make her any less of a drunk." Rory brushed Czpaka's hindquarters in a circular motion.

"Guess not." Ben put his hands, cold, into his coat pockets.

"We saw right through her. She couldn't stand it." Sam lifted a small bucket from the floor.

The smell of Absorbine filled the air, a strong but pleasant odor. Czpaka opened his eyes from his reverie.

Sam sponged some Absorbine onto Czpaka's back.

"That feels so good." The horse groaned.

Sam smiled as he worked his fingers along the big guy's spine.

"You two have been very helpful." Ben glanced back to see Crawford on the phone. Lowering his voice, he said, "We miss you."

"It's a five-boarder," Rory replied.

"Beg pardon." Ben, an Ohio boy, didn't recognize the expression, which referred to the number of boards in a fence panel.

"Bad. More to fix," Rory answered.

"Yeah, I think it is, too," Ben replied. He turned to leave, paused, walked across the center aisle, and knocked on Crawford's door. Crawford looked up through the large-paned window from which he could observe activities in the stable. He motioned for Ben to enter.

The sheriff patiently waited while Crawford finished his call.

When Crawford had touched the off button, Ben stepped forward. "I'm sorry to bother you again. Did you ever try to buy Iffy's farm?"

"Once. She refused." Crawford's voice was even.

"It'd be nice to have Iffy's farm, since it touches yours."

"It would. She was adamant."

" 'Course, it's close to town. Be a great development site."

Crawford, irritated, declared, "Not my forte."

Once Ben had driven out, Crawford called Jason. He'd heard Jason had gone back out with Jefferson Hunt.

Before he had a chance to rip him apart, Jason coolly circumvented the anger. "I know, I hunted with JHC. Crawford, one of us needs to be on the good side. If we can go forward at Paradise, some of those members will be resource people."

"They won't buy."

"No, but they might have a friend in California who will. We can't burn all our bridges."

"Have you talked to the sheriff?"

"He called on me concerning my patient."

"Oh, say Iffy, for Christ's sake. I know perfectly well it was about Iffy," Crawford erupted. "Why else would he see you? Did you say anything about Paradise?"

"No, of course not." Jason was angry now.

"He asked me if I wanted to buy Iffy's farm and develop it."

"I didn't say anything."

"You and I need to talk about Jefferson Hunt. Face-to-face."

"We will. It's been hectic." Jason begged off.

CHAPTER 25

Iffy's remains provoked slight controversy among her distant relatives, none of whom felt sufficiently close to pay for interment. Garvey, pity overtaking anger, paid for cremation and picked up the shoe box of her earthly remains, an I.D. sticker on the sides. His wife, horrified at the idea of baked bones in the house, told him to dump Iffy on the rosebushes, reminding him that ash is good for roses.

As the bushes slumbered under the snow, the tops visible, it made no sense to squander the ash on the snow.

For all his troubles, Garvey retained his sense of humor. He gave the ashes to Gray and asked him to scatter Iffy on Hangman's Ridge: "For if we dispensed justice as once we did, she'd have probably been hung."

Iffy, placed on a shelf in the kennel feed room, awaited Sister and Gray's return from today's hunt, Tuesday, January 17.

Gray had brought her to Roughneck Farm Monday night, and neither he nor Sister wanted to go up to Hangman's Ridge. They told each other it was because the farm road was icy. They couldn't use darkness as an excuse, since the moon was just past full.

Slapping Iffy on the shelf, they promised to scatter her ashes and read a prayer. They would not speak ill of the dead.

At this exact moment, this impending pathetic ceremony didn't enter Sister's mind.

Riding Matador for the first time in a hunt, she thought this would be a good day to try him. Usually hunting was slack for a few days after a full moon, animals weary after the heightened activity of the time. It affected humans, too, hence the term "lunatic." Tuesdays the fields were small, another good reason to test Matador. He wouldn't be overwhelmed with other horses.

After the visit last summer by Sister and Walter, Franklin Foster up in Fairfax had said yes to allowing the Jefferson Hunt on his land. Since the hunt would clear trails, build attractive jumps in old fence lines, and keep an eye on this one thousand acres without charging him a penny, it didn't take a genius to see the advantage to himself. The land abutted Paradise on the north and west; it was rough but rich in game.

Sister hadn't pursued this fixture during the years when Binky and Alfred's disagreements had flared up. One would say the hunt could use Paradise; the other would say no. She'd steered clear. There was no point in hunting Mr. Foster's land if hounds ran into Paradise. One brother, at least, would be mad at Jefferson Hunt. Last year, Margaret, working as hard as a shuttling diplomat, had secured Paradise once more for foxhunting. That's when Sister and Walter drove to what they considered Occupied Virginia: northern Virginia.

The Jefferson Hunt now had a fixture of seven thousand acres, counting both places together plus odd pieces surrounding those two large parcels of land. This more than made up for the loss of Beasley Hall except that Crawford had groomed his estate, built all the jumps, and been a generous host during his years of membership.

It takes a year to learn your foxes on a new fixture. It takes years to cut the trails according to the manner in which your foxes run. It's a foolish master who rushes into a new place, squandering people's time, energy, and money, opening trails, cutting brush and trees, and building jumps only to find that the foxes use a different highway.

That meant today she rode in thick woods, ravines unfolding before her. The deer trails proved useful. Discarded farm roads, saplings lacing through them, could be followed slowly.

Out for an hour. Nothing. Matador, walking along calmly, swiveled his ears each time Shaker blew the horn. She felt disgust about Iffy's murder. She wondered, too, about the mound of frozen blood she'd found on Crawford's land. Gave her the creeps.

Tootie rode Keepsake. Apart from wanting Tootie to hunt, Sister thought Matador would feel better if a stablemate rode with him. She had horse sense.

Tootie finished her term paper, but no one else at Custis Hall could keep up with her. Bunny wasn't going to trailer one student and her horse to a hunt, so Sister had picked Tootie up Monday night. She and Gray laughed at Tootie's stories; she laughed at theirs. Even better, she rose at five-thirty in the morning without being called three times. Tootie readied the horses while Sister made a light breakfast.

Listening to the horn, appreciating the silence behind her,

Sister realized she loved Tootie. She loved being a mother again, even only a part-time mother.

Tedi and Edward, those stalwarts; Gray; Ben; and Tootie constituted the field. Walter usually worked on Tuesdays.

The mercury wouldn't budge over thirty degrees.

"What kind of foxes do you think live here?" Trinity asked Asa.

"Lots of rabbits. Lots of everything. Both. Grays and reds," he answered, his nose down.

"Hard day," Delia said.

She'd put on a little weight, thanks to her extra rations. Sister and Shaker thought she could get back into the game today, as it appeared the pace would be slow.

Nothing is sure in foxhunting.

"Look at it this way, if we do find anything in this cold, it will be red hot. We'll be on good terms with our fox," Diana, always pushing for scent, said optimistically.

Dasher, who had stepped up to the plate, driving very hard now that his brother, Dragon, was laid up in sick bay with his wound, opened his mouth. *"Yes."*

Cora ran over to Dasher and inhaled deeply. *"Rock and roll."*

Hounds opened. Shaker blew three short notes three times. Given the thick covert, he couldn't see whether all the hounds were on. He didn't blow "Gone away." He fought his way through the brush.

Matador, a little up now, listened to Sister. She possessed the gift of soft hands, imparting confidence to her horse through light contact with the horse's mouth. Nor did she clamp down her legs in a vise. She had an educated leg. Matador appreciated that, too.

Both Betty and Sybil battled the rough territory.

They emerged onto an untended field, sumac sticking up out of the snow, spikes of broomsage visible. That was easier going, and the little group ran as hard as they could.

Surprised by hounds, the fox would learn in time what all this meant. Today all he wanted to do was reach his den. As he headed for it he leaped logs but otherwise kept a straight course.

As the small red plunged down into a steep ravine, a fine place against harsh winds, Darby lifted his head. *"What's that?"*

Even Cora didn't know what the sweet odor was. She slowed, waiting for Asa to come alongside. As the senior dog hound he might know, she thought.

"Don't know," he said as he kept running.

Delia, the oldest hound there, ran at the rear of the pack. *"Hold up."*

Her wisdom went unheeded as the second-year entry shot past even Cora, who paused for the senior hound. Cora then stretched out to catch the pack.

By now Sister had caught the deep sweet odor. "Shit," she thought to herself.

Gray recognized it. Tootie did not. Tedi and Edward, swept along with the run, glanced nervously at each other.

Five seconds passed. Then a terrible crash rising out of the deepest part of the ravine told the tale.

Shaker blew three long notes. "Come to me. Come to me," he called.

A shotgun blast shattered the air. Matador leaped straight up.

Sister, with her years of training, didn't even think about it. She sat deep, leaned forward, and pulled one rein down to bring Matador back down. She kept a tighter rein on him so he wouldn't put his head down and buck after standing up.

"They're going to kill us." Matador sweated.

Nonni, Ben Sidell's been-there-done-that trooper, calmly said, *"Steady, young feller. Hounds will get shot before we do."*

Keepsake leaped straight forward but settled right down as Tootie remained calm.

Sister slowed Matador. "Ben, you'd better come up here with me."

Gray rode on one side of Sister, Ben on the other.

Tootie, Tedi, and Edward rode behind.

Clouds of condensation billowed from mouths and nostrils. Sister passed a jutting ledge to behold a large still, broken glass and bottles everywhere.

Alfred DuCharme, shotgun pointing at Shaker, cussed a blue streak.

Tedi uncharacteristically blurted out, "Guess Alfred's not such a lazy sod."

"Get the hell out of here!" Alfred bellowed.

The hounds—unhurt, thank God—bundled around Gunpowder and Shaker.

Ben Sidell calmly rode forward. "Alfred, put that shotgun down."

"Goddammit!" Alfred recognized the young sheriff. "Goddammit to hell!" He lowered the shotgun.

"Break it open, Alfred."

Alfred did break open his shotgun.

The smell of fermenting corn nearly knocked Tootie off her saddle.

"Anyone have cut pads?" Sister rode up to Shaker as Betty and Sybil rode in, quite shocked at the scene.

"No." His face was pale.

"Alfred, you're operating an illegal still, and you're trespassing on . . ." Ben turned to Sister.

"Franklin Foster."

". . . Foster's land."

Dejection overcame Alfred. "Will this be in the papers?"

Canny, Ben dismounted. Tootie rode up to take Nonni's reins. Ben removed the shotgun from Alfred. "Now, Alfred, things don't look good for you. If you help me, I'll help you."

A fleeting look of hope crossed Alfred's craggy features. "What can I do?"

"The first thing you can do is destroy this still. Remove all traces of it. You wouldn't want Mr. Foster to find out and nail you to the cross, now would you?"

"No."

"The second thing you can do is promise me you will not do this again."

"I do." Alfred almost sounded believable.

"There's more. Are you listening?" Ben kept his voice low.

"I am."

"Did you sell to Iphigenia Demetrios?"

He cleared his throat. "I did."

"Did she come out here to you two Saturdays ago, January 7?"

"Yes."

"Was she a regular customer?"

"Yes. She'd pour my stuff in other bottles. She drank bourbon, too, mind you, but when she needed a real pick-me-up, she came to me."

"I see. Did you kill her?"

"No!" He stepped back, frightened.

"It's not so far-fetched, Alfred. She could have threatened

to expose you, and from the looks of this, you've profited greatly from illegal liquor."

"I would never kill anyone. Even for that. Because I break one law doesn't mean I'd break all laws." Alfred's wits were returning.

"I believe you. Thousands wouldn't," Ben joked. "Any idea why she was so upset that Saturday?"

"Work. Said work wasn't going right. Said she had no love life. Said she felt betrayed."

"By whom?"

"She didn't say."

"Does a cell phone work down here in this hollow?"

Alfred nodded. "If you climb up there on that rock ledge, it does."

"All right, here is what we are going to do. I'm going to call the fire department. Tattenhall Station is the closest volunteer station. I'm going to tell them that I'm performing a controlled burn here. I won't give the circumstances. But this way, if they get calls from anyone, they won't respond. I won't arrest you, and I will swear these people to secrecy." Ben nodded toward the field. "Are you with me?"

"Yes." Alfred sighed deeply.

Not only was Ben saving his face, he was saving him lawyer's fees, possible jail time, and significant damages to the state.

Ben walked over to Sister. "Sister, you are to never speak of this. Shaker, Betty, Sybil."

They agreed.

He walked over to Tootie, Tedi, and Edward.

"Edward, do you have room on your trailer to take Nonni back with you? I don't know how long it will be before I can pick her up."

"Be glad to do it," Edward replied.

"Tedi, Edward, Tootie, you must promise not to reveal what has happened here." He stopped a moment and hoped Tootie, despite her youth, could resist telling the story. "This may have a bearing on Iffy's murder. I need full cooperation."

Each pledged not to tell.

He spoke louder. "Alfred, when next you see any of these people, do you swear not to speak of this or treat them rudely?"

"Of course." Alfred might hate Binky, but he treated other people with respect.

"You're going to drive me to After All once we finish business here," said Ben to Alfred.

As the little group left, the fox, den up on the ledge within hearing distance of the clear creek below, thought this day memorable.

The hounds passed right under his nose.

"He's up there," Asa said.

"We must go in," said Delia, now up front, as they were walking.

"How'd you know?" Dasher asked Delia, his mother.

"Long before you were born there was a still hidden in a stone springhouse not far from Tattenhall Station. Fox ran into it and so did we. Once you get a whiff, you don't forget. The humans use different grains, so it can smell different, but it's always sweet and thick."

Trident, finding the smell gross, asked, *"How can they drink that stuff?"*

"If they eat spinach, I reckon they can eat or drink just about anything," Asa laughed.

As the happy group of hounds walked up and out of the ravine, Matador asked Keepsake, *"Is it always like this?"*

The gelding replied, *"No, you just had a special initiation."*

"*Whew.*" The gorgeous flea-bitten gray exhaled, which made Sister laugh.

Ben and Alfred smashed up what was left of the equipment with axes. Once Ben felt the horses were far enough away not to become frightened by the smell, he lit a match, and the place blew up like a tinderbox.

Alfred sighed deeply. "Best damn country waters in the state of Virginia, if I do say so myself."

"Do it legally, then, Alfred."

"Ah shit, Sheriff, I'd choke in laws like kudzu."

Ben didn't reply, but he sure did think life had become overregulated. He couldn't enforce much of the law; he'd need an officer for every five people.

Enlisting Alfred in his search for the killer was one reason why Ben had let him off the hook. The other reason was that he wanted Alfred's tacit blessing as he courted the old man's niece.

Margaret didn't know it yet, but Ben meant to win her. For him it had been love at first sight.

Once back at Roughneck Farm, Tootie took Sister's Matador. As she and Gray cleaned the horses, Sister and Shaker checked each hound.

"Let's give them a treat," Sister said as she walked into the feed room to put down the troughs. She noticed Iffy's ashes all over the feed room, the box chewed to bits. "Great day, Shaker." She used the old Southern exclamation.

He walked in, the hounds were in the draw pen. "Jesus."

"I expect she's with him now if forgiveness comes as advertised." Sister burst out laughing. "What a sight. Iffy all over the kennel floor. Who did this?"

"Oh, that's not hard to figure." Shaker walked through the

swinging doors to the special medical runs, as they called the sequestered housing and runs for an injured hound.

Dragon, bored, had lifted the latch on his gate with his nose. He knew well enough where the feed room was, so he pushed through the doors. Couldn't find any extra feed, since it was all in tightly closed zinc-lined bins. But the toasted bones were a treat. He's chewed up the box, chewed up some of Iffy, and then sauntered back to his special quarters.

Shaker, in a fog this morning, had forgotten to put the pin through the latch that prevented it from being lifted up.

He apologized to Sister as she swept up what was left of Iffy.

"Look at it this way," Sister said. "It may be one of the few times Iffy provided genuine pleasure."

Dragon, hearing this on the other side of the swinging doors, said, *"Bones were a little too dry."*

CHAPTER 26

What remained of Iffy lifted into the air under the huge oak tree at Hangman's Ridge. Gray dust and bits of bone that Dragon had passed over rose upward, then scattered as a great gust from the north sent ashes flying.

"Ashes to ashes, dust to dust." Sister pulled the collar of her coat up.

Shaker watched the dispersal of Iffy's remains. "Sorry little life."

"So it would appear."

"Should we say a prayer, anyway?" Shaker, a good Catholic boy, folded his gloved hands together.

"You do it."

"Heavenly father, into thy hands we commend this spirit. She didn't do much in this life. Iphigenia Demetrios was a thief.

But since Christ pardoned a thief suffering with him on the cross, perhaps you will pardon Iffy. Amen."

As they climbed into the Chevy 454, both shivered.

"Iffy's made contact with the other criminals," Sister joked as Shaker slid behind the wheel.

He turned on the motor, heater cranking up again. "They're here." He lightly touched his toe to the accelerator and headed toward the farm road on the southeast side of the wide flat ridge.

"Feast day for St. Prisca, a Roman lady from the first days of Christianity. She's attended by the two lions who declined to eat her or even take a swipe. Ah yes, those Romans thrilled to entertainments that make the NFL and the NHL look like Tupperware parties."

He laughed as he carefully descended the side of the ridge. The farm road, frozen, demanded attention.

"Where's the real January thaw? The big one?"

"Damned if I know." She looked up at a light blue sky. "Too bad Gray couldn't be with us for Iffy's decanting. Electrician's coming to his place, so he's there."

"Sam's making a good recovery."

"Yes, he is. He's invaluable, too, telling us when and where Crawford will hunt. Sam has said he's seen an abundance of fox at Beasley Hall. I feel sorry for the hounds even if there are a lot of foxes. Hounds need a good huntsman. They need to trust the person with the horn. That's why we have such a good hunt. You."

He smiled. "You, too." He slowed even more as a big ice slick glittered on the farm road. "Think he'll tire of it? Disperse the pack?"

"Not any time soon." She reached for the Jesus strap when the hind end skidded. "Some pumpkins yesterday."

Shaker laughed out loud. "Alfred's face crumpled. Did you ever see anything like it?"

"No." She laughed, too. "What a rogue."

"Shrewd, not putting the still on his property."

"He'd risk Paradise if he did that."

Sister felt her toes warming. "I expect he shipped most of it out of the county."

"Could Iffy have organized that for him? Shipping?" Shaker asked.

"She probably could have. Iffy was smart, organized."

Shaker breathed out once they reached the bottom of the ridge. "Whew." Then he said, "Think Garvey is in on this somehow?"

"Moonshine?"

"No," Shaker replied. "In on whatever Iffy was doing. She'd fake purchases, say, and they'd divvy up the money."

"I've thought of that, too. Be a good scam."

Shaker drove slightly faster. "Garvey doesn't seem like the type to loot his own business, but I guess you never know."

"Ben said there wasn't one incriminating article in Iffy's house, old barn, car. No hidden account books. Even her computer was innocent. Ben said it was so old he thought it was slowly dying of fatigue. Now, on the other hand, Garvey has been on a buying spree these last years, snapping up smaller companies. Still . . ." Her voice trailed off.

"Reminds me, you said you were going to buy a new computer for the kennels."

"Yes, once Christmas was over. Know what you want?"

"Same as yours. The iMac G5."

"By now they're probably better than mine. Take the farm credit card and buy what you want."

"Great." He smiled as they passed the apple orchard, the kennels coming into view. "We've got a drop-in."

"Damn. That's one I'd like to drop-kick." Sister recognized Jason's mighty Range Rover.

They pulled beside the white SUV. Jason kept the motor running as he talked on his phone. The Rover was wired for a phone, so he spoke up toward his rearview mirror, where a tiny microphone was located. He signed off as Sister stepped out of the Chevy.

"Hello, Sister, Shaker." He closed the heavy door behind him. "I called but no one answered, so I thought I'd take a chance and run by." He paused. "Long night at the hospital."

"You must be able to sleep on your feet." Sister motioned for him to follow her and Shaker into the kennel.

They filed into the office. Sister sat behind the desk.

"Boss, I'll see to Dragon."

"Fine. Sit down, Jason. It's basic but comfortable."

"Feels good. If I can get fifteen minutes of sleep here or there, I can power through. It's my feet that hurt. I've caused you trouble, and I'm sorry for it."

"You've already apologized." She wondered what he wanted.

"As you know, I have a friendship with Crawford."

"Yes."

"If I walk out hounds with you, learn your routine, it will imperil that relationship. As it is, he's trying to make me resign from the hunt. I won't do it. I'm hoping over time I can lower the hostility threshold." He smiled, pleased with his choice of words.

"Thank you for coming to tell me."

"If you have any weakness, any crack in your armor, he'll find it."

"I expect he will." She did have one, which she sidestepped.

Peter Wheeler's will, which had bequeathed the Chevy 454, his estate, and fifty thousand dollars a year to the club, had been made in 1976. She had been forty-three, and Peter, having a bout of illness, thought he might be leaving the earth. He recovered. But he put in his will that she couldn't take a joint-master. He'd realized his mistake in the last year of his life, but with so many other concerns, he hadn't revised his will in time. She saw no reason to speak of this.

"Hopefully, Crawford will find a positive outlet for his energies," she evenly replied.

He noticed the chewed-up ashes box, whose remnants were in the large wastebasket at the side of the big teacher's desk built in the 1950s. He'd seen enough of such boxes. Peering down, he made out part of Iffy's name on a typed label. "Iffy?"

She said without being asked, "It is. Was."

"What happened?"

"No one would take her. We said a prayer for her at Hangman's Ridge."

"What happened to the box?"

"A hound grabbed it." She declined to give the full story, which was funny to her but perhaps not to Iffy's physician.

As he walked to the door, Sister threw this out. "Do you think Iffy wanted to live?"

"She did," he replied, and left.

Felicity walked across the quad from the infirmary. Talking with animation to Howard on her cell phone, she planned their weekend date. This wasn't easy, since neither had a car.

She ended the conversation as she went up the stairs to her dorm floor.

Tootie came into the hall when she heard Felicity's footfall. "Are you contagious?"

"No." Felicity smiled.

"So?" Tootie held her palms upward, flaring out her fingers.

"Food allergy. Mrs. Norton called in an allergist, and they scratched my back with all kinds of stuff. Dog dander, grass, things you don't even want to know about." She rolled her eyes.

"And?" Tootie leaned against her doorway.

"Bleached flour." Felicity leaned against the other side of the door, crossing her arms over her chest.

"Wouldn't you have gotten sick before now?"

"That's what I asked, and the doctor said sometimes these things don't show up until a person is older. So she gave me this." Felicity pulled stapled sheets from her voluminous handbag. "If I follow the plan, I won't be nauseated."

"Well, that's good. I was worried."

"I was, too. It's an awful feeling. And when I listed what I ate those mornings, what I could remember, I mean I don't think about what I eat, but I ate white bread or rolls, stuff like that."

"Can you eat any bread?"

"Dark. Pumpernickel. It's weird."

"You're weird." Tootie punched her.

CHAPTER 27

The party wagon swayed slightly as Shaker turned from the Roughneck Farm road right onto the state road.

"Wrong direction," Cora wondered.

Ardent, who along with Asa and senior members of Sister's "A" line was resting on the top tier, said, *"Changed the fixture."*

"How do you know?" Delight asked, not impudently.

"Heard Shaker when he called me out of the Big Boys' run. Trouble at Little Dalby."

"What kind of trouble?" Diana, curious, lifted her head off her paws.

"Human trouble," Ardent responded.

"That's better than rabies." Dasher, eager to hunt, paced in the medium-sized trailer.

"True enough," Cora said, *"but human trouble has a way of rolling back on us."*

Sister, with Betty in the cab, pulled the horse trailer to Foxglove Farm.

Straight as the crow flies, the distance was two and a half miles, a booming run on a straight-necked fox. Going around the land by available roads, it took fifteen minutes to arrive at the lovely farm, where nothing was done to excess, all in proportion.

"I hate to overhunt my foxes." Sister slowly cruised round the big circle in front of Cindy Chandler's barn. She parked, truck nose out, so other trailers could park alongside.

This crisp January 19 morning, Thursday, more people came than Sister expected. She had a very respectable midweek field of twenty-five.

Pleasing as that was, being forced to shift the fixture at the last minute plucked her last nerve. Anselma Wideman had called at nine last night to inform her that Crawford Howard had chosen to hunt Little Dalby on her, Sister's, day. Crawford knew full well this would inconvenience Jefferson Hunt.

She changed the information on the huntline, simple enough. She sent out e-mails, also simple enough, and she called her staff to make certain they knew. Hunt clubs have phone lines that members call two or three hours before the appointed time in case a fixture needs to be changed because of weather or other events.

Needing all her wits to chase foxes, Sister held her emotions in check. She was wondering whether she could get away with murder. Crawford would be such a juicy, satisfying target. However, one murder was enough.

Walter juggled last-minute questions from visitors. He lent one an extra stock tie. The Custis Hall quartet along with Bunny, their coach, and Charlotte, the headmistress, were there.

Sister led Rickyroo off the trailer. Betty followed with Outlaw.

Sybil helped Shaker so Betty could assist Sister if she needed help.

Folding back her deep green blanket with dark orange piping, Betty, to lighten the mood, asked, "Perhaps we'll have an epiphany, late as usual."

"January 19 is a big day. Feast days of Branwalader, Canute, and Henry of Finland."

"Think we might have to call on them?" Betty folded the blanket over, then stepped into the tack room to place it over an empty saddle rack.

"We might need to do that, but none of them are called upon by hunters."

"I don't have your head for dates, but I am a Virginian. Birthday of Robert E. Lee, 1807."

"Yes, it is. And Edgar Allan Poe, 1809, and Cézanne in 1839. A lucky day."

"Think there was an epiphany?"

"I do." Then Sister laughed, her gloom lifting from the fixture problem. "But the Wise Men didn't find Jesus. Their camels did."

"Ha. Imagine hunting from a camel."

"Think I'd throw up. Couldn't take the motion." Sister checked her horse's girth and gathered the reins in her left hand, holding the left rein shorter than the right so if Rickyroo should take a notion he'd turn inside toward her instead of outside, which would throw her out like a centrifuge.

Betty did the same, and both women mounted up without a grunt.

Sister rode over to Cindy Chandler, who was on her tough

little mare, Caneel. "Thank you so much for allowing us here on short notice."

Cindy, a true foxhunter, smiled. "I love having you here." She stepped closer to Sister, which pleased Rickyroo, as he was fond of Caneel. "Would you like me to speak to Anselma and Harvey? If you do it's official, and you scare people sometimes." Cindy could say this, being a trusted friend. "The Widemans don't know hunting. They might finally understand territory conflict, but they won't grasp overhunting foxes."

"Do talk to them. Use all that deadly charm." Sister joked gratefully. "I'm not upset with them."

"I know that. It's Mr. Ego."

"We seem to have a few of those." Sister cut her eyes toward Jason, resplendent in a hacking jacket made expressly for him by Le Cheval in Kentucky so it fit perfectly.

"Peacock."

"M-m-m," Sister touched Cindy's arm. "Thank you many times over for everything. I always feel better when I see you or talk to you."

"Go on." Cindy smiled at her.

Sister saw that hounds were ready and everyone was mounted except for Ronnie Haslip, usually one of the first up. He'd dropped his crop and dismounted, and was swinging up again.

To give Ronnie one extra second, Sister quietly said to Walter, facing her, "You ride tail today. Do you mind?"

"Not at all."

"Take Jason with you. If he wants to learn, then he can learn service first."

"Ah." Walter sighed, but he didn't argue.

How could he? She was right. The look on Jason's face was

not one of a man being honored by a position of responsibility. It was that of a spoiled person who wants to ride right up in the master's pocket.

Millions he might have, but Sister was damned if she'd be bought. She had kept Crawford in line for ten years, succeeding in getting him elected president—a good place for him in many ways. The boob ball, which is how she thought of the hunt ball, had put an end to all. Bobby Franklin, who had resigned his presidency, submitted to an emergency general election. Bobby, a good leader, had accepted with grace, tabling his ideas of a long vacation this coming summer. Betty was thrilled. Vacations bored her to tears.

There they were. Frost heavy on the ground. The sun kissing the horizon. Puffs curling from horses' nostrils, hounds eager.

The horrid cow, Clytemnestra, and her equally enormous offspring, Orestes, had been bribed and barricaded in two stout stalls in the small cattle barn. Sweet mash liberally laced with decent bourbon contented the holy horror, who had gleefully smashed fences and chased people in times past.

Given the heavy frost, the mercury still below freezing, Shaker walked hounds up the slow rise to the two ponds, one at a lower level than the other, a long pipe and small waterwheel between them. Cindy had added the waterwheel in the early fall. Formerly the water had cascaded from the pipe in the upper pond to the lower pond. Now the pipe fed directly onto the wheel, whose sound as it turned was one our ancestors had heard for centuries untold, one lost now to the roar of turbines and internal combustion engines.

Those who had never before heard the mating of gears, the slap of the paddles, the sound of the water rising and falling off the paddles discovered the peacefulness of it. Those who had ridden at Mill Ruins had heard it before in deeper register.

The cascade produced a spray of droplets, arching out over the pond and turning to thousands of rainbows as the sun rose high enough to send a long, slanting ray to the wheel.

The moving water crystallized at pond's edge here and there, but until frosts stayed hard and deep for many days the ponds wouldn't freeze.

Grace, the beautiful resident red fox, returned before sunrise to her den behind the stable. Given the wealth of treats, especially the hard candies that Cindy put out for her, Grace had lost her motivation to hunt afar. Occasionally she provided a bracing run. Today wasn't the day.

Grace glanced up and back. A blanket of thick clouds massed on the mountaintops. In front of her, the east, the sky was crystal clear. Very interesting. Very tricky.

Hounds picked up Grace's scent at the waterwheel. The beautiful red liked fishing, a hobby she'd taught to Inky. The two girlfriends would sit at pond's edge for hours watching the goldfish, big suckers. Every now and then, Grace would grab one or Inky would. The squirming fish sometimes gained its life by flopping right out of their paws and back into the pond. Occasionally they were successful and enjoyed sushi.

Today, a tall male heron, motionless, stood on the far side of the upper pond. With a jaundiced eye he watched the hounds. He wasn't going to budge unless someone approached him. He was here first. Furthermore, he was hungry. He tilted his head, and an orange flash caught his eye. Fast as lightning he uncoiled his snakey neck and plunged his long, narrow, terrifying beak through the thin ice at pond's edge into the water, pulling out an extremely healthy fish.

"Wow." Diddy's soft brown eyes widened.

"He's an old crank," Ardent jibbed.

"Sure can fish, though," Asa whispered, since Shaker was within earshot.

Grace's scent lingered enough for hounds to feather, the rhythm of their tails seemingly connected to the intensity of the scent.

Moving upward away from the ponds, hounds reached a higher meadow, where for fifteen minutes the sun warmed the remains of the snow, bare patches of slicked-down pasture also visible.

About a half mile away rested an old schoolhouse by the farm road. Aunt Netty had once lived there until Uncle Yancy filled the den up. Their former addresses littered three fixtures.

Cindy hadn't noticed, since she hadn't been riding her property in the cold, but a huge, leggy, red dog fox, Iggy, had recently taken up residence. The lure was not only the abundant supply of mice, moles, rabbits, and grain tidbits but Grace. He meant to have her. At this point, she was coy. Another week, and she might be in season. He was patient. She wouldn't be so coy then. As it was, she maintained warm conversations with him.

Hounds walked up the pasture and jumped over the fence line, trotting down into the woods where an old springhouse still stood.

Most of the old farms kept their springhouses because they remained useful.

Human reasoning would predict that a fox moving down into the woods, coursing through a narrow creek, and going through the springhouse would produce no scent because the springhouse water would be that much colder, which it was.

However, foxhunting rarely follows the book. Expect the

unexpected. Perhaps this is why foxhunting prepares people for life.

Dana, second year, gaining confidence, flanked the pack. She lifted her head, and a tantalizing odor wafted into her nostrils. She moved in that direction, going away from the main body of the pack. As Sybil was on the other side of the creek, deep covert between her and Dana, the whipper-in didn't notice.

"I have something," she spoke once but clearly.

"I'll check," Cora told the others as Dasher pushed up to take the place of strike hound. *"She might be right."*

"Gets too far from the rest of us," Asa noted.

"Shaker will think she's a skirter." Ardent seconded Asa's concern, for both dog hounds thought Dana showed promise.

Skirters don't stay in good packs for long.

Cora reached Dana and put her own educated nose to the ground. *"Bobcat."*

"Can we chase him?" Dana wanted to be right.

"Sure can. Bobcat and mountain lions count. But here's the thing, Dana. If we pick up good fox scent, we have to leave off and go to the fox."

"Over here," Cora called, and the others honored her.

The pack roared alongside the creek.

Sybil couldn't keep up through the underbrush. Wisely, she pulled farther west to a cleared path so she could run parallel. Familiar with the country, she knew the places where she could cut back to get closer to hounds.

Sister at first thought hounds were on a gray running in tight circles. She, too, couldn't follow closely, given the rough terrain.

Hounds sounded fabulous, the echo of voices ricocheting from the steep terrain.

Tootie, Val, Felicity, and Pamela rode at the back of first flight. Out of the corner of her eye, Val perceived movement. She turned her head just as the bobcat shot out from under the thick mountain laurel.

"Oh, m'God," she gasped.

Tootie followed Val's eyes, and she, too, caught sight of that unique bobtail, a forty-pound cat, booking along. He then slid into more heavy cover on the other side of the trail. Had the hill-toppers been closer, they would have viewed him.

"Say something," Pamela ordered. She'd caught a brief sight of the bobcat.

"I don't know what to say," Tootie replied irritably.

"Staff!" Felicity shouted for she saw a flash of red heading for them at a right angle.

"Shit." Val, in tight quarters, wondered how to get out of the way.

"One dollar," Felicity gleefully announced.

The whole pack thundered behind them.

"Shut up, you two." Tootie, passionate about hunting, thought they'd all talked too much already.

Val urged Moneybags into the bushes.

Unhappy though he was at the idea of getting scratched up, he did as he was told.

Iota, Parson, and Pamela's Tango, a stunning bay, battled their way into the brush in the nick of time, for Shaker hurtled toward them.

Tootie had the presence of mind to remove her cap and swivel in the direction the bobcat had taken, since she couldn't turn Iota any more, given the tight quarters.

Shaker, face scratched by thorns, sat upright as Showboat soared over a cluster of mountain laurel.

Seeing Tootie's arm extended, cap at the end, he called out, "Gray?"

"Bobcat," Tootie called back as Shaker disappeared on the other side of the deer path.

Ahead of them they heard Walter, obscured by the covert, but they couldn't hear exactly what he said, given the sound of the hounds drawing away from them and the rattle of dead brown oak leaves clinging fast to branches. Certain oaks retain most of their leaves until the bud swells in spring, finally pushing them off.

"Are we lost?" Pamela asked.

"No. I know this territory," Felicity said. She'd hunted it more than Pamela had.

"They must be reversing." Tootie strained to hear up ahead. "Let's get out of here."

"All we have to do is stay to the side, then fall in the back." Pamela couldn't cede anything to Tootie, whom she considered a rival.

"There's no room. We can't get any farther off the path than we are now," Felicity observed.

"I'm following the huntsman. The hell with it." Val shot out of her tight quarters and turned Moneybags to the spot where Shaker had plunged into the brush again.

"Val, don't," Tootie admonished her.

Val disappeared.

Pamela, hearing the field approach from one direction, the hilltoppers from the other, groaned, "We'll be squished."

"Pamela, jump the mountain laurel, where Shaker jumped into the deer path. Do it. Everyone can get by, then we can jump out and bring up the rear."

Pamela studied the formidable obstacle less out of fear than to plan her approach. Tango was facing in that direction, so she clucked to the sleek animal, then squeezed with purpose as she slid her hands forward.

Tango, a scopey fellow, meaning he could jump wide as well as high, took three trotting strides and soared over. A small clearing provided enough room for him to move forward before he smacked into a copse of black birch, the trees close together. He stopped in time as Iota cleared it, followed by Parson.

The three girls sat there, silent.

Sister trotted by. Three velvet hunt caps appeared on her right, although she couldn't see the girls clearly. Saying nothing, she pressed on. Soon the sounds of Bobby Franklin and the hilltoppers getting out of first flight's way filled the air.

People shouldn't talk during a hunt except on the way back when hounds are lifted, but in such tight quarters a word here or there did escape lips. The crashing about in the bush amused Iggy the schoolhouse fox, who had watched the drama from under a mass of junipers on a rise in the land, their thick scent masking his.

He stayed upwind. Hounds blasted one hundred yards beneath him, but the bobcat scent, heavy, kept them from even catching a hint of his, for potent as the junipers were, a tendril of fox musk might have reached them.

As Charlotte Norton and Bunny Taliaferro rode past, Bunny craned her neck to see her three charges in there. Pleased at their perfect manners, she smiled broadly, as did Charlotte Norton. At that moment it didn't register with either woman that they counted only three caps, not four.

Once Jason and Walter had passed, Tootie clapped her leg on Iota. He cleared the mountain laurels again with ease. Felicity and Pamela followed, as Tootie had quickly moved up the deer path to give them room.

Before they could trot on, out popped Iggy. He grinned ear to ear.

"Tally ho," Pamela called out.

"Won't do any good." Iggy sauntered next to them, using their horses as a cover and a foil.

"Oh, my God; oh, my God." Felicity, overcome by Iggy following them like a dog, could scarcely breathe.

"He'll duck out when he's ready," Tootie predicted.

"Smart for a young human," Iggy remarked to the horses.

"She has all the instincts to make a great hunter, this kid," Iota bragged on his human.

"Mine has no game sense at all," Parson sighed, as he loved Felicity.

"Doesn't need it," Tango replied. *"Mind like a steel trap. She'll run a company someday and have more hay than anyone else."*

"Ever notice how some humans can learn and others can't, whereas we always learn from what's around us?" Iggy mused.

"Curious." Iota had noticed this because Tootie absorbed everything, whereas the others, not unintelligent, only picked up what they were looking for in the first place.

"They need systems," Parson, named for a practitioner of such a system, said.

"I think they're born that way." Tango turned his head slightly to avoid a hanging vine. *"Damn thing."*

"I don't. Heredity is stored environment. This fear, this need to believe, overrides their heredity. They don't listen to their bodies anymore except for sex. They're making a real mess of it, too." Parson had strong opinions.

"Well, you must observe natural phenomena without judgment," Iggy shrewdly noted. *"That's the only way you can flourish."* He stopped for a second. *"Coming back. He won't break into the open. If he gets bored with it, old Flavius will climb a tree. Mind you, he's ferocious."* With that Iggy disappeared, calling over his shoulder, *"I'll cross his line and get you all out of this ravine."*

Old Flavius, the bobcat, shot in front of Iota, who shied for a second. Tootie, tight leg, stuck like glue. Her heart pounded to be so close to such a beautiful yet fearsome beast.

"Hold hard."

The other two had caught sight of the big cat, too.

Two minutes later the whole pack crashed in front of Tootie and charged into the brush.

Confusion overtook them as Iggy's scent crossed Flavius's line.

Seconds later, Shaker, more scratches on his craggy face, appeared.

Pausing in the deer path, right in front of Tootie, he listened intently. "Two lines."

She remained silent. He smiled at her and turned his horse toward the north, staying on the deer path. "Girls, follow me."

Thrilled, they did as they were told. Not four strides down the deer path, Val fought her way through the brambles to fall in behind Pamela.

Pamela turned to see Val's gorgeous face crisscrossed with scratches like tic-tac-toe. She stifled a giggle and pressed on. Val was displeased to be following Pamela.

Shaker kept close to his hounds as they milled about. Once he thought he knew which was the fox scent, he put his horn to his lips and, doubling the notes, urged them on to the scent.

First to figure it out was Diana. "*Dog fox. Don't know him.*"

The hounds swung to her except for two couple of the second-year entry. The bobcat scent—hot, hot, hot—fooled them into thinking they were closing on their quarry.

Shaker couldn't count all his hounds in the thick covert. He blew again, feeling his shirt stick to his back from sweat despite the cold. Hounds opened again.

Dana froze as Betty Franklin and Outlaw blasted into the bush.

"Hark to 'em." Her voice, firm and clear, bided no stragglers.

The two couple squirted toward the sound of the horn and the cry of the pack.

As they scooted away, Betty paused one moment and said to her beloved friend, "How in the hell do we get out of this mess?"

"*Leave it to me.*" Outlaw lowered his head and pushed through tight cedars, brush, and vines. Tarzan would have felt at home here except for the cold.

Steady as a rock, the quarter horse moved forward until he broke through to the creek again.

He leaped down into the creek; it was a two-foot drop, but the footing wasn't rocky in the creek.

Betty, trusting him, let him pick his exit spot. Little blue cedar berries, round, had slipped behind her coat collar. They drove her nuts, but there wasn't a thing she could do about it. A few had found their way into her boots, too.

"*We can fly from here.*" Outlaw blew air out his nostrils, waiting for her command.

"*I love you.*" Betty patted him on the neck, then galloped forward, for they had real estate to cover.

Flavius, free of the hounds, walked to the springhouse, where he'd stashed some kill. He paid no attention to Sybil on Bombardier. The horse shied as Flavius bared his fangs for effect. Sybil flew off. Bombardier stood still, and she remounted, amazed that the bobcat sat and watched her. Sybil felt like prey.

Iggy led everyone on a merry chase. Needing the exercise, he didn't head straight for the schoolhouse. He boogied to the twin ponds. The heron, livid that Iggy circled both ponds, lifted wide his huge wings.

"Scares me to death," Iggy sassed him.

Athena and Bitsy reposed on the topmost limb of a towering sycamore denuded of leaves.

"It's been quite a show," Athena chortled.

And it wasn't over yet, for hounds, finally out of that heavy covert, sped over the patchy ground, tiny bits of snow and mud shooting off behind them. Cora, first, flat out, circled the upper pond, leaped down to the lower, and circled that.

Iggy, a secure four minutes ahead—given his speed, he was in the prime of life—veered into the manicured woods, called "parked out" in this part of the world. Making no attempt to foil his scent, he then raced in a large semicircle. As he reached the woods' edge, he kept to it, knowing it would be full of scent from edge feeders like rabbits.

Just as the field came out by the upper pond, Iggy came into view.

Sister, seeing him, did not make the mistake of an overenthusiastic field master. Her task was to follow the hounds, not the fox. She didn't cross the huge expanse of snow-covered pasture to get on terms with him. That would have cut off her hounds. She stuck behind the hounds, which she could finally see as they launched themselves off the bank to land next to the lower pond, the waterwheel paddling away.

As "Tally-hos" sounded behind her she fought the urge to turn and tell them she wasn't an idiot, she might be old but she wasn't blind, she had seen the fox. Better yet, hounds, heads down, were on. No need for "Tally-ho." Well, it was a large field. Not everyone knew her, as many were cappers. She pressed on, wondering how people can foxhunt yet remain ignorant. That flew out of her mind as she launched off the upper bank, a tidy drop jump onto the slick surface by the lower pond.

That would part a few riders from their mounts, thereby enriching the club bar. Off you go, and a bottle must be produced at the next hunt. If a junior you had to deliver a six-pack of soda.

The music, spine tingling, swelled, and she now saw Shaker come out of the woods followed by Tootie, Val, Felicity, and Pamela.

Jumping off the upper bank, Bunny also beheld her students. She'd get to the bottom of this when the hunt was over. What were those girls doing behind the huntsman? She was going to skin them alive.

Iggy, in the open now, treated everyone to a view as well as an appreciation of his blinding speed.

The pace began to tell. People fell behind. Gray, riding in the middle of first flight, moved up behind Tedi and Edward, who rode right up behind Sister. He didn't feel it was proper for him to ride with Sister on days when there were large fields. It would smack of favoritism. When fields were small, he'd be close.

As Sister thought, five people came a cropper on the drop from the upper bank to the lower. Ronnie Haslip, a good rider having a bad day, broke his collarbone. Walter stayed with Ronnie, sending Jason forward in case anyone else went down hard.

"I'll ride back to the trailers with you," Walter offered. "Or if you want to stay here I can drive up here for you."

"It's only my collarbone. Tie my arm up with my stock. Hurry, Walter, hurry."

Walter unpinned the long white four-fold tie and wrapped it around Ronnie's shoulder, careful not to make it too tight as he looped it under Ronnie's forearm resting across his chest.

"There."

"Give me a leg up, Master." Ronnie grinned.

Walter, strong as an ox, practically lifted the lighter man up and over onto the other side.

They lost ten minutes but caught up with the field in time to see Iggy dart under the schoolhouse.

Bobby put the hilltoppers just to the side of first flight so they could see everything.

Ben Sidell, riding with Bobby, felt his cell phone buzz in his pocket. He'd pick up the message later.

Shaker, blowing "Gone to ground," effused over his pack. "Picking up the right scent, what good foxhounds. What good hounds."

"We were good, weren't we?" Diddy's tail flipped like a windshield washer.

"I made you look good." Iggy laughed. *"Hey, I'm one smart fox. I live under a schoolhouse."*

Cora called back, *"Okay, Professor."*

This would be his name ever after: Professor.

Shaker walked over to Showboat. The footing was slick as an eel. He slid, nearly falling flat on his face. Tootie held Showboat's reins.

"Thank you, Tootie."

"Thank you. I've never had so much fun in my life. Thank you." Tears filled Tootie's eyes.

He took the reins, patted her hand, "Tootie, neither have I." He swung up, then said to the other girls, "You all can go back to Sister now."

"Thank you." They beamed and rode past Sister, all smiles, and joined Jason, Walter, and Ronnie at the rear.

"Let's pick 'em up." Sister would have searched for another fox had the footing been better.

They'd had a bracing day, been out for two hours. Best to stop.

The clouds reached them at last, the only clear sky being a thin, brilliant, blue stripe in the east. Pines rustled. Branches started to sway.

By the time they reached the trailers, the first snowflakes were dotting their velvet hunt caps.

Val, on hearing of Ronnie's mishap, volunteered to cool out his horse. He offered her money, which she quite properly refused. She wanted to help. Tootie took care of Moneybags for Val.

"Mr. Haslip, if Coach lets me, I'll drive your rig home and do everything. I'd like to do that. I'm really a good driver."

"Thanks, honey." He melted at the sight of the girl, even though he was gay. Val was breathtaking. "I think Walter will drive and leave his horse here with Mrs. Chandler."

"Well, if that doesn't work, I'll do it."

Jason strode over. "All right, Ronnie, let me get you up in the tack room."

He, too, melted at the sight of Val, but most men are wise enough to not dally with minors.

Ronnie stepped into the tack room. Jason untied the makeshift sling.

Ronnie, feeling the pain once the adrenalin of the chase had worn off, joked, "Hey, at least you don't have to cut off my boots."

"I'd never do that," Jason joked back.

Sister stuck her head in the trailer tack room. "Need a belt? Say bourbon and branch?"

"When it's over." Ronnie grimaced as Jason wiggled the coat off his left arm.

Sister stayed outside, holding a flask carrying Woodford Reserve mixed with 25 percent pure water.

Ronnie unbuttoned his shirt with one hand. What hurt was having Jason pull over his head the silk and cashmere long-sleeved undershirt he wore on the nasty cold days. Tears ran down his eyes. The cold hit his lean naked torso, and he shivered.

"All right, Ronnie." Jason felt the collarbone. "Not my specialty, but it's a poor doctor who can't set a bone."

Walter joined Sister at the tack room door. Val worked on Ronnie's nice mare. She didn't want to see the bone being set. People in pain upset her, made her feel helpless.

"Ronnie, with those abs you ought to be a cover boy." Sister made light of the situation.

"Right." He gritted his teeth as Jason put his right hand on one side of the break, left on the other, then snapped the bones back.

"Oh, shit," Ronnie blurted out. He nearly crumpled.

Jason put his hand under Ronnie's elbow, helping him to lean on the raised section in the tack room, the nose of the trailer.

Walter stepped in. "May I?"

"Sure," said Ronnie, lips white.

Walter lightly ran his fingers over the collarbone. "Good job, Jason."

"What'd you expect?" Jason smiled. "Ronnie, as you probably know, it doesn't do much good to set a collarbone. Keep it in a sling. That's the best advice I can give."

"He's broken that left collarbone twice before." Sister handed up the flask. "First time was at our hunter pace when he was twelve."

"You didn't give me bourbon and branch then." Ronnie's color was returning.

"I would have if your mother hadn't been hovering." She noticed his shiver. "Boy, you aren't going to get that pullover back on. I don't have anything I can give you."

"I have an old flannel shirt in my bag," Walter said. "Better than nothing. It'll be six weeks before you can get a sweater on."

"Three," Ronnie resolutely replied.

Jason pulled a Montblanc ballpoint pen out of his coat pocket. He produced a prescription pad, for he'd first gone to his own trailer and changed coats, picking up the pad, too. "I'm giving you a prescription for 800 Motrin. Take one in the morning. One at night. It'll help."

"Thanks." Ronnie took the small white paper.

"Nice pen." Sister admired the Montblanc.

"If you use the best equipment you have fewer problems." He stepped out so Walter could come up to help Ronnie on with the shirt. "Walter, you want to tie him up?"

"That doesn't sound right." Walter reached for Ronnie's stock.

Despite the short notice, Cindy Chandler had put together

a breakfast. People brought in dishes. Most wanted hot coffee or tea more than anything else at that moment.

As Sister walked to the farmhouse, a little jewel, she had her own epiphany.

So did Ben Sidell when he called back the number displayed on his cell phone. Lyle Aziz was jubilant that the results had come in so quickly on Angel Crump.

"Her death certificate said heart attack. Her heart stopped beating all right, Ben. She was loaded with scopolamine."

CHAPTER 28

Following hounds on horseback is an early-morning activity. On weekdays people clean their horses, clean themselves, and report to work. In hunt country, many employees use flexible schedules not only for parents but for foxhunters, deer hunters, fishermen. The ways of the place might be altered by modern life but not utterly transformed.

Ben kept Nonni with Betty and Bobby Franklin. He enjoyed tending to his sturdy mare, no beauty basket but honest and wise. Three years ago the sheriff had known nothing about foxhunting. Now he couldn't imagine life without it, nor could he imagine a day without Nonni. It was a love match.

He changed clothes in the tack room, his uniform crisp, then drove to the hospital. The snow, falling heavily now, worked its magic on the countryside. The brown patches were turning white; tree branches were outlined by a silver-white line on top.

Margaret DuCharme met him in her office.

"Please sit down, Sheriff."

"Call me Ben."

"This is an official visit, right?"

"It is." He sat in the high-tech aluminum chair, the back and bottom a mesh that looked hard but wasn't.

Margaret walked out from behind her desk and sat opposite him on a duplicate chair.

Noticing his wiggle in the seat, she inquired, "I hope that's not uncomfortable."

"No. It's actually very comfortable." He noted the décor of her office. "Funny, I would have thought you'd be, uh, I'm not very good at styles and periods, but, you know, traditional."

She smiled. "Paradise takes care of that. It's so traditional it's falling down." She indicated a slender Italian desk lamp, the dome over the halogen bulb a deep green. "I'm crazy about Italian design."

"Sleek." He crossed one leg over the other. "I hope you can help me."

"Am I under suspicion?" She folded her hands together, leaning slightly forward.

"Technically, yes. Realistically, no. If you were a killer, you'd never be stupid enough to leave the evidence in your vehicle."

"Thank you." She smiled, her symmetrical features relaxing. "What can I do to help?"

"How easy is it for a doctor, a nurse, or even an orderly to steal controlled substances?"

She exhaled deeply. "In theory, it's difficult. Medicines that need to be refrigerated are in locked refrigerators. Those which can be stored at room temperature are in steel cases, locked.

Years ago they used wooden cases, but a desperate junkie could pry or smash them open."

"Do you think things like morphine, say, are taken?"

"Not morphine so much. The drugs of choice are cocaine and OxyContin. Prozac, Valium, mood elevators have a street value, but the real prizes are coke and OxyContin. As you know, all hospitals have some pure cocaine as well as morphine for extreme pain."

"Steroids?"

She shook her head. "It's much easier to buy those on the black market than to fool around with the hospital supply, which isn't that large."

"Has anyone been caught recently?"

"You would know."

"Only if the hospital prosecuted. It's in the administration's self-interest to let them go quietly, just as it's in a bank's self-interest to write off an embezzler. Prosecute; it makes the papers, and the public loses confidence. I may not like it, but that's the way it is."

Her eyes leveled on his. "True."

"So, have drugs been stolen?"

"I don't know, but common sense tells me, yes." She smiled. "There's no wall that can keep out a lover or a cat. If a staff person is hooked on Percodan, they'll find a way. The higher up they are on the food chain, the more ways they can cover the theft—sometimes for years."

"Do you think there are doctors who are addicts?"

"Yes. It's not that uncommon. Do I know who they are? No."

"What about you?"

"No. I got through my residency drinking enough coffee to float a battleship." She smiled. "That's another thing: most doctors drink far too much coffee. The OB/GYNs have the worst of it because babies always seem to appear at three in the morning." She smiled again.

"They do, don't they?" His face felt particularly hot. "Another question. Were Iffy and your Uncle Alfred close friends? Do you think it was a passionate relationship?"

She rubbed her chin, an odd gesture that somehow seemed very feminine. "There was a connection there, but I don't know how deep. It's not the kind of thing Uncle Al would tell me."

"An affair? Maybe when Iffy was more attractive, less bitter. Sometimes people can become friends afterwards. Most times not, I guess." He kept the questioning conversational.

"Iffy?" She pondered this. "I doubt it."

"Do you know much about your uncle's business activities?"

Struggling, she swallowed. "He fiddles with stocks. He keeps a few fighting cocks. I stay out of it." She quickly added, "He seems to be doing better this last year than years prior."

Ben didn't press it. "How's your business?" He smiled broadly.

"Good. People will always tear up their knees." She laughed.

"Tell me about the drug scopolamine."

"Commercially it's called transderm scope. In therapeutic dose, 0.3 to 0.6 milligrams, it's often used to combat motion sickness. Usually a patient wears a small patch behind the ear."

"How long does it take to work?"

"Two hours. So if you're seasick and your cruise leaves the dock at noon, you'd put the patch on at ten."

"Does it have other uses?"

"Arthritis. Then it's usually in a cream. And it may be used in combination with other drugs—atropine, for example." She paused. "I don't have much use for it. My work generally is on ligaments and muscles. But people have such different chemistries. There may be a patient who responds better to scopolamine for chronic pain than another drug. Why?"

"An autopsy report has crossed my desk. The corpse had extremely high levels of scopolamine."

She tapped her finger on the chair arm. "It can kill you."

"How—I mean how could you administer it, and what would be the symptoms?"

"Mix a lethal dose and put it on a patch. Patches come four in a package. Any physician could easily mix up a dose. It's not difficult at all."

"Any other way?"

"Sure, put it in a cream. Depending on how quickly you wanted it to work, you'd alter the dose, obviously. But it will kill you in twenty-four hours if that dose is over the line."

"Let's say I've mixed up cream, arthritis cream. It's full of scopolamine. What happens to the victim?"

"Depending on their age, current health, they'll become confused, then sleepy. They can't keep their eyes open. The heart will beat arrhythmically. Death."

"Looks like a heart attack."

"Yes."

"If the victim were quite old, the heart failure probably wouldn't arouse suspicion?"

"Probably not. Most elderly people have heart problems. The pump shows signs of wear and tear."

"Anything else about scopolamine?"

"If you pulled up the victim's eyelids, the pupils would be dilated, the opposite of narcotics, where they are pinpoints."

"So a really clever killer could tell the victim to wear a patch, then pull it off before the corpse is examined?"

"Could."

"Is Walter a good cardiologist?"

"Yes."

"If he pronounced—is that the right word?" She nodded, so Ben continued. "If he pronounced a patient dead would he know they'd been killed with scopolamine?"

"No. I wouldn't either, especially if the patient had a heart condition. There are no outstanding signs. You'd only know by autopsy. The technical term for the manner of death is supraventricular tachycardia. You'd have to see the heart. Now, any of us could have that type of heart attack, but the scopolamine will blow out the heart that way. The tissues, the blood work would tell the tale. It's an ingenious way to kill someone."

"Yes, it is. Someone would need to be a doctor, pharmacist, nurse."

"Or a very bright chemistry major." She folded her hands together.

"This is a different line, but it may have some bearing on Iffy's case. How easy would it be for a doctor to falsify insurance claims?"

Margaret's eyes, light hazel, opened wide. "All too easy, Sheriff."

"And temptation is high?"

She folded her hands together. "People don't realize what it costs to be a doctor. Oh, they know those years after college are expensive, but they don't think about the costs once you are on your own. Salaries. Office space. Hospital privileges. Constantly updating your computers and software. The courses you must continue to take throughout your life to keep your certification. And the real killer is insurance."

"It raises by specialty?"

"Well, there's no cheap insurance. Mine is thirty-six thousand a year."

He exhaled in sympathy. "No competition to lower rates?"

"Not really."

"So there is incentive to cheat?"

"Yes."

"How?"

"Create problems that don't exist. For instance, I treat you for a bruised patella, kneecap. You're fine. I fill out the paperwork. The insurance company sends me a percent of my fee."

"I'd have to be in on it. You need my signature on the form."

"I suppose patient signatures could be forged, but it's cleaner if we're in it together."

"I see. Is it possible to fake an operation?"

"It is, but then everyone in that operating room has to be in on it. It's easier to do this for in-office procedures." She focused her lustrous eyes on his. "Iffy?"

"I don't know. It's possible." He couldn't help telling her.

She sat back up, putting her right forefinger to her temple. "I hate Jason Woods. If this is true, I hope you can make it stick."

"Like I said, I don't know. I shouldn't have told you. It's not professional." He stammered for a moment. "I find it difficult to refuse you."

"Then I'd better ask for something big." She smiled broadly.

Heart pounding, he blurted out, "May I take you to dinner Saturday?"

"How about Sunday? College games are Saturday. There's bound to be at least one torn ACL."

"Sunday it is."

He left the hospital far happier than anyone going into it. After stopping by headquarters and assigning another officer to direct traffic at a particularly obnoxious intersection, he drove out to Roughneck Farm, where Sister awaited him.

Rapping on the mud room door, he heard, "Come in."

"There you are." She took his coat, hanging it on a peg as Raleigh and Rooster sniffed him.

"What a day today. And hey, what a big field for Thursday."

"Was good." She'd made sandwiches, which she put on the table. "You probably didn't eat enough at the breakfast."

"Actually, I didn't. Usually I make a pig of myself, but I was trapped between Ronnie, Walter, and Jason all telling war stories. You're always feeding me." He inhaled the rich coffee aroma. "You make the best coffee."

"Thank you." She poured him a cup, sat down, and picked up her sandwich so he'd pick up his. "I rarely eat at the breakfasts. For one thing, I can't eat standing up. I mean, I can, but I don't like it. For another thing, I usually don't reach the table."

"Must be hell to be popular."

"I suffer." She laughed.

They ate, chitchatting about the drop between the two ponds where Ronnie had broken his collarbone, the swirling wind currents down in the ravine, and the footing that alternated between hard ground and packed snow.

"Weatherman says three inches." Ben dabbed his mouth with the napkin.

Golly, on a kitchen chair, head above the table, watched every move. *"I'll accept a votive offering, given that I denned a fox."*

"No fair. You get to sit on the chair," Rooster complained.

"You get enough treats. In fact, Rooster, diet time."

"Nasty—you can be so nasty." Rooster put his head on his paws as he lay by Sister's feet.

Raleigh, silent, sat on her other side. If he looked noble and patient, she might weaken.

"Here." Sister tore a bit of ham for Golly, then gave some to the dogs. Raleigh's ploy had worked.

"I'm closing in, Sister. If I make one wrong move, I'm going to lose our killer."

"Yes. He's highly intelligent. I suspect most killers aren't."

"Actually, most people in jail, men and women, are what's called low-normals. Some are borderline retarded. A few truly are evil, but most of them can't control their impulses. No sense of delayed gratification on any front."

"Pity. We can't afford the cost of incarcerating them, but we can't afford them on the streets, either."

"They'll do it again." He accepted a brownie. "That's not what some people want to hear, but that's the way it is. And always was."

"I suppose so, but our killer doesn't fall into that category."

"When did you figure it out?"

"It's been building. I had a vague feeling once we found Iffy. He never figured on a coyote. He's not country." She paused. "Today, we started on a bobcat. Think of Iffy. She's your bobcat. Legitimate game and guilty as sin. Naturally we'd follow the scent."

"Yes." He realized he was holding the coffee cup to his lips but hadn't drunk some, as he was intently listening.

"Then down in the thickest part of the covert, our true quarry crossed the line of the bobcat. Some second-year entry didn't come right to the horn when Shaker swung the pack onto the fox. Betty pushed them back, and we had all on and a terrific finish. Our killer is the fox. We've got to swing onto his line. We can't let him go to ground. He's fooled us by using a bobcat to divert our attention."

"I don't have enough to convict him." He appreciated her insight. "Do you think we can turn our fox?"

Occasionally a whipper-in will turn a fox. This takes a smart whipper-in because one can turn the fox back into the hounds, a dreadful thing to do. Usually, a fox should be turned if it, too, is heading for a major highway or if it is running out of the country. Betty Franklin could do it. The trick is to turn the fox at an angle, but not back to hounds. Then the whipper-in has to stay on the outside of the fox until the danger has passed. It's extremely difficult to do because the fox isn't trained to obey, whereas the hound is.

By turning the fox, you save your fox, your hounds, and your master, who might be facing an irate landowner.

"We can try," said Sister. "Do I have your permission to inform Shaker, Betty, and Sybil?"

"Yes."

"May they put .22 in their pistols instead of ratshot—just in case?"

"Yes." He paused. "Who will be the bobcat?"

"I will."

"Sister, I should do it. It's dangerous."

"So is foxhunting. Please don't take this as an insult, Ben, but I ride better than you do." She paused for a moment, then reached over to cover his hand with hers. "I take my chances. It's the only way to live, and I really want to get this bastard. Forgive my French." She added, "I suppose I should tell Gray. They meant to kill him, you know."

"Don't. I appreciate your concern, but the more people who know, the more chances for our fox to pick up the tension. Shaker, Betty, and Sybil are out there as staff. Gray will be in the field."

"I understand." She breathed in. "Saturday's fixture is Paradise."

"Funny, isn't it?"

CHAPTER 29

Seven river otters played early Saturday morning on the feast of St. Agnes, January 21. Their philosophy of life contrasted sharply with that of the virgin martyr of Rome, dying in 305 AD. She refused marriage, for at thirteen she had consecrated her body to Christ. Her reward for such a gift was a sword straight through the throat. Like a lamb, *agnus* in Latin, pretty Agnes met her Maker.

The otters felt life should be frolic with a bit of sex in early spring. Mating, delightful as it could be, paled before running hard, flopping on one's belly before reaching water's edge, then sliding down at top speed to crash into the swift current, riding the little waves.

Bruce, the largest of the otters at thirty pounds, father of the brood, hit the cold water with a boom, sending two waves up at his sides. He bobbled along for fifty yards before swimming and scrambling out at an easy place.

"Whee!" One otter after another squealed as he or she roared toward the large creek's edge then down the steep, slick slide they'd made.

Out they scrambled, each one hurrying to reach the starting place only to barrel down, hit the side of the bank, and fold forelegs next to the body. Down they'd go, furry toboggans loving every minute of life.

Crayfish, rockfish, all manner of delicious edibles swam in the deep, wide creek. Then, too, a berry now and then aided the digestion. The family, in splendid condition, had little competition for the food they prized.

Earl, a gray fox in his second year, sat on a log, the orange half moons of fungus protruding from the snow, more light snow still falling.

Trite though the phrase may be, it was a winter wonderland. As everyone sported thick fur coats with dense undercoats, the temperature was bracing.

Also watching the nonstop otter celebration were Athena and Bitsy, sitting high in a majestic spruce. Flying from Sister's took them twenty minutes. For humans, hauling horses and dealing with roads that weren't straight, the time from Roughneck Farm took forty minutes.

"Come on," Bruce invited Earl.

"No, thanks. I only swim when I must," the handsome fellow replied.

"You don't know what you're missing," Lisa, the mother, revving her motors, called out.

"Do you think they're simpleminded?" Bitsy asked Athena.

"No, just silly."

"You'd think they didn't have to work for a living," Bitsy, fond of stirring the pot, remarked.

"They don't. This place is one big supermarket for them." Athena opened and closed her beak with a clicking sound.

Squirrels in the tree scurried along the boughs, snow falling off as they ran. They were not overly fond of Athena, who could kill and eat them if she wanted to. But they knew she was full, since she'd given everyone within earshot her menu. They leaped to the oak where they lived.

"Flying rats," Bitsy giggled.

"Come on!" Bruce called Earl again.

"Nah, I need to save my energy."

"You looking for a girlfriend?" Bruce thought keeping a mate the better course.

He thought a minute. *"If I find the right vixen I have to help with food. I guess I can do it. I'm finally ready."*

"And a healthy young fellow you are," Bruce complimented him, turned a flip, and reached the runway, speeding to zoom over the side.

Athena, eyes half closed, opened them wide. Swiveling her head, she listened closely. Bitsy, her ear tufts at full attention, mimicked the big owl.

"Trotting," Bitsy said.

"Short stride, but hooves, yes, hooves. Every now and then you'll hear the hooves hit a stone. The wind blows some places clean."

"Deer." Bitsy fluffed.

"No. Different cadence." Athena thought hard, then said, *"Haven't heard that in many a year."*

"What is it?"

"A wild boar. A big one," Athena replied.

"I thought wild pigs traveled in herds," Bitsy commented. *"Not that I've run into any, mind you."*

"Sow and her young, they do. They join up with other sows; but no, this is one boar alone. It's mating season. Actually, it's mating season for just about everyone. I heard you threatened to lay an egg or two at the end of the month."

"It's so much trouble. Laying the eggs isn't so bad, it's feeding them." Bitsy, having never been a mother, thought it might be an enchanting experience and then again, it might not. She had bragged to Target and Inky that she intended to lay two eggs. She wished she'd kept her beak shut.

Athena chortled, a raspy sound. *"True, so true."* Her deep voice filling the snow-covered woods, she informed the animals below, *"There's a boar heading this way at a fast trot. One boar, so I expect it's a male."*

"He's not going to eat us." A saucy little otter raced for the slide.

"Root, hog, or die," Earl remarked. *"Guess it's hard to root in the snow."*

"He can smell what's underground, snow or no snow. He likes potatoes, turnips, and acorns." Athena respected wild pigs, finding them highly intelligent—not in her class, but intelligent.

Way in the distance, two miles away, the piercing note of Shaker's horn sounded "Gone away."

Athena swiveled her head again, eyes black and full. *"Foxhunters."*

"You mean they'll shoot me?" Earl asked, horrified.

"No, you silly twit. They'll chase you with hounds, American foxhounds to be exact. Very logical animals, but you're far more clever. Run

about, use water, foil your scent. If hounds get close, zigzag. And above all, don't run into deep snow," Athena counseled.

"In fact, you can crisscross this otter scent should hounds come this way. They're on a fox now." Bitsy loved the chase.

"How come I don't know about this?" the young gray asked, troubled.

"Haven't used this fixture for years. Problems with the DuCharme brothers. Foxhunters were here two weeks ago, but way on the other side of Paradise. You haven't been prepared by cubbing. That's when the humans in charge train the young hounds and young foxes, too. But if you do as I say, you should be fine. Duck into a den, any den, when you've had enough. Oh, hounds will dig and sing and curse you, but they can't do squat. The huntsman will dismount and blow a funny, wiggly sound, and then they'll leave. It's harmless, really," Athena reported.

Bitsy, eager to dispense information, told the gray fox, *"There's a tall, slender lady who rides up front. She leads the humans. Silver hair, even more silver than yours, and if you make friends with her, she'll feed you."*

"How can I make friends with her if she's chasing me?" Earl sensibly asked.

"She'll be back, now that they have this fixture. She'll probably be on horseback or in an ATV, and she might be with the huntsman, who has dark red curly hair, or she'll be with her friend, Betty, who rides on the edges. It's complicated, this foxhunting." Bitsy puffed out her little chest.

"It's a sacred thing to the humans." Athena opened wide her fearsome beak. *"Holy. You do your part and Sister will care for you."*

Way off, all the animals could hear hounds, a ghostly sound at this distance.

"Sounds like they are coming our way." Bruce glanced at his family.

"Will they hurt us, those nasty hounds?" a youngster inquired.

"Hounds stick to fox scent. They won't fuss you up." Bitsy used a colloquial expression.

"It's not the hounds you need to worry about; it's the humans." Athena burst out laughing. *"The horses will be slipping and sliding. The humans will be lurching around up there, and you might even see a few go splat."*

"Oh, my, my, yes," Bitsy seconded her heroine.

Hounds moved closer.

Lisa called to Bruce, who was still bodysurfing, *"We'd better go home."*

"One more slide!" He quickly climbed out, graceful in his fashion.

"No, I don't want to take any chances," she insisted.

"You're right." He genially agreed, having learned it's better to agree with your spouse.

Earl watched as the happy group walked to their den, which had overgrown entrances near the base of a large tree hanging over the creek. Thick roots, eight to twelve inches in diameter, burst through the banks where the water had eroded the soil. Entrances and exits were hidden under the roots on the bank side, too.

"You might want to head toward your den or a den you've seen along the way. The hounds track your scent. They don't need to see you," Athena told Earl.

"How far away do you live?" Bitsy asked.

"Mile and a half, southwards."

The horn sounded closer now, perhaps a mile away.

"If you're lucky they're on a vixen, and she'll duck in somewhere between here and where she is now. Then you won't have to go far to find her." Athena looked on the bright side. *"But Bitsy is right; you'd best be going."*

"Thanks for the advice." Earl used the otters' slide and swam across the creek. Given the current, he climbed out thirty yards downstream.

"Worried about him?" Bitsy asked.

"A little." Athena frowned, opened her wings, dropped off the branch, and with one downward sweep of her enormous wings glided over Earl. "*If you encounter problems, run with deer. Use any other animal. You can't mask your scent. It's a good day for scent.*"

Bitsy, needing many more flaps, caught up with the great horned owl. *"Maybe we should stick with him?"*

"Might bring those damned crows. You know how they like to mob foxes. Of course, I'd be happy to kill a few."

Bitsy, saying nothing, stayed with Athena. She'd not forgotten her close call at pattypan forge.

Athena and Bitsy passed over a gray vixen, who raced through a large expanse of running cedar, much of it partially exposed from last night's wind. Although it was calm enough now, with gentle flakes coming down, the scent would be true, not blown yards off. The vixen made use of the terrain, then ducked into a den, a few bones on the low pile outside announcing her gourmet tastes.

Cora reached the den first, and within half a minute everyone else crowded around.

Betty, on the right, stayed over in the meadow to the edge of the woods where the den was located. Sybil, on the left, stopped on ground level with the den as Shaker rode up.

The field, seventy people, enjoyed the spectacle of thrilled hounds, the blowing of "Gone to ground," and the happy knowledge that hounds had accounted for their fox.

Sister, on Aztec, smiled.

The Custis Hall girls rode in the rear with Walter. Sister had asked Tedi and Edward whether they would mind if Jason rode behind her. She wanted to observe him to see whether he knew as much as he said he did. If nothing else, she'd be seeing his hunting manners close up.

Knowing that the club always needed money, the Bancrofts graciously rode behind Jason. As one of the main benefactors of the club, the Bancrofts hoped others would come through, especially now that Crawford had bagged it.

Sister nodded to Shaker when he remounted to go forward, then quietly turned to ask Jason behind her, "What do you think, red or gray?"

"Gray," he replied, a smile crossing his handsome face.

"I do, too." She smiled back.

If one studied fox tracks it didn't take too much to discern the difference between a red's foot and a gray's, especially in winter. The red's prints could be about two and a half inches long. The hindprint might be smaller, but the heavy fur around the paw would register on the ground or on snow. The toe marks and lobe of the pads would be a little indistinct.

The gray's prints were an inch and a half long for a mature fox, the print sharper. The toes dug in deeper, it seemed, and if it weren't for the toe marks, one could mistake the print for an overfed, much-loved pet cat like Golly.

She gave Jason credit for making the right call, but if he had studied prints all he had to do was look down at the snow. Still, thousands foxhunted and couldn't recognize footprints or fox scat. He had done some homework.

She twisted all the way round to see if the field was together. They were, thanks to Walter and the girls pushing them up. If someone straggled, Walter sent them back to Bobby. No one in the field would disobey a master's command if they wanted to keep hunting—not just with Jefferson Hunt but with any hunt. The masters would pass on who was a butthead as readily as they passed on who was a true foxhunter.

Bobby, hands full with green riders, green horses, and occasionally treacherous footing, just joined them as Shaker moved off. It seemed to go in spurts, the numbers of green riders or green horses, but shepherding them always fell to the hilltoppers' master, the most unsung staff position in foxhunting.

Few would dream of going first flight if they couldn't ride, especially at Jefferson Hunt. Sister enjoyed a formidable reputation—and who wanted to look a fool under her eyes?

The whippers-in usually rode hardest, but they were alone, an advantage under the circumstances. If they weren't riding hard or trotting forward, they'd be immobile at a prime spot, and that spot always seemed to be the coldest damned place on earth.

The huntsman stayed with hounds as best he could. He, too, rode hard, but he rode straight behind the pack. Chances were, the whippers-in covered more territory than he did. This wasn't to say he didn't do things that Sister and the field would not. He did, but often no one saw him take a four-foot drop off a creek bed into the water. He stayed with his hounds if possible.

While Sister could do anything on a horse, her first responsibility was the field, not the hounds. Very few fields today were well mounted enough, with fearless riders, to do things that were routinely done thirty years ago. The reason was that so many people had taken up foxhunting who hadn't grown up with horses. It wasn't that they couldn't clear the four-foot jump if they had the right horse, but only a few had the right horse. The right horse, nine times out of ten, was a thoroughbred or a thoroughbred cross, depending on territory. Those arriving late to the glories of riding often feared thoroughbreds. If you knew the animal, you loved its sensitivity and forward ways. If you didn't, you thought you were on a runaway that would spook at a white stone pebble. The change in the field was as big a shift in foxhunting as the rise of the automobile, the sickening encroachments of suburbia.

As hounds searched for fresh scent, Sister looked behind again, noting that Gray was in the middle of the field, Ben back with Bobby. She was glad Ben had asked her not to tell Gray. He was right; Gray would have inched forward, sticking too close to Sister.

Athena and Bitsy peered down from a leafless sycamore, its distinctive multicolored patchy bark noticeable in a palette of white, gray, beige, and black.

"They'll pick up Earl's scent soon enough if they keep going in this direction," Bitsy fretted.

"M-m-m." Athena noticed Diddy tossing snow with her nose, then leaping up for it.

"This isn't playtime," Asa reprimanded the happy girl.

"Sorry." Diddy reapplied herself to the task.

The treetops waved slightly as they dropped down a steep path to walk along the creek bed, flat and wide, the rushing water drowning other sounds.

"If we fly with the hounds, we won't signal Earl's position." Athena was more worried than she cared to admit. *"The crows will stay put. If Earl does need direction, we can move up to supply it."*

"Yes, yes." Bitsy agreed, then lifted off to slowly fly along. No need for speed at this point.

A quarter mile down the creek bed they reached the otter slides.

"Gray, dog fox." Dasher inhaled.

The otters, peeking out from under the big roots in the bank, listened as the hounds chimed in after Dasher.

They watched the whole pack go down their slide and hit the water, swimming across the frothy creek in one body.

"Bet they've made the slide bigger and slicker." Bruce couldn't wait to return to his game.

Darby, at the rear of the pack, heard Bruce's voice and turned to see the otters looking at him. *"You're funny-looking,"* the young hound blurted out.

"Not as funny as you are," Lisa smartly replied as Shaker on Gunpowder jumped off the bank six feet away from the slide, where the grade was better for a horse.

The pack in full cry flew through the flatland on the other side of the creek and climbed up the gentle rise to higher ground to run southwards, wind at their rear, scent blowing away from them.

Earl knew enough to use the wind, but scent was strong and hounds were closing.

He kept on straight through the woods, but the pine needles, under snow, couldn't help dissipate his scent. Hounds moved faster than he thought they could.

Nothing looked promising, so he picked up the pace, his brush now carried straight out. A rotted log ahead provided a break in his scent. He ran inside, straight through to the other end. He kept going.

A pocket meadow needed to be crossed quickly before he could escape into denser woods on the far side. He knew a few dens in there that could be used. If someone was in them, too bad. They'd be crowded for a time.

Snow lay eight inches in parts on the pocket meadow. He didn't relish going across. At the last minute Earl skirted back into the woods, heading northeast, at a right angle to his former line of scent.

Old deer bones protruded from the snow. He ran into the middle of them, then sped away, turning again toward the meadow.

Hounds checked briefly at the bones.

Sister picked her spot and her moment.

"Jason, come up here beside me for a minute."

He rode next to her, then stopped. "This corpse helped our fox, the reverse of Iffy's corpse, which points her finger at you."

Jason shrugged, laughing. "Sister, you have a good imagination."

Hounds sped away. Sister followed. Jason fell in behind. Had she gotten it wrong?

This time Earl did go into the meadow, and it was his bad luck to founder in a deep spot that lay deceptively flat on the meadow. Struggling to extricate himself, he heard hounds draw closer, much too close. He could see them bursting into the meadow, clouds of snow churning up in front of their forelegs.

He finally clawed out of the hole, but the going was deep.

Athena and Bitsy flew over him now.

Athena saw the boar, all four hundred and forty pounds of him, yellow tusks long and sharp, arrive in the little meadow at a trot in the opposite direction.

"Go right!" Athena called down.

Earl, running for his life, pounded through the snow as the huge boar trotted straight at him.

"Duck around him. He'll swing his head in that direction. Make a wide circle, then run like hell, Earl!" Athena commanded.

Shaker, up behind his hounds, saw the danger and blew three long notes to call hounds back, but not before half the pack was face-to-face with one ugly brute.

The boar lowered his head. He stopped. He paid no attention to Earl, who circled him, reaching the woods and freedom.

"Go back!" Ardent boomed, barely managing to pull back the pack.

Shaker, blowing his hounds to him, galloped away from the boar, pulling hounds back into the woods from whence they had come but far to the right of the field, who did not know what lay ahead. The field did, however, pull up at woods' edge.

Jason rode up to Sister, already in the meadow, before she could turn to follow Shaker. He wedged his knee under hers, throwing her over the saddle. Aztec trembled in front of the boar, then turned, racing back through the field. He was only six, but even a seasoned horse would be scared once it got a whiff. Horses were blowing up behind Aztec.

Jason then bellowed, "Reverse."

The field, not able to see over the meadow's rise, obediently turned in the woods.

The only person who had a clear view of what had happened was Betty, on the right at the edge of the woods.

Aztec stopped at the rear of first flight. Walter reached over and grabbed his reins.

Tedi and Edward turned, but Edward stopped turning back.

"Jason passed us—but where's Sister?"

They waited a moment, their horses becoming more restive.

Betty bolted out of the woods toward Sister.

Luckily, Sister had fallen on her right side. Her .38 rested in a holster on her left side under her jacket.

Slipping in the snow, she tore open her coat, black horn buttons popping off, to reach for the gun as the boar charged. No time.

"Roll, then run!" Athena directed, hoping the human might understand.

Betty, hurtling toward the boar, said to Magellan, "We might get hurt, but we have to do this."

"I will," the thoroughbred replied, all heart.

The boar turned his big head for a moment upon hearing Magellan.

Sister had rolled. Then she ran as fast as she could. The snow slowed her.

She turned while Betty occupied the brute by circling him. Betty'd drawn her gun. Sister at last drew hers.

Betty, cool, didn't fire. "Get to the woods, Janie. I'll pick you up there," she hollered.

"No. What if you fall?"

"Dammit!" Betty rode in the opposite direction of Sister, the boar charging after her. Then she wheeled and spurred Magellan. The horse flew past the beast, who though large had quick reflexes. Betty reached Sister, who stuck her gun back in the holster.

Slowing Magellan, Betty leaned down, her left arm straight.

Sister grabbed Betty's arm, ran alongside Magellan for two steps, gained speed, and swung up.

Thank God, Betty was strong. She held Sister's weight as the older woman flung her right leg over Magellan's hindquarters. Mounted, the two galloped into the woods. Tedi and Edward followed on seeing them.

Walter was moving forward with Aztec. He had no idea what was up ahead, since Jason hadn't told anyone. Most had turned to follow Jason, thinking he was temporary field master.

The boar had no desire to chase the horse or the people. His mission was to find the female whose perfume had reached him a half hour ago.

Sister, not dismounting, slid from Magellan to Aztec, who had calmed down next to Clemson, Walter's bombproof older hunter.

"Where's the field?"

"I don't know," Walter said.

"Jesus!" Sister's face reddened. "Listen!"

Hearing Shaker's horn, Sister said, "Tedi, kick on. Edward, too. Take the field. Don't listen to Jason."

Walter turned to the horn, but he waited a moment for Sister and Betty.

Sister reached over to Betty. "It's not over."

"I know."

With that, both women left Walter in the lurch. Angry, he squeezed Clemson to catch up, but their horses were younger and faster, so he followed Tedi and Edward, also moving fast.

Sister reached the hilltoppers first as Betty pulled away to go to Shaker, who didn't know anything had happened.

"Ben, he got away," Sister said, voice low.

Ben reached into his pocket and plucked out his cell phone to call the deputies on the road.

"Bobby, you have one hell of a wife." Sister then blew by the rest of them, calling out, "Tedi and Edward will lead you. They're coming up behind. Wait for them."

She rode up to Shaker and filled him in. Betty had not done so, feeling it was more important to take her position at ten o'clock from the hounds. She was right in this, as there was nothing any of them could do about Jason at the moment.

"Let's pick them up. He'll kill anyone or anything in his way, and we don't know where he is." Sister told her huntsman, "Hold hounds for a moment."

Trudy sat on her haunches. *"What was that ugly thing?"*

"Big old fat wild pig, that's what," Asa informed her. *"He would have cut us up like flank steak."*

"Quicker than you think, those pigs," Cora commented.

"How come we haven't smelled them before now?" Diddy asked a good question.

"They keep to themselves except during breeding season." Ardent hated boar.

"And they're in the mountains. Paradise runs into all that billy-goat land we hunted last week. You won't find them at Tattenhall Station or Tedi or Edward's." Diana studied game just as Sister and Shaker did.

"Well, they'll come down if food is scarce. They'll trot fifty miles and not think a thing of it." Ardent thought it odd that a wild pig will hurry along to a foraging spot, then, when close, slow way down.

"Hope I don't see another one." Trinity had been scared out of her wits.

"Gather round." Sister waited as the field made a semicircle around her. "Ben, do I have permission to announce our suspicions, which I believe are now confirmed? Everyone's safety is at stake."

"Yes."

The sheriff's one-word answer riveted everyone's attention.

"We believe that Dr. Jason Woods killed Iphigenia Demetrios." She waited while that sunk in. "He is armed, extremely dangerous, and highly intelligent. I want everyone to stick together on the ride back. In those places where it's tight and you go single file, look to the person in front, then back. If anyone falls out of your sight line, holler. Loud."

"Why won't he just ride back to his trailer and take off?" Henry Xavier asked.

"Since he now knows that we know, he'll assume I have officers at the trailers and on the crossroads in every direction. He's going to keep clear," Ben replied. "I will ride tail for the hilltoppers. I'll be the last person in the line. I think we'd better move along."

"Shaker . . ." Sister meant to tell him to move on. Then she suddenly exclaimed, "Where's Sybil?"

"Still on the left, I hope," Shaker, worried, replied.

"Did you blow her in?" Sister asked crossly.

"Of course I did."

"I'm sorry, Shaker. I know better. I'm on edge."

"If I'd nearly been gored by a boar, I'd be on edge, too, and we don't know where that bastard is—the human, I mean." Shaker removed his cap to wipe his brow, the cold air sharp on his sweating head.

"Blow again."

Shaker put the brass horn to his lips and blew the notes that sounded like "Whipper-in," two medium notes followed by one shorter one.

Nothing.

"We need to move on, Sister," Ben firmly told her.

"I can't leave her there, Ben." Sister's voice was low, soft.

Shaker spoke up. "I'm going with you."

Tedi and Edward came to them, realizing their daughter had not come back to the horn. Walter also rode up.

"Tedi, you stay with the field. I'll go," Edward gently ordered his wife.

"No. This is my fault. He was quicker and more ruthless than I thought. I should have known better."

"He was lucky," Shaker said.

"Yes, but smart. He used the boar." Sister respected her foe.

She had underestimated him and desperately prayed that Sybil wouldn't pay for it.

"I'm going. I'm a doctor." Walter spoke firmly. "Edward, please help with the field in case someone makes a mistake."

"What if he comes back to snag a hostage?" Betty had ridden in, since hounds rested.

"Ben's with them." Edward wanted to go.

"We'll have too many people. We can't risk him shooting all of you. You, too, Shaker."

"I'm not letting you go!" Shaker noticed Gray riding toward them.

"We can't risk the pack because I was stupid. He'll shoot my hounds. No. You, Betty, go back. Edward, get Gray, and get him turned around before he knows what's happening. Go back. I can outfox this son-of-a-bitch."

"I'm going with you." Walter, accustomed to command when necessary, faced her.

"I'm an old woman. If I die, so what? Walter, you're young. Go back with the others."

As the others turned, Shaker called the pack, and Betty floated out to the side.

Walter said, "I'm going."

"I'll see you back at the trailer, Betty. I owe you." Sister realized that Walter would not be dissuaded.

Betty, deeply distressed, fought back the tears and nodded.

"Walter, unbutton your coat. You're wearing a shoulder harness. Make sure you can get to your gun fast."

He did as he was told. They cantered to where the riders were pulled up and circled until they found Jason's tracks.

"I'm worried sick," Walter confessed as they followed the tracks.

Sister replied, "With good reason. This is my fault."

Before he could protest that it could have happened to anyone, she picked up the pace.

The deer paths were wide. She slowed at one point where fox dens were near a thread of a creek.

She noticed a glob of frozen blood, footprints.

She pushed Aztec from a canter into a gallop, pointing at the blood with her crop.

Walter looked down as he passed. A grim determination filled him. Sister had been caught off guard. He'd been duped by a colleague. He wanted to strangle Jason for that as well as for the harm the other doctor had done.

Jason, moving south toward Chapel Cross, slowed after a half-mile gallop. A sense of direction wasn't his strong point, so he carried a small global positioning device, which he checked from time to time.

He knew the closer he got to Chapel Cross the more wary he needed to be. There'd be cops everywhere, but he thought he could elude them by dismounting and smacking Kilowatt on his hindquarters. That might divert them long enough for him to cross the road. Once on the other side of Chapel Cross he knew he could steal a car or truck from a farm as the county became more populated.

He'd change cars along the way. Arrogant, he felt he was smarter than everyone. He believed he could lay low, angling toward the Canadian border. He had his passport with him, a habit he'd learned when overseas. He also had a forged Belgian passport. He thought ahead. In time he figured he'd fly out of Canada. The money was safe in a bank in Zurich.

Jason hadn't thought it would reach this point, but he always had backup plans. Iffy had screwed up the original plan by panicking and, worse, insisting they run away together. She'd paid for it.

He walked along, not realizing that Sybil shadowed him a quarter mile behind. She could have shot his horse when he galloped past her as she sat on a ridge.

She couldn't do it. She couldn't kill a beautiful animal who happened to have a criminal on his back. She knew she was wrong in terms of human justice, but she felt in her heart that she was right.

She knew Jason wasn't a country boy, smart though he was. Tracking him would be easy enough. If she had a chance for a clear shot at him, she'd move up and fire. Her advantage lay in surprise.

The thick undergrowth forced them both to stick to deer trails. She stopped abruptly as Bombardier snorted when a deer approached downwind, their usual approach when their curiosity was aroused.

The doe stopped, looked at the horse, then bolted into the brush.

She had heard Shaker blowing for her. She wondered how Jason had gotten away. She told herself that one great thing about being a whipper-in was you became resourceful.

A soft flutter of wings startled her. She looked up to see, right over her head, Athena, low, followed by Bitsy, flying silently as only owls can do. Bombardier didn't flick an ear. The owls were so close that the variations in feather colors showed clearly.

Jason, senses straining, also did not hear the owls, who gained altitude while staying behind him. The thick forest gave way to a rolling hay field. The only route to Chapel Cross was over that field. Fortunately, it was far off a state road—but still, how long before the helicopters would be looking?

Jason figured Ben had called in all the resources he had, but it would take the helicopter team at least forty-five minutes to reach him because the small airport was thirty-five miles away, and the team would need to suit up, mount up, then fly to Paradise.

He had a comfortable window of time to reach Chapel Cross. Even in his black frock coat he'd stand out crossing the white hay field, but if he skirted the edges he'd tack another fifteen minutes onto the ride.

He pushed his horse into a trot and risked it.

On reaching that same spot, Sybil pulled out the cell phone Sister insisted she carry in case of injury. She punched in Sister's prerecorded number, which was 7.

At the vibration, Sister grabbed her phone out of her pocket.

"Sister, I'm at the edge of Binky's southernmost hay field. Jason's crossing it at a trot, heading for Tattenhall Station, I expect," said Sybil in a low voice.

"Thank God, you're all right. Don't take any chances, Sybil. Walter and I are behind you, moving up. Half mile. Tops."

"Right." She clicked off the phone.

Jason heard a human voice, very faint. He turned to see Sybil at the edge of the woods. He wheeled Kilowatt, pulled out his gun, and rode hard straight for her.

Sybil slipped back into the thick woods. She rode off the deer trail to dip down into a swale. It would take him a minute or two to find her. She noticed boot prints at the edge of the swale.

Conventional wisdom would have dictated she run, but her

entire back would be exposed. Steeling herself, she clicked off the safety of her .22, six bullets in the chamber instead of ratshot. Small though the caliber was, in the right place that .22 could stop a person cold.

She held the reins in her left hand, her right arm extended. All she needed to do was swing her arm to her target.

Jason assumed she would run away. Kilowatt, fast, would get so close to her that he could drop her. Then he would turn and race like mad across the hay field. He couldn't lose more time.

He stopped to listen for the sound of her hoofbeats. Silence. Then he heard the rustle of leaves as Bombardier moved a little. Walking deliberately toward the sound, he, too, readied his .45.

Athena quietly flew ahead of him. As she passed over the lip of the swale she called, *"Hoo, Ho Ho, Hoo."* Athena saw Donny Sweigart Jr. in camouflage fatigues, crouched in the bushes by the edge of the swale.

Bitsy, on the same vector, emitted one screech, her little beak agape. They circled and landed in a treetop.

Sybil looked in the direction from which they had flown. Three seconds later, Jason appeared at the edge of the swale from that same direction.

He had a smirk on his face that said, "Like shooting fish in a barrel."

Donny pushed through the brush and startled Kilowatt, who took a step back. Jason steadied himself and turned as Donny threw a round ball of frozen blood. It hit Jason hard in the chest. His right arm jerked up. He squeezed the trigger.

Sybil fired as the blood hit Jason, that split second saving her.

Hit in the shoulder, feeling the sting that soon followed,

Jason had to decide who to shoot first. Donny, a country boy, knew that running made him a target. If he stayed and fought, he'd have a chance. So would Sybil. Donny grabbed Jason's leg.

Jason fired, just missing Sybil.

This time she rode toward him as he attempted to smash the butt of his gun into Donny's face. Sybil patiently took a deep breath, making certain of her target since she knew two lives depended on her—or three lives: Jason might shoot Bombardier.

She fired, squeezing the trigger gently. Jason slipped backward off Kilowatt, who didn't move, oddly enough. Nor did Jason.

Sybil reached him. His eyes stared up at the sky. A neat hole over his right eye testified to her marksmanship.

"Thank God for you, Donny. Thank God."

She fired in the air three times, the universal signal of distress. Then her heart pounded and she shook.

"Steady girl, steady. We did it." Bombardier nickered as he nuzzled Jason's marvelous horse.

Three minutes later, flying through and over all obstacles, Sister and Walter reached the two humans and two horses.

Seeing the round frozen ball of blood, Sister understood. "Donny." She half smiled.

Sheepishly, he smiled back, for Sybil had dismounted and was hugging him fiercely, a most thrilling feeling.

CHAPTER 30

Personal cataclysms take many forms. All provide the same result: you're tossed into the air. Some people fall hard, others hit the ground but rise and learn, a few land on their feet, and fewer still bounce back higher than they had been cast down.

Sister usually fell into the last category. Yesterday's event, though distressing, energized her.

"People are like teabags. You never know how strong they are until you put them in hot water," she said to Shaker as they finished power washing the feed room. "Betty and Sybil are strong."

"Hell of a way to find out," Shaker grunted. "I should have been with you when he first knocked you off Aztec."

"First of all, honey chile"—she used the Southern nomenclature with warmth—"how could you know? You pulled the hounds from danger. You did the exact right thing. From the safety of the woods, there's no way you could know. It all turned out right." She paused. "He used an old dirty polo trick, actually. He put his knee behind mine and kicked my leg up high and hard. Over I went."

"No polo where's he gone—unless they play with pitchforks."

"By the grace of God."

"I will lift up mine eyes unto the hills from whence cometh my help," Sister smiled. "Sybil, Betty, and I are lucky, lucky women." She shrugged, tears filling her eyes.

Shaker misted over, too. "You never know, do you? You never know what's around the corner." He rolled the power washer back to the corner. "We could eat off the floor."

"That's a thought."

"Boss, I didn't get a chance to really talk to you yesterday, what with the police and all. I did pop my head in last night to see that you were okay."

"Three-ring circus, wasn't it?" She rolled up a hose.

"How did you know?"

"At first, I didn't. Iffy's behavior kept me focused on her. I'm convinced she tried to shoot Gray. Wasn't a hunter catching the last days of deer season. Can't prove it, but I believe it to be so."

"Gray was on to her."

"Well, he was on to someone cooking the books. He couldn't discuss it, but I knew something was amiss. I thought maybe Garvey was stealing the cream. That idea soon faded, but Iffy could have worked with Garvey and discovered she was going to take the fall. A lot of thoughts flitted through my peabrain."

"But she was guilty?" His thick eyebrows moved upwards.

"Yes, she was—and what's even more disgusting is she killed Angel. Jason gave her the scopolamine, the stuff that's used for motion sickness and arthritis." She walked into the kennel office, Shaker following. "Tell you one thing, Ben Sidell is good. He put his nose down and followed every scent trail."

"Thorough."

"That he is. He figured out the insurance scam. I had no idea about that. Ben and his staff interviewed every living patient on Jason's roster. Jason did save lives, but there were people on his roster who feigned symptoms, including Alfred DuCharme. They were never sick in the first place. Jason wrote up treatment in collusion with the phony patient, and the money rolled in. When Ben went through his patient roster, since some called Jason, that tipped him off to the fact that he was under suspicion, but he was confident he'd covered his tracks."

"Two crimes?" Shaker dropped in the chair by the desk, turning it so he could face Sister as she sat behind the desk.

"More than that. One attempted murder. I'm counting Iffy shooting Sam. One murder: Angel. Then Iffy's murder. A brilliant insurance scam, two million dollars pilfered from Aluminum Manufacturing. The insurance companies will get involved with their own investigation, but Ben's estimate is that Jason sucked up about nine million dollars."

"Nine million!" Shaker exclaimed.

"It's obvious you haven't seen a hospital bill in a long time. Jason specialized in cancer. The diagnostic tests, the chemo and radiation if needed, the operations if needed, the aftercare, the pharmacy bills. It's insane. Really, it's easier to die. It's certainly cheaper."

"I'll remember that." His wry smile was engaging.

"Here's the thing I don't understand. By all accounts Jason

was a good doctor. Why wasn't that enough? Doctors make a good living. But he must have had some kind of instinct, some sixth sense of who could be corrupted. Someone might have a few cancer cells on the skin. He'd talk them into letting him invent a major cancer, and they'd split the insurance money. He even went so far as to perform some operations, not cut-open-the-chest stuff, but still, in-office procedures on healthy people. Mostly he threw patients into a fake radiation and chemo program and raked in the money. Walter—who is tremendously upset, by the way—said it's not that hard to acquire x-rays and records. He thinks Jason took those of deceased people. He'd x-ray his 'patient' later, and lo and behold, the tumor or the cancer would be in remission. The cleverness of it, the attention to detail—it's almost admirable."

"Nine million dollars." Shaker fixated on the loot.

"Think what we could do with that money?" Sister sighed, then glanced out the window. "Sun's up."

"Clearing up." He rose and walked to the hot plate. "Tea? Coffee?"

"Tea."

"Angel loathed Iffy. How could Iffy kill her without Angel knowing? I mean, Angel wouldn't take motion sickness stuff from Iffy, I don't think." Shaker returned to the main subject.

These two, working cheek by jowl for decades—for Shaker had been hired as a young man to whip-in—had long ago divested themselves of connecting every sentence to the one prior.

"Angel had some arthritis, common enough in someone eighty-four. Walter suggested an over-the-counter remedy. Remember, Ben had questioned him thoroughly when the news about Angel came back from the labs. First he visited Margaret DuCharme. Later, after he saw me he questioned Walter, and

Walter said he'd recommended cream with scopolamine in it. No big deal; we could go down to Rite Aid and buy a jar. Iffy mentioned to Angel that much faster relief could be had by putting a patch behind her ear." Sister gratefully accepted her tea, the bag steeping. "She said this in front of Garvey. I mean Iffy was smart, and she was bold. Garvey told Ben that Iffy told him to try it if he stiffened up, and also to take shark cartilage pills."

Shaker blushed. "I take them. Glucosamine and chondroitin, too. Works."

"The things I find out." She put the teabag on her teaspoon and wrapped the string around it to squeeze out the excess water, then dropped the spent bag into the wastebasket.

It landed with a plop.

"Try it."

"Long as it isn't a lethal dose."

"Doesn't it have that stuff in, soopy—"

"Scopolamine." She pronounced each syllable. "There's no way to know, but the logical conclusion is that Iffy brought in a patch loaded with the stuff and told Angel to put it behind her ear. If she didn't, no one would know it was murderous. Who else would use it? Iffy would have to find another way to kill Angel as Angel's suspicions of Iffy's stealing intensified. But Angel did put the patch on. Iffy timed it, walked into Angel's office forty minutes later—remember, Angel's age played a part in the speed of this stuff—and she removed the ear patch."

"But where'd the two million go? Iffy was tight as a tick."

"Went to Jason, who obviously wasn't."

"Jesus. She killed for that bastard?"

"She was in love with him. We'll never know what he promised her. Marriage?" She shrugged.

Shaker absorbed this. "Iffy in love."

"Hard to imagine."

"He must have really played her." Shaker shook his head in disbelief and disgust.

"We can all be fools in love. I guess it just proves that Iffy was human."

"I guess." He sipped his tea. "Lorraine's got me off coffee completely now. She says tea is better for me."

"Reckon it is." She rose and looked outside the window up to the house. "Gray's still asleep. Light's not on upstairs. Poor guy; he's exhausted. First he finds the coverup at Garvey's. Then Sam gets shot. Then he's in the dark until I nearly bought the farm yesterday. I was lucky Jason didn't shoot me. He was slick; I'll give him that."

"Why wouldn't he shoot you?" Shaker quickly amended that. "Not that I wanted him to."

"Ha. You say." She teased him and sat back down. "Ben only had him on insurance fraud. Iffy was the embezzler, not Jason. He received the proceeds of her ill-gotten gains, but he was technically innocent. If he'd shot me yesterday he'd have had a much tougher time in court."

"He shot Iffy."

"We know that, but Ben still would have to prove it. And it wouldn't be easy. Jason's big bucks could have hired a lawyer that would make Sherman's march look like trespassing."

"That's a fact." Shaker appreciated the wiles of high-paid lawyers, thanks to a divorce many years earlier.

"That was my first clue that Jason was our man."

"Damn. I sure didn't have any idea. All I knew was that Iffy had been planted over Jemima Lorillard. How do you get to Jason from that?"

"He thought he was clever, but he was no fox. He didn't know squat about hounds. I mean the man hunted with us and not once during the season did he really study the hounds at work. No, he was a run and gun." She held up her hand as if holding off a protest. "I know, I know, they pay their dues and I am grateful so long as they don't interfere with hounds or staff, but really, how can you foxhunt and not study hounds? I will never understand it. If they want to run and jump all the time they should take up three-day eventing."

"That's not easy."

"Didn't say it was." She sat back down. "But it's not foxhunting. You need to appreciate hounds a wee bit. Wouldn't hurt to know something about quarry."

"How did that get you to Jason?"

"The fox knows how fabulous hound noses are. You and I know. Jason didn't. He stupidly buried Iffy over Jemima, but he only dug down about three feet. He knew Sam and Gray's schedule. He was smart about that. And he was smart enough not to just throw her over a ravine somewhere because the vultures would circle round soon enough. His one bit of luck was the twenty-four-hour thaw. Guess he would have kept her in the freezer until there was one otherwise."

"Ugh."

She laughed. "I know; that was mean. Anyway, he was lucky there. But hounds can smell six feet down. Not even snow is going to stop them if the ground isn't frozen deep. I suspect by planting Iffy at the Lorillard graveyard he thought to throw suspicion on Gray should Iffy come to light—which she did, a lot earlier than Jason expected. Since Iffy didn't like Gray, the reverse could also be true. It's not locked down, but I do think

Jason was shrewd enough to do something like that. He had to get rid of the body somewhere; might as well create confusion with it."

"He showed he couldn't be trusted when he whipped-in to Crawford, pardon the expression." Shaker meant that Jason's performance couldn't be called whipping-in.

"Oh, and wasn't that a moment?" she gleefully recalled. "Crawford called Ben last night to say he knew nothing about Jason's crimes. Ben called me, and we had a good laugh."

"He didn't. I mean I hate his guts, but I don't think he was part of it." Shaker grimaced.

"Never underestimate the greed of the rich." She drank a large gulp. "But I agree. I don't think he knew anything. Couldn't really be part of it, anyway. Too busy chasing hounds all over Jefferson County."

They both laughed.

She got up again to check the bedroom light. "Still out. I'm glad he stayed last night."

"I was shook up. You really must have been rocked."

"Jason thought the boar would kill me. He would still be clean of murder if he was caught. Like I said, I was lucky. It's funny; you know, it didn't really hit me until I finally got home. Gray came with me, and I walked into the kitchen. Golly ran up with Raleigh and Rooster. Hit me like a brick."

"That would be a hard way to die, gored to death."

"Even if I didn't die; imagine the damage?" She exhaled. "Scares me, those pigs. Always has."

A pair of headlights shone into the windows.

Shaker stood up, holding his heavy cup. "Betty."

"What's she doing out here? She should be primping for church." Sister stood up, too.

Betty cut her lights, got out, hurried through the cold, and knocked three times on the kennel door, which she then opened. "I couldn't sleep." She threw herself on Sister. "We almost lost you."

Sister hugged Betty. "Honey, we might have lost you, too, or that beautiful Magellan."

They were all crying again, wiping each other's tears, then laughing.

"Big girls don't cry," Shaker laughed as he reached in his pocket for a clean handkerchief and handed it to Betty.

"You need it as much as I do," she sniffled as she laughed.

"I'll be manly and use the back of my hand."

This sent them into fits of laughter—the laughter of relief, companionship, and deep love.

Betty hugged them both, then clicked the hot plate back on.

"You really came for tea," Shaker kidded her.

Betty sat on the edge of the desk. "My legs are still shaky."

"Know what you mean," Sister confessed.

"Gray asleep?"

"Yeah. Rory stayed with Sam last night. It will be another three weeks before he can lift his arm up to get a shirt on. Wound stopped draining, though."

"Absence makes the heart grow fonder. At least that's what they tell us." Betty hopped off the desk to rummage through the teabag box, filled with odds and ends of tea. "What's this?" She held up a gray packet.

"Pickwick. Strong. Don't sell it in America," Sister informed her.

"Are you going to miss church?" Shaker asked.

"I left Bobby a note to go without me." Betty poured hot water into the cup, the Pickwick bag already releasing dark color. "Wasn't Sybil incredible? Cool as a cuke."

"Two toughest whippers-in in North America," Shaker bragged.

"I'll remind you of that when you tear me a new one out there."

"Now, Betty, it's been a long time since I cussed you."

"I believe when we return you refer to it as a blessing." She smiled. "But it has been a long time."

"I'm lonesome," Dragon howled from his sick bay quarters.

"I'll see to him." Shaker left.

"I spoke to Sybil last night," said Sister. "She's all right. She said what ran through her mind is that her boys no longer have a father, and she didn't want to leave them motherless. She knew she had to aim true."

"You know some women give up foxhunting when their children are small. Too dangerous," Betty mentioned.

"Why would you want your child to grow up seeing you shy off from a little danger now and then? Teaches them to be wimps." Sister had firm opinions about these things.

"Come on, you big baby." Shaker opened the door to the feeding room, Dragon at his heels.

"You're healing up nicely," Betty complimented him.

"I want to hunt." Dragon sat down.

"And I hear you ate some of Iffy's bones." Betty gravely pointed a finger at him.

"Dry as toast."

Betty didn't know what he'd said, but he made her laugh.

"I almost forgot. Gray gave me a titanium stock pin!" Sister said, excited. "Garvey had it made."

"No kidding." Betty was impressed.

"I'll wear it next hunt."

"Whose feast day is it? If I'm not going to church I want to know in case anyone asks."

"You're an Episcopalian," Sister dryly replied. "However, it's the day of St. Vincent of Saragossa, who was roasted on a grid-iron, among other tortures, and died in 304 AD." She thought a moment. "Awful way to go."

"Think of Angel. Although it wasn't awful. Peaceful really—but still, she was murdered."

"She was, but when it's your time, it's your time. Iffy was the agent of her murder, and were she alive, she could be punished. But still, it was Angel's time." Sister took a deep breath, then handed her cup to Betty for more tea.

"Wasn't Donny Sweigart a surprise?" Betty returned to yesterday's drama. "When I heard back at the trailers I was surprised. He's not but so smart, and I never took him seriously. I was wrong. He has courage. He helped save Sybil."

"True enough. He could have stayed hidden. After all, he had two strong incentives." Sister reached for the refilled cup.

"To save his life, you mean, since Jason didn't know he was there. If he'd known there was a witness he would have shot him."

"Good reason." Shaker blinked.

"The other reason being that our dear Donny has been baiting foxes. He hasn't set traps yet. He's been putting out frozen globs of blood," Sister told them.

"What good does it do frozen?" Shaker snorted.

"Well, that's just it, but he figured the fabled January thaw has to happen. They enjoy the treat. He'll put out more in the same place, but in a trap. Voila." She paused. "He's even using the discarded blood he picks up from the hospital. To save money buying chickens."

"Sister, what the hell is he doing trapping foxes?" Shaker sat upright.

"Crawford," she replied, one eyebrow shooting upwards.

"But he's supposed to keep an eye out on dens for us!" Betty found this almost as scandalizing as Jason's crimes.

"After I profusely thanked him, after Ben took a statement, I walked him away from the group and asked him. He said Crawford was paying one hundred dollars a fox."

"Highway robbery." Shaker's voice rose.

"So what, now we buy back our own foxes? The ones originally in our coverts?" Betty's face was flushed.

"Had a little talk with Donny. I said I'd give him a monthly stipend, find more work for him, but he absolutely must never remove one of our foxes."

"Where will we get the money?" Betty knew the inner workings of the club.

"I have no idea, but I'll find it somewhere," Sister said with resignation.

"Dammit, he has a job at Sanifirm," Shaker cursed.

"Which Crawford is trying to buy," Sister replied.

"Oh, that's great, just great." Shaker rolled his eyes.

"But Donny likes us. If we give him regular part-time work, I think all will be well."

"How regular?" Betty stared at her teacup.

"Reading the leaves," Sister laughed.

"I'd have to tear open the bag."

"One thousand dollars a month," Sister announced.

"Christ." Shaker, although not bearing the weight of financial need, since he was a club employee, nevertheless cared for Jefferson Hunt and identified with it in every respect.

"Like I said, I'll find it somewhere. And it won't be this

minute. The other thing"—she smiled—"he wants to go to court to change his name."

"He wants to be called Jude," Betty giggled.

"Brad," Shaker laconically added with a twinkle in his eye.

"No. He wants to drop the junior. He said he hated being called Junior as a kid. I said I'd help."

"Funny what affects people," Betty mused. Then she changed the subject. "Forgot to ask you. I remember, then it slips out of my mind."

"Old age." Shaker lifted one eyebrow.

"Balls. We're the same age. Too much going on," Betty fired back. "How many spoons?"

"Sixty-one," Sister immediately answered.

"What are you two jabbering about?" Shaker raised his eyebrows as Betty handed Sister another cup of tea.

"Every New Year's I count all the spoons in the house. Mother used to do it. Now I do."

"Aren't you supposed to have an even number of spoons?" Betty pretended this was serious.

"Yes, you nitwit. Haven't you ever lost a spoon?"

"Never," Betty lied, face angelic.

"Spare me." Sister laughed.

"It's someone's time. Sometimes I believe that and sometimes I don't." Betty looked from her master to her huntsman, returning to the deeper subject.

"Somerset Maugham wrote this in one of his books. I like Maugham," Sister smiled. She was an avid reader. "A master and his servant were riding toward Mecca, and they met Death with a surprised expression on his face. The master turned his horse away from Death and raced to Samarra. The servant said to Death, 'Why were you so startled to see my master?' Death said,

'I was surprised to see him here, as I have an appointment with him tonight in Samarra.' "

Both Shaker and Betty thought about this.

Shaker finally said, "You can't outrun Fate."

"Or old age," Sister remarked. " 'Course, you can slow old age down, throw marbles under his feet."

Another set of headlights shone on the wall. The sun now cast long beautiful shadows over the snow. The stable and farm buildings glowed.

Dragon stood up.

Two doors slammed, although the second one took longer than the first.

A knock on the door soon followed.

"Come in," Sister beckoned.

Tootie, Val, and Felicity trooped in.

Betty naturally assumed they were still upset over yesterday's events.

"Sister, can we talk to you?" Val asked, ever the leader.

"You can, and you can talk in front of Shaker and Betty. Whatever you say stays here. We're full of secrets." She smiled.

Tootie looked at Shaker, then Betty, then Sister. "We need your advice."

"We have a problem," Val jumped in.

"No, we don't." Felicity showed a new, rebellious streak.

"Felicity, I can't believe you're saying that." Val was ready for an argument.

"It's not exactly a problem, it's"—Tootie struggled—"new information."

"It's a goddamned problem," Val blurted out, forgetting she was in the presence of adults, then quickly realizing it. "Sorry."

"You owe me one dollar." Felicity's jaw set as she held out her hand.

"I can't believe you." Val pulled money out of her pocket, peeled off a dollar, and slapped it in Felicity's hand, hard.

"Girls, it's first light. This must be important." Sister gently pushed them along.

"Felicity has lied to us." Val seemed stricken.

"I didn't lie. I didn't know until I went to the doctor." Felicity defended herself.

"Sure. You said you were allergic to flour!" Val's face turned crimson.

"Val, put yourself in her shoes," Tootie counseled.

"I'd rather not." Val crossed her arms across her chest, then noticed that Dragon was observing every move.

Felicity finally said, in a calm voice, "I'm pregnant."

Shaker stood up and offered Felicity his chair. That surprised her, for she hadn't thought through all the consequences of her condition.

Betty, motherly, put her arm around Felicity's shoulders.

Sister also stood, put her arm around Tootie, and pulled Val to her for a hug. Then she gave Felicity a big hug. "Everything will be fine."

Sister burst into tears not because of Felicity's news, not because of yesterday's drama, but because deception, truth, death, and life were happening all at the same time. It was exactly as it should be.

SOME USEFUL TERMS

Away—A fox has "gone away" when he has left the covert. Hounds are "away" when they have left the covert on the line of the fox.

Brush—The fox's tail.

Burning scent—Scent so strong or hot that hounds pursue the line without hesitation.

Bye day—A day not regularly on the fixture card.

Cap—The fee nonmembers pay to a hunt for that day's sport.

Carry a good head—When hounds run well together to a good scent, a scent spread wide enough for the whole pack to feel it.

Carry a line—When hounds follow the scent. This is also called "working a line."

Cast—Hounds spread out in search of scent. They may cast themselves or be cast by the huntsman.

Charlie—A term for a fox. A fox may also be called Reynard.

Check—When hounds lose the scent and stop. The field must wait quietly while the hounds search for the scent.

Colors—A distinguishing color—usually worn on the collar but sometimes on the facings of a coat—that identifies a hunt. Colors can be awarded only by the master and can be won only in the field.

Couple straps—Two-strap hound collars connected by a swivel link. Some members of staff will carry these on the right rear of the saddle. Since the days of the pharoahs in ancient Egypt hounds have been brought to the meets coupled. Hounds are always spoken of and counted in couples. Today hounds walk or are driven to the meets. Rarely, if ever, are they coupled, but a whipper-in still carries couple straps should a hound need assistance.

Covert—A patch of woods or bushes were a fox might hide. Pronounced *cover.*

Cry—How one hound tells another what is happening. The sound will differ according to the various stages of the chase. It's also called "giving tongue" and should occur when a hound is working a line.

Cub hunting—The informal hunting of young foxes in the late summer and early fall, before formal hunting. The main purpose is to enter young hounds into the pack. Until recently only the most knowledgeable members were invited to cub hunt, since they would not interfere with young hounds.

Dog fox—The male fox.

Dog hound—The male hound.

Double—A series of short, sharp notes blown on the horn to alert all that a fox is afoot. The "gone away" series of notes is a form of doubling the horn.

Draft—To acquire hounds from another hunt is to accept a draft.

Draw—The plan by which a fox is hunted or searched for in a certain area, like a covert.

Drive—The desire to push the fox, to get up with the line. It's a very desirable trait in hounds, so long as they remain obedient.

Dwell—To hunt without getting forward. A hound who dwells is a bit of a putterer.

Enter—Hounds are entered into the pack when they first hunt, usually during cubbing season.

Field—The group of people riding to hounds, exclusive of the master and hunt stuff.

Field master—The person appointed by the master to control the field. Often it is the master him- or herself.

Fixture—A card sent to all dues-paying members, stating when and where the hounds will meet. A fixture card properly received is an invitation to hunt. This means the card would be mailed or handed to a member by the master.

Gone away—The call on the horn when the fox leaves the covert.

Gone to ground—A fox who has ducked into his den or some other refuge has gone to ground.

Good night—The traditional farewell to the master after the hunt, regardless of the time of day.

Gyp—Another term for a female hound.

Hilltopper—A rider who follows the hunt but does not jump. Hilltoppers are also called the "second field." The jumpers are called the "first flight."

Hoick—The huntsman's cheer to the hounds. It is derived from the Latin *hic haec hoc,* which means "here."

Hold hard—To stop immediately.

Huntsman—The person in charge of the hounds in the field and in the kennel.

Kennelman—A hunt staff member who feeds the hounds and cleans the kennels. In wealthy hunts there may be a number of kennelmen. In hunts with a modest budget, the huntsman or even the master cleans the kennels and feeds the hounds.

Lark—To jump fences unnecessarily when hounds aren't running. Masters frown on this, since it is often an invitation to an accident.

Lift—To take the hounds from a lost scent in the hopes of finding a better scent farther on.

Line—The scent trail of the fox.

Livery—The uniform worn by the professional members of the hunt staff. Usually it is scarlet, but blue, yellow, brown, and gray are also used. The recent dominance of scarlet has to do with people buying coats off the rack as opposed to having tailors cut them. (When anything is mass-produced, the choices usually dwindle, and such is the case with livery.)

Mask—The fox's head.

Meet—The site where the day's hunting begins.

MFH—The master of foxhounds; the individual in charge of the hunt: hiring, firing, landowner relations, opening territory (in large hunts this is the job of the hunt secretary), developing the pack of hounds, determining the first cast of each meet. As in any leadership position, the master is also the lightning rod for criticism. The master may hunt the hounds, although this is usually done by a professional huntsman, who is also responsible for the hounds in the field and at the kennels. A long relationship between a master and a huntsman allows the hunt to develop and grow.

Nose—The scenting ability of a hound.

Override—To press hounds too closely.

Overrun—When hounds shoot past the line of scent. Often the scent has been diverted or foiled by a clever fox.

Ratcatcher—The informal dress worn during cubbing season and bye days.

Stern—A hound's tail.

Stiff-necked fox—One who runs in a straight line.

Strike hounds—Those hounds who through keenness, nose, and often higher intelligence find the scent first and press it.

Tail hounds—Those hounds running at the rear of the pack. This is not necessarily because they aren't keen; they may be older hounds.

Tally-ho—The cheer when the fox is viewed. Derived from the Norman *ty a hillaut,* thus coming into the English language in 1066.

Tongue—To vocally pursue the fox.

View halloo (Halloa)—The cry given by a staff member who views a fox. Staff may also say "tally-ho" or "tally-back" should the fox turn back. One reason a different cry may be used by staff, especially in territory where the huntsman can't see the staff, is that the field in their enthusiasm may cheer something other than a fox.

Vixen—The female fox.

Walk—Puppies are "walked out" in the summer and fall of their first year. It's part of their education and a delight for puppies and staff.

Whippers-in—Also called whips, these are the staff members who assist the huntsman, who make sure the hounds "do right."

ABOUT THE AUTHOR

RITA MAE BROWN is the bestselling author of (among others) *Rubyfruit Jungle, Six of One, Southern Discomfort, Outfoxed,* and a memoir, *Rita Will.* She also collaborates with her tiger cat, Sneaky Pie, on the *New York Times* bestselling Mrs. Murphy mystery series. An Emmy-nominated screenwriter and poet, she lives in Afton, Virginia. She is master and huntsman of the Oak Ridge Foxhunt Club and is one of the directors of Virginia Hunt Week. She is also Visiting Faculty at the University of Nebraska, Lincoln.

ABOUT THE TYPE

This book was set in New Baskerville, a typeface based on the design by John Baskerville. The original was cut by John Handy in 1750. Noted for its high contrast and sparkly look, it saw a renewed popularity when the Lanston Monotype Corporation of London revived the classic Roman face in 1923. The Mergenthaler Linotype Company in England and the United States cut a version of Baskerville in 1931, making it one of the most widely used typefaces today.